Echoes of the Forgotten

Book 1 of The Raknari Trilogy

THE RAKNARI TRILOGY

Returning readers to the ancient world of *The Ancestors Saga, The Raknari Trilogy* takes us back to Khalvir's beginnings.

Journey with the young Khalvir as he navigates the dangers of his new life amongst the Cro.

Caught in the grip of the terrifying chieftain, Eldrax, a man who covets Khalvir's unpredictable and deadly powers for reasons unknown, Khalvir must face the threats posed by friend and foe alike and survive long enough to grow from a lost boy with no memory, to one of the most fearsome warriors to walk the ancient Plains.

About the Author

Lori Holmes is the author of the bestselling *Ancestors Saga* and the companion series *The Raknari Trilogy*.

The idea for the Ancestors Saga first came to Lori in 2008 when her mother made a passing comment, 'what could the human race have become if only we had followed a spiritual path, rather than a technological one?' The comment set off a chain reaction. Two main characters came to life. The first was a young woman whose people had rejected technology and evolved a spiritual connection to the living world around them. The second was a man. This man was half ordinary human and half 'spiritual' human.

For a time, that was all there was, two characters sitting in a pool of light, surrounded by a mysterious darkness. This went on until one day, having a keen interest in prehistoric and ancient history, Lori was reading an article outlining evidence that our modern human ancestors interbred with the other human species we once shared our planet with. And that, as they say, is history. An ancient and icy world opened out around the two main characters, a changing world filled at once with danger and possibility, where the fate of man, in all its known and unknown forms, had yet to be decided.

Adding a dash of legend, myth, and Sumerian theories on the creation of mankind, *The Ancestors Saga* was born.

Lori's debut novel, The Forbidden, begins the epic journey into *The Ancestors Saga*, combining history, mystery and legend to retell a lost chapter in humanity's dark and distant past.

Lori currently lives in Shropshire, England. When not lost in the world of *The Ancestors Saga*, she enjoys spending time with her family (three children, two whippets and her husband - it's a busy house!). Lori can usually be found outdoors walking and exploring the great British countryside.

Find out more at www.loriholmesbooks.com

ALSO BY LORI HOLMES

The Ancestors Saga

Book 1 | *The Forbidden*

Book 2 | *Daughter of Ninmah*

Companion Novel To Book 2 | *Captive*

Book 3 | *Enemy Tribe*

Book 4 | *The Last Kamaali*

The Raknari Trilogy

Book 1 | *Echoes of The Forgotten*

Book 2 | *Call of The Warrior*

Book 3 | *Whispers of Fate*

ECHOES OF THE FORGOTTEN

BOOK 1 OF THE RAKNARI TRILOGY

LORI HOLMES

VISUAL 8 PUBLISHING

To my beautiful son, Jonathan, and the cheeky smile that somehow makes mommy forgive you for waking her up at 5am each morning.

CONTENTS

ACKNOWLEDGEMENTS

A huge thank you to the team at *Writing.co.uk Literary Consultancy*, for all their hard work and endless advice on editing this manuscript and helping me shape this book into what it is today.

Another big thank you goes to the team at *Damonza.com* for their incredible design skills in creating the wonderful book covers for *The Ancestors Saga* and *The Raknari Trilogy*.

PROLOGUE

TAKEN

Juaan paced back and forth inside the giant *eshaara* tree. The ill-fitting, woven leaves covering his body chafed against his shoulders as he glared around at the reddish-gold space. It was empty but for him. Outside, the light was waning fast. It would be dark soon. A shiver of anxiety ran down his spine, stoking his anger.

Where is she? The thought cut through his mind. *She promised to be home before dark.*

Juaan ceased pacing and stood in the entranceway to the great tree, staring down at the ground far below, but there was no sign of the one he sought.

Nyriaana.

For a moment, he watched the movement of the people beneath as they went about their lives, oblivious to his observations. Juaan's lips twisted; he was glad they couldn't see him from his vantage point. If he had to suffer one more scornful glare from any of them, he was going to do something he would regret. And that would not be good.

The constant hatred he suffered from his mother's tribe was easier to bear on some days than on others. Today was not one of those days.

The knot of foreboding in his stomach, a companion Juaan had lived with his entire life, was tightening.

The time was drawing close. He could feel it. Thirteen Furies had passed since his birth. He was approaching manhood, the time when the Ninkuraaja Elders' promise to the tribe's formidable Kamaali would bind them no longer. When that time came, they would finally expel him from their borders, banishing the Forbidden half-breed heresy at last. Juaan imagined the look of satisfaction on the Elder's hated faces, and wondered if a simple expulsion would slake their prejudice, or whether they would seek a more permanent end to the insult he presented to their goddess, Ninmah.

Juaan's thoughts flickered to the spear hidden within the tree he and his dead mother had once shared. His mother had known he would need it one day. She had killed a Cro man with it once to save her own life, leaving it buried deep in the man's gut. Juaan remembered the courage it had taken for her to steal back out of the protection of the trees to retrieve it, smuggling it back to her home in the dead of night, where she had kept it hidden. Just for him.

Juaan wondered if he should just take the spear, steal some food, and leave the forest and the lands of the Ninkuraaja People of his own volition. Juaan smiled. It would certainly rob the Elders of their satisfaction.

But even as he contemplated it, a spasm of pain strong enough to steal his breath tightened his chest. His captured heart writhed as he saw Nyriaana's trusting face in his mind's eye.

She did not know the power she held over him. From the moment they met, his heart had been hers. The day his mother had died, Juaan had been a child of only eight Furies, left lost, drowning. In her innocence, Nyriaana had not seen a Forbidden heresy to be feared and avoided. With the power of her tiny, infant arms, she had reached out and drawn him back to the shore; the only being since his mother who could look upon him without flinching. Sometimes, Juaan felt the Ninkuraaja girl had become his only reason for living.

He could not leave her. Not willingly.

He only wished she felt the same way about leaving him. Juaan hissed. *Where* was *she?*

As the light of Ninmah dimmed above the ever-rippling canopy above, he could bear it no longer. Juaan descended the tree and set off. He ignored the looks of disgust and abruptly turned backs with an effort and forged headlong out of the *eshaara* grove that sheltered the tribe, and into the thick trees of the outer forest.

She had gone off to play with the other Ninkuraaja children. Juaan had no idea which direction they had taken. He paused, temporarily stymied. He could search all night if he didn't have a general trail to follow. It was now too dark to read the ground reliably.

There was, however, another way.

He was half Ninkuraaja, after all. Drawing a long breath, Juaan rolled his eyes closed and clenched his fists. He did not know if he could do it. He fought to grasp that extra sense, the dull echo that always lay just on the edge of his awareness, just beyond his full control. His mother had tried to teach him the skill. The tribe's Kamaali, Sefaan herself, had attempted to guide him in the subtle powers of Ninmah's Gift, the connection all Ninkuraaja shared to the energy of the earth; the Great Spirit of KI, himself.

The results of their guidance had always been haphazard. Only when Juaan was scared or angry did the power come easily to him, and then the results were often... frightening.

There. Snatches of thought and flickers of life brushed against his outer awareness. Sweat beaded upon Juaan's brow as he concentrated as hard as he could, throwing out his higher sense as far as it would go, focusing on his fear for Nyri, on the danger she might be in if he was not there to guard her side.

The thought had no sooner crossed his mind when a distant scream wrenched at Juaan's gut. *Nyriaana!* It was the catalyst he had needed and his senses exploded forth.

Ah! Juaan put his hands to his head in a futile attempt to shield himself from the onslaught. All around him the forest buzzed, sang, whispered, everything talking together at once. *Focus, focus.* He battled to control the Gift within and sift through the whispered messages that bombarded him from all sides.

He found what he sought. The presence of the children glowed against his mind's eye, off to his right. Juaan's muscles uncoiled. They were not in danger. Their auras flared with the light of excitement. A game was in progress. Juaan ground his teeth together, swallowing the blaze of jealousy. Was she having so much fun with her own kind that she had forgotten all about him? The thought added to that little knot of ever-present fear in the pit of his stomach.

Nyriaana was growing fast, the shine of innocence he had always loved waning in her eyes. Juaan knew she would inevitably be drawn to her own blood in the end. It was only natural. How long did he have before they made her see him as all the others did, as a Forbidden monster? He knew it would be better if it happened sooner rather than later. He could not watch over her for much longer. It was only right that she should make other connections. But the thought of losing her that way, of seeing hate stamp out the love in her eyes, ripped agony through his heart.

The darkness gathered in strength as his pain drove his ire. Juaan cut through the forest, stalking toward the cause of his upset. He would bring her home. She was still his, not theirs.

Thrusting aside the last of the undergrowth, he revealed his target at last. The Ninkuraaja children were breathless and flushed, engrossed in their game. Juaan scanned the group and spotted Nyriaana. The carefree happiness on her face only made him feel more retched.

"Nyriaana!" he burst out, closing the distance between them in a matter of strides. "Nyriaana! You come here right now!"

Silence fell, the children growing as still as the surrounding trees, dumbstruck by his audacity. Only Nyriaana moved, her head shrinking defensively into her shoulders. Juaan watched as another girl, her rare silver hair standing out in stark contrast to the rest of her black-haired brethren, lean in and whisper in Nyri's ear. Nyri stiffened. Her usually open face grew cold, freezing like stone, but not before Juaan witnessed the profound grief flicker in her eyes. He knew that look; it was the one she wore whenever she thought of her lost mother. Juaan clenched his fists, imagining what that spiteful girl had said. But his anger gave way to uncertainty as Nyri lifted her chin, a gleam in her eyes that he had never before seen directed at him. Defiance.

Juaan tried not to recoil and lose his hold on his bad temper. When he heard the silver-haired girl hiss '*monster*' in Nyriaana's ear, he suddenly had little problem with the latter. He came toe to toe with Nyri and she tilted back her head to meet his gaze; her eyes like indigo flint.

"You promised me you'd be home before dark." He needn't have growled. A full Ninkuraaja, Nyri's higher senses were far stronger than his. Her connection to the Great Spirit was unsullied. She would know without words how upset he was with her. Juaan just hoped she couldn't feel his desperate fear at the flat look in her eyes. "What are you still doing out here?"

But with his churning emotions heightening his own latent senses, even Juaan felt the wave of hot indignation that rolled at him from his left.

"Just who do you think you're talking to, Forbidden?" a boy spat. Juaan knew that hated voice. Daajir. "Why should she keep promises to you? She is Ninkuraaja, beloved of Ninmah. You..." a mocking laugh, "what? We don't even know what *you* are."

Juaan turned his head, keeping his eyes upon Nyri until the very last moment before fixing them on Daajir. He became aware that he was trembling faintly and knew he was approaching the edge of his control. Angry, frightened, he would snap if this hated boy opened his mouth just one more time. Did this cruel child hope to win Nyri's affections? His balled fists tightened.

Daajir did not miss the deadly message in his eyes, and Juaan watched with satisfaction as the smaller Ninkuraaja boy took a quick step back. The fool could not keep his mouth shut, however. "You can't do anything to me, you a-abomination," Daajir blustered. "I'll—"

The red mist descended. A lifetime of torment and humiliation at the hands of his adopted tribe came boiling to the forefront, and Juaan snapped. Before he was even really aware of it, he had Daajir's leaf coverings clenched in his left fist, the bully dangling off the ground at eye level before him. He hadn't spared one thought for the consequences. It was too late for that now. Daajir had been *begging* for this moment.

Since he was damned anyway, Juaan was going to enjoy giving him what he had deserved for so long. He tightened his grip, watching the smaller boy's eyes bug. "You'll what?" he hissed into Daajir's face.

"Juaan! Put him *down*." Her panicked voice cut through the red haze. Blinking, he turned his head to her. Frightened tears were standing in her eyes, but she set her jaw. "I don't wanna go home yet! You can't make me!"

Juaan forgot the stupid boy in his hand in an instant. He had ceased to matter. He lowered Daajir to the ground, but still felt malicious enough to shove the pathetic fool onto his backside.

It was a mistake. The Ninkurra boy leaped to his feet, furious and shamed enough to charge into an attack. Juaan set his feet, his lips curling in invitation. *Go for it,* he thought. *Come on. I'm waiting.*

But the smaller boy seemed to keep one last shred of sense and held his ground. "I'll kill you for this!" Daajir snarled. "You do not belong, *Forbidden*. One day, I *will* kill you!"

Juaan saw the consternation flash through Nyri's eyes and stepped forward to drive the other boy away from her. He had had enough. "Nyri," he growled. "We're going home right *now.*"

"No!" her cry reverberated through him and his limbs grew numb as she continued to scream. "I'm not going! Leave me alone! You're not my mama!" Her lip trembled with the strength of her emotion. "You don't belong here! Leave. Go away. You're no one!"

And the hand that had held his heart together so carefully through all the turning of the seasons since his mother's death squeezed mercilessly, crushing it into dust. Juaan felt detached, as if he was floating away, bereft once more of a centre. He saw the shock cross Nyri's face as she clapped a hand across her mouth, the angry tears turning to remorse. But it was too late to trap the words behind her lips and they both knew it. She reached out to him in desperation, but he pulled away. Her touch would bring no comfort now.

"You heard her," Daajir's voice hummed with triumph. "She does not want you anymore. You have no place here. Leave."

Juaan continued to stare into Nyri's eyes. He could not let their audience see the agony he felt. His lips formed the words without him feeling them. "Alright," he heard himself say. "Stay out here and freeze. I don't care. Woves take you." Wrapping his long arms deeper into his ill-fitting coverings to hold himself together, he strode away and did not look back.

So, the moment he had so dreaded had come to pass. And it was far worse than even his darkest imagining. Lost in a haze, Juaan paid little attention to where he was going as he threaded his way through the undergrowth. He had thought himself prepared, but he could not have anticipated just how deeply it would shatter his world to see the ultimate rejection in her eyes.

Tears threatened at the corners of his eyes. He blinked them angrily away. Thirteen Furies had come and gone since his birth. He was too old to cry like a helpless babe. His breath plumed in the air. It was growing cold. The trees passed, getting larger as he approached the heart of the *eshaara* grove.

As the shock of her rejection receded, his mind caught up with all that had passed beyond the breaking of his bond with Nyriaana. Juaan's breath came faster. He had just attacked Daajir. There would be no simple expulsion now. The Elders had wanted to kill him as a baby for simply daring to exist. Now he had attacked one of their own. Such a trespass was unheard of among Ninkuraaja. Juaan knew well that his mother's People could inflict punishments far worse than death. Punishments that could tear one's mind apart. His heart pounded hard against his ribs. He needed to get out. His time was up.

But even with the threat of death, or worse, hanging above his head, a shiver of reluctance pulled on his heart. He was betraying her. Juaan growled and increased his pace, trying to outdistance the pain. She had made her choice. She had chosen *them*. It was the only choice she could have made. She could not come with him. It was better this way.

It was.

Juaan stopped when an immense tree loomed out of the gloom before him. Without even realising it, his feet had brought him right to the far edge of the *eshaara* grove. To the very base of his mother's old home. His hands reached out to grasp the familiar red-gold bark. He concentrated on the feel of the tree, letting it block all other thoughts as he climbed, committing the texture of the tree's skin to memory, remembering all the times his mother had climbed it with him cradled in her arms. A lump lodged in his throat. After tonight, he would never see this place again. The last tie to his mother.

Juaan reached the opening in the twisting boughs high above the ground and crawled inside. Blinking as his eyes adjusted to the dimness, he looked around. There wasn't much left here. A bear skin sling lay moth-eaten and abandoned on the leaf-strewn floor. His mother had borne him inside this sling when he was a newborn, fleeing across the Plains to return to her own People following the destruction of his father's Cro clan. Juaan's throat closed as his fingers brushed through the sparse hairs of the skin. But this was not what he had come here to seek, and he tore himself away.

Thrusting his hands into the pile of leaves in the far corner of the space, he pulled out the spear he knew was waiting for him. A Thal weapon. The last gift from his mother. Juaan studied the strange carvings at the top of the haft. Thal markings of protection, his mother had said, made by the Thal who had pledged her life to him even before his birth. Juaan hoped the weapon and the spirit of the one who had made it would protect him on his journey into the unknown. He imagined the mighty hands that had long ago worn it smooth.

Swinging the spear experimentally in his own hands, Juaan was reminded sharply of performing the same motion on the night his mother had gifted him the weapon. The night she had left him forever. Back then, his hands had been too small to fit around the thick haft.

Now they were large enough to wrap snugly around the wood. But far from feeling mighty and fearless, he felt as clumsy, afraid, and unsure as he had on that terrible night. He did not know how to use this weapon. Tears of hopelessness threatened to fall, but Juaan sniffed loudly and forced them back. He would learn somehow. His mother had survived beyond the forests. She had been brave. He would not shame her.

Letting the weapon fall to his side, Juaan looked once more at the faded and nearly hairless bearskin. He could not suffer the thought of leaving it behind and stooped to pick it up, then slung it around his shoulders. He could use it to carry food.

Food. The thought shuddered through him. There was no chance he could risk going to the store trees and helping himself to the tribe's meager gatherings. Daajir would surely have returned by now and told the Elders that his true nature had surfaced at last. The monster in their midst had emerged. Juaan gritted his teeth.

What was he going to do? Were there trees that would feed him beyond this forest? Somehow, Juaan doubted it. Unlike the Ninkuraaja, his mother told him that the Thals and the Cro mainly lived off the flesh of animals. He looked at the spear, seeing it with fresh eyes. Could he kill with this? He nearly dropped the weapon at the very thought.

Juaan tightened his grip on the haft. He was wasting time. They would come for him soon. He would not let them find him and perform their punishments. Clutching the long spear in his fist, he climbed awkwardly with one hand back to the forest floor. He touched his mother's tree in silent farewell as the tears escaped. *Goodbye.* He did not know if the silent being could heed his farewell. He fancied it did feel sad, in its own way.

Juaan squared his shoulders as he turned to the outer forest and quailed. Now he was standing there at the foot of his tree for the last time, his gathered courage fled. The journey ahead suddenly seemed very real and very terrifying. He was leaving all that he had ever known behind. As unwelcome and as hated as he was here, this was the only home he knew.

Stop being a coward, he told himself. This was his home no longer. It was time to find another. Drawing a deep breath, Juaan stepped away from the tree and set off into the dark with only the sound of his own footsteps and the rustle of the undergrowth around him for company.

He no longer had a home. He was not wanted. But Juaan could not prevent his heart from splintering, tearing further and further down the middle the farther he travelled away from the *eshaara* grove. Every step away became a tremendous effort. *You always knew this day was coming,* he repeated to himself. *Why cling to a home you never had?* He knew why. The space at his side yawned wide. *Nyriaana. You promised to never leave her.* He quashed the thought before it could fully form. *She doesn't need you anymore!*

Nevertheless, Juaan's steps became slower and slower as his anger towards her and their confrontation drained away. Juaan imagined her face when she returned home and realised that he was gone. She would blame herself. The thought of her pain almost had him turning around. Would she search for him? Almost certainly. The thought of Nyri's desperation, as she ran fruitlessly from tree to tree, brought him to a full stop.

Juaan leaned heavily upon his spear, regathering himself. He could not go back. It was his own fault. In a flash of temper, he closed that possibility forever. He told himself over and over she was safe with her People. She belonged there. She would forget and have a life without him. What would she have had with him but a life on the fringes? Even the Elders were poorly fed as their precious forest slowly deteriorated around them. An outcast would not survive. Even his mother, who had overcome so much, had succumbed to such a life. He would *not* let Nyriaana share the same fate for him.

Juaan thought instead of their earlier confrontation, remembering the defiant look in her indigo eyes as she rejected him, recalling the words she had spoken: *You don't belong here! Leave! You're no one!* The pain of betrayal flared once more at the memory of them and Juaan drew it around him like a defensive cloak, letting it give him the strength he needed.

He struggled on, tears streaming down his face, when something in his crushed and empty heart stopped him dead in his tracks once more. Juaan stood swaying on the spot as he tried to make sense of what he was feeling. It was akin to a shiver on the air. A disturbance. He frowned. He had not been trying to concentrate on his unpredictable higher sense. He shouldn't be feeling anything out of the ordinary. But there it was. The air quivered again. This time it was stronger, clearer. A call. A cry of terror.

Juaan.

He spun to face the direction from which he had come, back towards the *eshaara* grove. He gasped and clutched his chest, knees almost buckling as the cry doubled in strength, reverberating through his body. Juaan blinked into the darkness. In the distance, on the very edge of his perception, he could just make out a red glow flaring between the trees.

Nyri!

He was running back towards the tribe before he was even aware of it. Elders be damned. Trees whipped by as Juaan ducked and wove between them. The red glow became clearer and the physical sound of the screams reached his ears. Screams of terror. Screams of pain. Screams of death. The bombardment of sensation, and his fear for Nyriaana nearly sent Juaan to his knees.

A body bolted from the dark, crashing into him. Juaan was knocked to the ground. Gasping, he saw the Elder, Pelaan, right himself and run on, his silver-haired daughter wrapped tightly in his arms. The terror in the man's eyes was beyond thought or reason. Juaan didn't think the Elder knew what he had collided with as he continued his flight without looking back.

Not feeling the pain of the collision, Juaan rolled to his feet, dodging as more and more of the tribe flew past him, fleeing into the dark as if the dark god Ninsiku himself was on their heels. *Woves, Woves.* He heard them cry. The moisture left Juaan's mouth. He knew what that meant.

A raid. Wove demons had come for the tribe. Juaan searched each face in desperation as they blurred past him, seeking the only one that mattered. But she was nowhere to be seen. "Nyriaana!"

"Juaan!" The sound of his name being called brought him up short. His eyes widened. The tribe's *akaab* healer, Baarias, was braced against a tree, clutching at his chest as he fought for breath. The man's lilac eyes raked the empty air at Juaan's sides, a terrible realisation dawning on his face. Pushing his prejudice for the healer aside, Juaan stumbled towards his uncle.

"Baarias?" He clutched at the leaf leather clothing covering the healer's chest, ignoring the man's flinch at his touch. "Where is she? Where is Nyriaana?"

The healer's eyes turned toward the red blaze. His expression was numb.

"No!" Juaan tore away from him. He gave no thought to it as he ran towards the burning light.

Baarias surprised him by catching his arm. "You can't go! It's too late. You'll be killed, boy!"

Juaan fought back. "You think I care!" he snarled. "She needs me!"

Baarias' hand fell away. Juaan watched a strange expression contract over his face as the healer stared into his eyes. A mix of dawning realisation and the whisper of regret.

Juaan disregarded him and turned back to the danger, gathering himself.

"Juaan..."

He glanced at the healer impatiently.

"I'll come with you."

Stunned, Juaan faltered, then his mind was racing. He was going to get Nyri out of there, but when he did, what then? If the demon raiders were still present, he would be surrounded by enemies. There was no way he could run fast enough once the pursuit started.

A large grey stag barrelled out of the gloom to his right, its eyes rolling with fear, and sudden inspiration hit.

"Catch him!" Juaan ordered the healer. He had no time to explain the plan forming in his head, so he grabbed the healer's wrist, pushing his thoughts to the surface. He hoped Baarias would hear and understand.

The lilac eyes widened. "But what about you?" Baarias breathed. "You'll—"

"It doesn't matter!" Juaan burst out. "It's too late for me. I know. I cannot go where she is going. Just do as I ask! Please. She is all that matters. Just promise me you will look after her. In my mother's name, keep her safe!"

Agony contorted the healer's face at the mention of his sister. A trembling hand reached out, almost, but not quite, touching Juaan's cheek. "You are her son," Baarias whispered, then he raised his chin. A look of hope, a kindling of redemption, flickered in his eyes. "I promise."

"Thank you," Juaan whispered. "Go! Meet me by the dead tree. I'll bring her there. Be ready!" Then he ran without a backwards glance, diving headlong into the midst of the burning *eshaara* grove.

The intensity of the heat nearly knocked Juaan back, stinging his skin and stealing his breath. He flung his hands up to shield his streaming eyes from the sear of blinding light. Red hot spirits were blazing all around. His mother had told him of fire, but he had never seen it with his own eyes. This was nothing like the warm, giving light of which she had spoken. This was terrifying. This was death and agony.

Strange, fur-clad figures with skulls for faces moved through the grove, blazing brands and cruel weapons clutched in their shrouded hands. Woves. Demons of Ninsiku.

The violence that Juaan witnessed in those moments made him want to close his eyes and hide, but he knew he would never unsee it. He had experienced the terror and loss of raids before, but this was different. This was wanton destruction.

A scream rose above all the rest, but he knew he did not hear with his ears. It shredded through his very mind. *Juaan, help me! Juaan! Nyri!*

Heedless of the heat, he plunged through the grove, dodging and weaving around the attackers and their helpless victims. The Ninkuraa had nothing to defend themselves with, but he had no time to help. The scent of his own singed hair and flesh filled his nostrils, the woven leaves covering his body blackened and curled, but Juaan ran on. Where was she? That brief sense of her had disappeared as quickly as it had come. His breath came in hitching gasps. If he was too late, if she was already...

Before the fear could incapacitate him, he saw her. Nyriaana was dangling from the fist of a Wove raider, much as Daajir had dangled from his own earlier that day. Her captor was a towering giant, thick-set with a wave of red hair flowing around a blank bear skull face. Juaan experienced a twist of pride as Nyri resisted and sank her teeth into the hand that held her, brave and spirited even in the grip of a demon. But the beast did not release her. Murder gleamed in the black eyes blazing from the skull sockets and they flicked towards a burning tree. It was clear what the monster was planning and a fury such as Juaan had never known seared through him.

"No, please." He heard Nyri whisper as the demon prepared to fling her into the flames.

"No!" Juaan vaulted forward and barrelled into the giant demon holding Nyri aloft. To use the spear in his hand never even crossed his mind. Blind with rage, Juaan simply crashed his whole body into his enemy at full speed. His bones rattled, but he didn't even feel the pain of the impact as he and the great Wove toppled, Juaan's legs tangling with his enemy's. The fingers loosed Nyriaana, and she rolled away as Juaan and the Wove hit the ground.

Breathless and dazed, Juaan fought to regain his senses and scramble back to his feet. Hate seared through him as he looked down on his fallen enemy. "Leave her alone!" he heard himself scream as he kicked the stunned demon hard in the side.

Nyri was still lying where she had come to rest on the ground, blood streaming from her mouth and nose. The beast had hit her. The red mist descended over Juaan's eyes. Crying out, he raised the spear in his hand, ready to plunge it through his enemy's heart.

"Juaan!" Her voice broke through his craze. "Juaan!"

She was staring up at him. Terrified. His senses returned. There was no time for vengeance. He would not become a monster in front of her. Grabbing Nyri's hand, Juaan yanked her to her feet, dragging her along in his wake. He had to get to Baarias. It was the only thing that mattered.

His ribs screamed as the injuries he had sustained from colliding with the beast made themselves known. His left elbow ached and his arm felt weakened. Juaan pushed the pain away. *Keep going. Keep going. Get her to safety.*

For a few strides, Nyri kept up, but she couldn't manage it for long. She stumbled and collapsed, gasping and choking. Her hand shook inside his. Juaan tugged at her arm. "Come on! Get up!" he urged. "You've got to run!"

"I-I can't," she moaned through the blood and tears. "Juaan, I c-can't."

Ninmah, help me. Blinking the moisture from his stinging eyes, Juaan tried to see through the smoke. The dead tree was nowhere in sight. Their flight was not over. The pain in his side was becoming unbearable, but Juaan bent and scooped Nyri up in his arms. She wrapped her own around his neck as he ran, burying her face in his throat, hot tears soaking his skin.

The fires raged on and the air was now thick with smoke; Juaan could barely see. His lungs burned. The air he breathed no longer fuelled his body. He choked; spots danced before his eyes. He pushed his legs as far as he could until they could take him no further, and he sank to the ground before he collapsed and fell on her. The smoke billowed and parted, revealing the dead tree crouched away in the gloom before him.

"Close enough," he breathed. There was no sign of Baarias. Juaan felt a shiver of apprehension. Could he trust the man who had abandoned his mother? *Where are you?* he hissed in the silence of his mind.

Nyri whimpered, and he drew her to his chest, cradling her against his heart as he willed the healer to appear. Despite the danger they were in, Juaan felt suddenly whole again. The pain that had existed since he had chosen to leave vanished. He drank everything in, knowing this was the last time they would ever be together.

Nyri shook in his arms as the smoke enclosed them in a bubble of fear and uncertainty. The shouts and the screams continued, swallowed up by the dark. Juaan rocked back and forth, wishing he could block the sound of the horror from her ears.

"Don't be afraid, Nyri, Nyri, Nyriaana," he half sang the rhyme that had come unbidden from his lips on the day of their first meeting. But the familiar words did nothing to comfort her this time. She sobbed, the tears flowing faster.

"What's going to happen to us?" she forced the words through chattering teeth.

Juaan could sense the shock catching up to her. He tightened his arms. "Shhh," he whispered. "You'll be safe, I promise. I promise to make you safe. Have I ever broken a promise to you?"

Her head shook in denial against his chest. She had given up hope. She knew them to be lost.

Baarias! Juaan cried internally. *Damn you to Ninsiku.* The healer had decided to save his own skin, abandoning them to their enemies. It was only a matter of time now before they were found.

"Why did you do it?" Her small voice drew him from his thoughts.

"What?"

"Come back for me?"

Juaan recoiled. "Why in Ninmah's name wouldn't I come back for you?" Did she think he would have abandoned her so easily? Did she really not know what she meant to him?

"I hurt you. I was cruel."

He could taste her guilt. Juaan sighed and shook his head. He had already forgiven her. "It doesn't matter now. You are my Nyri, and I will protect you to the end."

He felt her body shudder as she cried uncontrollably, clutching at him in desperation.

The sharp snap of a twig made them flinch. Their time had run out. Nyri's nails were digging into Juaan's skin. He tightened his grip on the spear he still held in his hand. He wouldn't go down without a fight.

"Please let's go. I want to go." Nyri pulled at him. "*Please.*"

"Shhh," Juaan hissed, then spoke in a breath. "We have to wait here." He had to cling to the hope that Baarias would come. It was the only thing left.

"Why?" she pulled harder. "Let's go! I wanna go! Please! Please!"

It was then that he heard it. The distant bellow of a stag. Juaan almost wept with relief.

He took Nyri by the shoulders, shaking her from her daze. She had to understand. For her own survival, she had to leave him now. "Nyri, listen. *Listen.* When I tell you, you must run that way." He pointed with his spear towards the dead tree. "Run as fast as you can. As *fast* as you can!"

"Why? No!" Panic cut through her confusion. "I wanna stay with you!"

I want to stay with you, too! But he could not say it. Not if he wanted her to live. Juaan hardened his will and pried Nyri's clutching fingers from around his coverings. He caught her small face between his hands, looking into her wide indigo eyes for the last time, burning them into his memory. "Run."

"Where?" a muffled voice mocked from the gloom.

Juaan bolted to his feet, spear raised. Nyri grabbed onto his free hand and was dragged up with him. He was careful to keep her between himself and the tree as ten hulking shadows emerged from the murk to form a loose semi-circle around them. Nyri huddled against Juaan's legs, her grip tightening on his fingers. Her hand shook. He hoped she could not feel the tremble in his own grip.

The giant leader of the skull-headed band stepped forward, red hair whipping in the breeze like the very fire he had unleashed. Juaan bared his teeth in response to the triumphant glint in the black eyes.

"Brave, boy." The voice was deep and halting, rough, like rocks cracking together. "You think you challenge me and walk away? Should have killed me. No get another chance." The beast stepped closer, only to draw up short, the black eyes widening in a flare of recognition. "You?" the skull-headed monster breathed before his gaze flicked to the spear in Juaan's hand. Juaan saw the brute's throat flash. "It can't be."

Confused, Juaan tightened his grip on the wooden haft, his palm slick with cold sweat.

The black eyes returned to his face and Juaan saw the demon had regained his composure with an effort. He was assessing him now, muttering words Juaan could not understand, before raising his voice again. This time, the tone was inviting. "You not these People. Let me take girl. Come willingly and I let you live."

Juaan felt as though his fury should burn the monster to ash right where he stood. "Never!" he spat. "I'm not one of you, either! I will not let you take her."

His opponent merely huffed, unimpressed. One of the other skull-faced demons stepped forward and spoke urgently to its hulking leader. More words Juaan could not understand flowed forth, but it was clear the other demon wanted the confrontation to finish. The fire-haired leader snapped back, and the subordinate bowed its head, stepping hastily back into place. Impatience lay heavy on the air.

"Stubborn boy. Seen it before. Always the same ending. Move. You not know how use weapon." The red demon took a menacing step forward, a dark promise in his black eyes. "I not ask again."

Juaan knew what would happen if he did not obey. The whole of his existence burned down to the small vulnerable hand within his as a dreadful epiphany shuddered through him. In that one moment, the reason for his very existence was laid bare before him.

He was meant to die for her.

And so it was without fear when he raised his chin in defiance. His hand on the spear grew steady. The demon's eyes sparked as he readied his own weapon; a stout club crowned with a heavy knuckle bone. Juaan drew a long breath.

An angry bellow and the drumming of hooves cut through the air, breaking the standoff.

Yes, Juaan exalted as confusion flickered around the circle of Woves. Then Baarias was there, bearing down upon their enemies as he rode the great stag, barrelling into their midst. Juaan barely noticed his enemies diving out of the path of the wicked antlers, lowered for the charge. He wasn't aware of anything except what he had to do. He spun around, lifting Nyri in his hands. Finding a strength he did not know he had, he threw her into the air just as Baarias swept past.

It was a single heartbeat of time, but to Juaan it seemed to stretch forever as Nyri realised too late what was happening. She tried to cling to his hand, but Baarias had already caught her and was tearing her away. In that terrible, eternal moment, Juaan watched her heart shatter in her eyes.

Then she was gone in a swirl of smoke and a thrumming of hooves.

"Goodbye," Juaan whispered.

He did not have time to turn back to his enemies, to face his death. As he gazed after the disappearing stag, feeling his heart go with it, something smashed into the back of his head.

The world hazed to black. Juaan did not even feel it when he hit the ground.

***

Chapter 1

AWAKENING

The boy awoke. His eyes stung and watered as he forced the lids open. He blinked to clear his vision. His stomach roiled, and he drew a deep breath against the wave of nausea. He immediately wished he hadn't. The air was thick and acrid in his lungs, and a sharp pain in his side lanced through him. The boy rolled onto his knees, coughing and retching until his throat felt raw.

Finally, he sat up. The world turned before his eyes.

"Ah!" he groaned, as his hand went to his head. A point behind his left ear throbbed painfully. He could feel a lump growing under his bruised skin. When he brought his hand back, red fluid stained his fingers. The world tilted again.

"You wake?" A rough voice demanded from close by.

Startled, the boy looked up. A large man was sitting upon a fallen tree, watching him. Hairy coverings swathed his bulky frame. A large skull dangled from one hand. The man's pale features were pale and coarse, marred by several scars. His forehead was high and sloping, the nose broad and his lips wide. But the most striking feature was a mane of fiery red hair erupting from his scalp. A powerful emotion stirred within the boy's heart as he met the glittering black eyes. Hate? Fear?

Should he hate this man? He frowned. Who was this man? The first fluttering of unease curled through the boy's stomach. Where was he?

"Where the woman who gave this?" the stranger interrupted his thoughts, as he thrust the long, thick spear that he held in his massive fist towards the boy. The boy took in the weapon dumbly. The wood was darkened with use and age, but at the top, deep carvings scored the surface just beneath the stone tip. Part way down the haft was a black ring of hardened material. The spear had once been broken, and the halves fused back together.

Nothing about it was familiar, and the boy shook his head, not knowing how to respond.

"Tell me!" The man shot to his feet with a speed that belied his bulk. Expression black with fury, he advanced on the boy, raising the butt of the spear high. "Tell me where!"

Terrified, the boy scrambled backwards. He raised his arms to shield his head, but even as he cowered down, a sudden wave of defiance arose from within. *No.* He pushed himself to his feet and met the stranger's eyes squarely, as he raised his chin. He would not bow.

But his actions only maddened his attacker further. With a snarl, the big man brought the haft of the spear crashing down. The boy found he could only stand there, watching as the weapon raced towards his face. He could not have moved, even to save his life.

A voice called out, and the spear halted a mere hair's breadth from his cheek. With a frustrated growl, the red-haired man turned to another of the strange men standing away in the trees. Smoke smouldered from the cracked and blistered bark.

Trembling, the boy sank to his knees again as his attacker moved away to speak with the one who had called for his attention. The world swam. He tried to clear his thoughts; tried to remember how he had got here while fighting the panic that was threatening to set in. The boy looked around. He was in a forest. Massive trees surrounded them, almost too large to be comprehended. Their branches twisted together in a way that was peculiar and yet oddly familiar. He felt the urge to climb into one of them, but could not understand why he should do that. The trunks of the trees were blackened and burned. Dead leaves rattled in the breeze. The sight brought with it an overwhelming wave of sadness... and emptiness. But more than anything else, the boy was aware of a pain in his chest. It was not the physical pain he felt. That would heal in time. This pain went deeper. He had lost something. Something important and its absence had left a hole in his heart. The space at his side yawned. He rubbed fretfully at his forehead.

The boy studied his body, desperate to find a clue, something to make him remember. He was dressed in woven green leaves and plant matter. The coverings felt tough and leathery and they fit too tightly, chaffing at his skin here and there. He shifted his attention to the men that surrounded him. They were all dressed in thick furs of varying shades of grey and black. A far cry from his own coverings.

A few of the men's eyes followed him as he staggered to his feet and limped forward. The boy kept his eyes on them in return, unwilling to turn his back. But in watching them, he did not give enough attention to the ground beneath his unsteady feet, and he tripped on something heavy and soft. With a soft cry of alarm, he came down on top of the object, only just catching himself on his hands. His left arm almost gave out beneath his weight. The elbow was bruised.

The boy looked down and blank, dead eyes stared straight back up at him. "Agh!" The boy threw himself back and staggered away from the body. Nausea clawed up his throat. Doubling over, he began to wretch again. Low laughter broke out from his fur-clad audience at his expense.

Bracing his hands on his knees, the boy forced himself to look back at the corpse upon the ground. The light red-gold skin of the fallen man, dulled with the grey cast of death, hung upon his bones. His black hair thrown was out around him, an expression of horror twisted forever upon his frozen face. He would have been small. Clearly an adult, the man would still have only stood level with the boy's ear. The blank eyes were large and his ears tapered to a subtle point. But what held the boy's attention was the man's attire. It matched his own. The boy quickly studied his own hands, and felt his ears, but his hopes of an answer were immediately dashed. His skin was a shade darker, the shape of his ears more rounded. He was not the same.

"Boy." The gruff command came from behind him. He turned to see the red-haired giant approaching. That wave of intense dislike swept through the boy again. "Tell me where others went. I need know."

Others? The boy glanced around. *What others?* His lack of an answer only aggravated the man. A large hand flashed out and caught him right across the mouth. The boy's lip split as he went down in a heap. Hot tears of anger prickled in his eyes as he sat up and wiped at his bleeding mouth. He glared up at the large man who loomed over him, and forced his tears away. He would not give this beast the satisfaction of seeing him cry.

"Tell me where went!" the man demanded again, raising his hand once more.

"I don't know!" the boy screamed back at him. "I don't know. I don't know!" He put his head in his hands and rocked back and forth. The pain in his skull throbbed. He felt his head would surely burst.

"Don't know?" The beast's voice lowered as he caught the boy's chin in his gnarled hand, forcing his face up. "What you remember?"

The boy's eyes flickered around again, trying to find something familiar, anything that would bring him comfort. His panic was rising again, threatening to choke him. The beast's eyes were cutting, cruel, and without mercy.

"You no remember anything!" It was not a question. "What your name?"

And the boy couldn't answer. He didn't even know his own name. The panic overtook him and he broke into helpless sobs. "I don't know." His head throbbed. The world spun, fading around him once more as he collapsed onto his aching side. "I don't know!"

***

CHAPTER 2

FOUND

"Rannac!"

The raknari warrior looked up as the Chief of the Hunting Bear clan barged his way into the hide shelter in which he waited. A body was slung over Eldrax's burly shoulder. Rannac rose to his feet as the Chief slung the limp figure onto the ground before him with a dull thump.

"Tell me, Rannac." Eldrax jabbed a thick finger at the skinny form wrapped in tattered leaves. "Tell me what you see."

Rannac's dark brow pinched together as he crouched over the unconscious form. An elf-witch boy? His eyebrows rose. Eldrax rarely bothered capturing male elves. But then the seasoned warrior's eyes moved to the slack face, and his heart skipped a beat. Not an elf witch. Not entirely. *To all the gods,* Rannac thought in dismay. *It* can't *be.* But he could not deny the truth of what was right before his eyes. A Forbidden hybrid. And not just any hybrid. Part Cro, part elf-witch. Rannac had only known of one such child in existence.

Before him, battered and unconscious, lay the son of Juran, Chief of the Black Wolf clan. Rannac's own brother. The last time he had seen his brother, Juran had lain dead among the remains of his destroyed clan. It had been countless seasons before that since Rannac had seen his brother alive. The last time being the day Juran had banished him from the Black Wolf. But time had not warped his memory. He could still see his brother standing clearly in the high plains of this boy's cheekbones, in the angle of his eyes. He could also see *her*.

Rannac envisioned the elf-witch standing before him as clearly as if it were yesterday. The fateful day he had lain broken in the foothills of the Mountains so long ago, watching her shield her babe from him as though his gaze alone would harm the child. He remembered the fierce flash of her indigo eyes.

"It's him, isn't it?" Eldrax was pacing the hide shelter like an agitated bull ox, raking a hand through his red mane. "The child of the witch that was denied to me. The son of my enemy."

The affirmation lodged in Rannac's throat. His once broken leg throbbed. After everything he had suffered to keep this boy and his mother from his Chief's clutches, here he was, lying helpless at his feet. Fate was a cruel master.

"Answer me!" Eldrax snarled as his pale face twitched.

"Yes," Rannac croaked. Then louder. "Yes. It is him."

"Of course it is! How could he not be? This was in his hand." A hint of old madness glinted in his black eyes as Eldrax thrust a long, thick spear towards Rannac. Carvings curled around the haft below the tip. Thal runes. Hardened pitch fixed two once-broken halves together. Like the boy at his feet, Rannac would know that weapon anywhere.

Do not *drop that spear again!* He had admonished her. *Never hesitate. Go!*

Eldrax spun the weapon in his hand. "I knew it was him. I just wanted you to admit it and know you failed, Old Wolf. Your misguided defiance that day came to nothing, and no punishment I dealt could be more cruel. I won." He barked a harsh laugh and continued pacing. "Green eyes, green eyes." Rannac heard him mutter, but he ceased listening.

I'm sorry, boy.

"Now. What to do with him?" The Red Bear was back at the boy's side, looming, unpredictable as a storm. "The son of Juran should die."

Rannac clenched his fists. "My Chief."

"He defied me, Rannac," Eldrax cut him off. "Denied me a desire, just as his cursed mother once did. It would be sweet revenge to take what *she* so coveted." The voice turned into a growl, the spear poising above the boy's exposed throat.

"Eldrax." Rannac had to seize upon all his vast experience as a warrior and a hunter to keep his voice low, when all he wanted to do was tackle the Red Bear to the ground. But that would not help either him or Juran's boy. "To kill him would be a waste. You wish to possess witch children. One lies before you."

Eldrax grunted. "He is not mine. Thanks to this raid, I have many elf women to Claim. I do not need this scrawny bag of bones." He jabbed the boy with a fur-wrapped toe.

"But you cannot guarantee the witches' survival, or their strength in magic. Not one has yet survived beyond their trees, Eldrax. Only this boy's mother has ever done so. It would be a folly to waste him. At least for the moment. If you do father a witch child of your own, then do with the boy as you please. Until then, keep him under your protection. He might have the power you desire."

"Still seeking to serve your brother, Rannac, or me?" The black eyes narrowed.

The boy's fate hung on a breath. "Yours, Eldrax." Rannac held his Chief's gaze without blinking.

The Red Bear snorted. "I cannot guarantee his loyalty. He is an outsider."

"So was I," Rannac reminded his Chief. "My brother banished me from my birth clan after my failed Challenge for leadership. Your father accepted me into his own. I owed him my life and served him well. As I now serve you."

"*Her* insolence burns in him," Eldrax said, as though he had not heard. "I can see his hate for me blazing from his eyes."

"We raided the only home he has known." Rannac said in an effort to placate his Chief. "It is to be expected. We can change—"

"No." Eldrax shook his head. "That is not the reason. He cannot remember. He can't even remember his own name." The wide mouth twisted. "I hit him too hard."

"He remembers nothing?"

"No."

Rannac absorbed that for a moment, letting his sorrow for the boy pass, before seizing the opportunity the situation presented. "Then the boy has no idea to whom he should be loyal. He is yours to mould, my Chief. His mother was strong. He could be everything you have hoped to find. You have had my guidance since you were a boy, Eldrax, and you still have it now. Let the boy live and serve you. If he betrays you... I will be the one to end him."

"You'll pledge your life to that, Old Wolf?" The Red Bear raised a ruddy eyebrow, but Rannac could see his will wavering as the desire for vengeance gave way to reason and desire.

"Yes." Rannac tipped his chin.

"If I allow him to live, he can know nothing of his past." The tip of the spear was suddenly at Rannac's own throat. The older warrior forced his bunching muscles to hold still as Eldrax growled his command. "To him, I am his saviour. He will be mine, as his mother should have been." The spear tip pressed harder against Rannac's jugular. "You will ensure he swears the oath of loyalty to me as his Chief before the turn of the seasons, Old Wolf, do you understand? I cannot suffer a rogue male in my camp." Very carefully, Rannac dipped his chin and the spear tip dropped. Eldrax's wide lips then lifted into a smile as the Chief appraised the unconscious boy. "Hmmm, yes. I think I prefer it this way. Juran's son growing to serve me." The smile vanished. "And I will not forget how he stood against me this day. There are more fitting punishments than death if one is patient. And I can be patient. Very well, Rannac, I will let him live. Watch him until I return."

With that, the Red Bear swept from the shelter, no doubt to gloat over his other new, doomed acquisitions.

Rannac blew out a breath, then sank onto his haunches next to Juran's son. "You had better prove to be extraordinary, boy," he growled. "For both our sakes."

***

CHAPTER 3

TRAPPED

"*Juaan?*"

He dashed away the tears that had formed in his eyes as he heard Nyriaana approach him, her feet rustling in the dried leaves on the ground. He was facing the outer forest, his back to the eshaara grove where his mother's tribe dwelt.

"Juaan, I've been looking everywhere for you?" her little voice chided. "What are you doing here? It's nearly dark?"

"I don't belong here," Juaan whispered, barely audible.

She either heard or felt the words, for Nyri was at his side in an instant, her wide indigo eyes searching his face fearfully. "Yes, you do," she said, a hint of desperation in her voice. "Mama promised to look after you. You are my *family."*

Juaan wanted very much to smooth her crinkled brow with his thumb, to ease her worry, but he could not. "Only because Sefaan gave her no other choice. I have no place here, Nyri. I cannot even grow one insignificant honey plant." Juaan kicked at the leaves in frustration. "Your papa is right. How is someone like me going to help feed the tribe?"

Juaan remembered the scorn in Talaan's eyes as he had failed to make the seed in his hand sprout. The Great Spirit would not come to him. He could not channel the energy of the earth to speed up the plant's growth. He could not perform tasks even the youngest of the Ninkuraaja children had mastered. "I should just leave."

A vibration against his latent senses told him just how much these words affected the little girl at his side. "Leave me?" He brought his gaze around in time to see her lips tremble.

"Oh, Nyri," he sighed, and closed his eyes so he would not have to see the pain on her face. She could not understand.

"Here." She bumped Juaan's arm with her fist. "I fetched these for you."

Juaan peeked down at her hand. In her small but strong fingers, Nyri held out a bunch of red berries. His favourite. Juaan's shrunken stomach snarled. He had not eaten since the previous day. After his failure to prove his use before Talaan, before the entire tribe, he had not dared to take a share of the tribe's meager gatherings.

"You shouldn't have risked taking them for me," he scolded softly. Furies were getting longer, harsher. The Ninkuraaja were finding it harder to influence their trees to produce enough to feed their tribe. "The Elders will punish you."

There was a flicker of apprehension in her eyes as Juaan said this, but she raised her chin bravely. "You need to eat, too."

Juaan sighed and took a few bites. The sweet taste exploded in his mouth and the soft flesh of the fruits eased the ache in his empty stomach.

"You're not going to leave?" Her small voice was uncertain.

"No one wants me here."

"I want you," Nyri declared and seized his hand in hers. Her fingers barely fitted around his, but he felt their strength as she let her unguarded emotions flow through their contact. Adoration, protectiveness and

an edge of proprietary. He was hers. Juaan's lips twitched. He would never understand what it was she saw in him that was worthy of such pure affection. Nevertheless, his heart warmed. Her presence drove out the hopelessness that lurked in the darkness of his soul.

"Will you stay with me, Juaan?" she asked.

There was only one answer he could give. By her side was where he belonged. Where he would always belong. Juaan folded his fingers around Nyri's and squeezed. "To the end."

Images flickered. They taunted on the edges of his awareness, shadows of a life. He reached for them, but they skittered back into the darkness of his mind, leaving him lost and utterly alone.

Someone prodded him in the side. Agony flared like a lightning strike along his ribs.

The boy shot upright with a cry on his lips. Fighting to focus, he twisted his head around, trying to make sense of his surroundings. The light was dim, but it was not the usual fading of twilight. Something was blocking the brightness of the day. A swathe of material that rippled and snapped in the wind enclosed him on all sides, stretching over his head, supported by wooden poles. He fought to control his breathing as the sensation of entrapment closed around him. The air was cloying, musty. He needed to get out. A fresh breeze ruffled over the boy's face, drawing his attention to an opening in the stretched material. An opening to freedom. He rolled over and crawled on his hands and knees towards it.

"Naruk, du mu," a voice barked.

The boy yelped in alarm. He whipped around to face the far end of the enclosed space and the presence he had hitherto missed. The shadows shifted and morphed into the figure of a crouched man who leaned upon a long spear. Intense grey eyes gleamed from a lined, brown-skinned face. The boy backed away. He had to get away from these fur-clad men. He had to get back to the trees, back to the forest. These new surroundings he had woken to were only adding to his panic.

The new stranger rose to his feet in one smooth motion. The boy rolled to his own in response and fled.

He did not make it two strides before a powerful hand closed around his arm. The boy thrashed against the hold, flailing his free fist as he tried to land a kick on his assailant. He was on the ground before his mind could even process what had happened. He cried out in fear and pain as the man forced his right arm up behind his back.

That was when he felt it. A ball of heat was growing in his chest, building, building. The boy ceased struggling, bewildered by the fire twisting inside him, begging to be unleashed. Some deep-set instinct told him he could use it to hurt the man who was pinning him to the ground, if only he knew how to loose it.

But the instant he stopped struggling, the stranger released his arm and stepped away. As soon as he did, the energy inside dispersed, melting away into the shadows of his soul as quickly as it had made itself known. The boy shuddered and rolled carefully onto his back, readying himself for the next attack. But the man had backed away and was now crouched at the far end of the space once more. He held both hands up, palms outward. A thrill of shock went through the boy at the sight of the two missing fingers on the man's left hand.

The gesture was placatory, but the boy did not relax his tense posture. He held still as he studied the man. This half-handed one was not as bulky as the red-haired monster from the forest, and the boy guessed he was not as tall. The body under the furs was wiry and lean. The boy's eyes drifted to the face. Sharp cheekbones cut across the harsh lines and crags that framed a long, crooked nose. Stubbly fur covered the defined jaw. Long hair bound in a twisting tail trailed over his left shoulder. Streaks of grey marred the deep brown at the man's temples.

The man's eyes were direct and piercing. A jagged scar slashed his right eyebrow, missed his eye, and trailed to an end just below his cheekbone. Even if the boy had not already experienced the ease with which this man could subdue him, he could see that before him was a man to be reckoned with. A thousand battles were scrawled into each line of his face.

The boy swallowed. "Who are you?" He hoped the red-headed giant had not sent this man to demand more answers from him.

The stranger simply pointed at him with a scarred and calloused hand, then at the opening on the far side of the covering that surrounded them. He shook his head firmly.

The boy took the meaning. He was not to escape. Despite his fear, he set his jaw and glared at the man. Who was he to tell him where he could go?

The brown skin at the corners of the grey eyes crinkled in amusement. It was not the same mocking amusement that had been in the eyes of the red-haired beast in the forest. This man liked his defiance, even though they both knew it would get him nowhere, hence the amusement.

"Where am I?" the boy demanded.

The man cocked his head, then pointed at his ear and made a swift cutting motion with his hand, shaking his head again. The boy was unsure of what to make of this. Did this gesture mean the man could not hear?

"He no understand elf speak," the rough voice came from behind.

The boy leapt to his feet. The red-haired giant was standing right behind him. He had approached so silently that the boy had not been aware of his presence. The man towered over him, his shaggy head bowed under the covering above.

"Let me go," the boy demanded as bravely as he could.

The red-headed giant regarded him for a long moment before cuffing him around the head with enough force to send him to his knees.

"I the only reason you alive, boy," the red-headed giant snarled. "Owe me life. You respect me, I protect and look after. You no respect me, I take away life just like that." He snapped his thick fingers.

The boy rubbed the side of his bruised face, but held his tongue. He had good sense. He was under no illusion that the giant meant every word he said.

The red-head sank into a squat before him. "I Eldrax," he said. "Chief of the Hunting Bear clan."

The boy had the feeling he was supposed to be impressed. He kept his face composed and his mind open, hoping to learn something that might help him break past the blank wall in his memory.

The lack of a reaction to the arrogant introduction irked the red-head. "You honoured to sit before me, boy," he growled. "You lucky Rannac there convince me he like you, give you chance to be part of clan. He tell me you be useful."

The boy frowned towards the grey-eyed man crouching in the shadows.

"You half elf-witch? You have power inside you?" Eldrax poked his arm.

The boy's eyes shot up before he could think to control his reaction, remembering the coiling heat building in his chest like a tide. The chief, Eldrax, caught the unguarded moment, and a triumphant grin split across his face. "Then Rannac was right. I keep you, boy."

"No!" the boy burst out before he could stop himself.

The ruddy eyebrows lowered and a dangerous glint came to the black eyes. "You no defy me, boy. Learn fast, no one defy me unless they want to die."

"Please," the boy begged, desperation driving out his pride. "Please, just let me go back to the trees. I need to go back to the forest."

"Why?" The red-headed chief cocked his head.

The boy opened his mouth to tell him, but no words would come. All he knew was that there was an emptiness inside his heart. He had lost something, and he needed to go back to the trees to find it. But he couldn't remember what it was he had lost or why he needed it so badly.

"Why you want go back?" Eldrax pressured, his thick lips twisting.

The boy dug his fingers into the ground beneath him, fighting the tears burning behind his eyes. "I don't know," he whispered into the ground.

The chief laughed, and the boy flinched from the sound. "You no want to go back. Believe me, boy. Elves kill you. I saved you from that fate. Elves hate half-breed like you. You Forbidden!"

Forbidden.

A shiver swept up the boy's spine. Blurred images flickered through his mind, overshadowed by fear and resentment. He thought he saw the shadow of a small black-haired boy, his sharp face twisted with hate. But the vision dissipated before the small boy's features fully formed. He shook his head and lifted his hands to press his palms to his aching temples.

"Come with me back to Hunting Bear camp on Northern Plain. Cro clan the only place you be safe. I protect you, boy. No one else accept Forbidden half-breeds like us." The big man pounded his chest.

No, no, that's not true, his mind screamed. He had been accepted, somewhere, somehow; his heart knew it and wanted to return to that.

He dashed the tears from his eyes and set his jaw. "No. I don't believe you. I don't want to be a part of your clan."

Eldrax shot to his feet, his pale face reddening. "You will serve me or I kill you now and throw your corpse to the wolves!"

The boy scrambled back, but he had nowhere to run. The monster's enormous bulk blocked the only escape, but he would not submit. He would not let go of this one piece of knowledge. The whole of his being knew it to be true. He had been loved, and this chief would not convince him otherwise. The pale fists balled.

Suddenly, the half-handed man, who had been waiting patiently in the corner throughout the entire exchange, was at his side. His movements were as lithe and sure as a tree cat. He raised his hands to his fuming chief. It was a placating, calming movement. The grey eyes held the black steady. The older warrior spoke to his chief in a deep, soothing voice that held an understated power. Even this most terrifying of men respected the one called Rannac, for the chief calmed and turned away with a snort, waving a hand dismissively.

"You lucky Rannac likes you, boy," he threw over his shoulder as he walked from the shelter. "But you better pray to the gods that you prove useful to me if wish to enjoy protection. Patience is not one of my strengths."

And with that, he was gone.

***

CHAPTER 4
NEW HORIZON

Rannac put his hands on the boy's quaking shoulders. The child flinched under his touch and tried to pull away. A low hiss emitted between his lips as the startling green eyes came around to warn him off. He was still ready to fight, despite being outmatched.

"Such a spirit will serve you well, boy. Now hold still." Rannac reached for the bleeding wound under the youngster's left ear.

The boy balked and made to bite his hand. Rannac whistled. "But too much spirit will get you killed. I'm not trying to hurt you." He held up a wad of furs, dabbing it to the back of his own ear, before pointing to the boy's wound.

A slender hand came up to touch the bruised and bloodied area. The boy winced, then frowned at the wad in Rannac's hand. Rannac watched as he deciphered his offer of help. Still scowling, the child turned away and gave no more resistance, ignoring him. Rannac assumed this meant he would allow Rannac to tend to his wound.

"That's better. Now hold still." Taking a water-skin from his waist, Rannac washed the wound clean. He probed lightly with his fingers. Thankfully, the Red Bear had not cracked the boy's skull, which was more than Rannac could say for his ribs. Bruising already forming over the ridges of the boy's chest beneath his scant garments. He touched the area experimentally and the boy let out a muffled mewl of pain. Yes, cracked.

"Take those leaves off," he ordered. "They're not doing much for you, anyway."

The child stared at him.

"Off."

A stream of what he thought might be curses flung at him as Rannac took matters into his own hands and tore the tattered leaves from the boy's back. *The gods.*

The youngster was just a couple of winters shy of entering manhood. His body promised a tall, rangy man. Not as tall as his father, thanks to his elf blood, but imposing enough. He should already fill some of that potential, but malnourishment had robbed him of it. He was little more than skin and bone.

"We need to feed you up, boy," Rannac said as he bound strips of hide tightly around the youngster's ribs. It must have hurt, but the boy stared stalwartly ahead, his jaw set, determined not to show weakness to an enemy.

Task complete, Rannac spied a pouch made from a single leaf dangling at the boy's hip. "What's that?" He reached out to touch it.

The speed of the youngster's reaction surprised even Rannac, and the boy scored a blow to his hand, knocking it away. He then spun, opening a wide space between them, lithe as a spear cat, then stood tense, one hand hovering protectively over the pouch.

Rannac blinked. Even if the boy had none of his mother's witch power, he would give the rest of his fingers on his left hand to train this boy in the arts of the raknari. Rannac had taught many boys to become defenders of the clan, but this youngster had just displayed a raw potential Rannac had rarely seen. It flowed through his veins.

"You would make your father proud, boy," he muttered, knowing the child would not understand him, then spoke louder. "Alright, I will not touch your treasure." Rannac raised his hands, watching the usual reaction to his maimed left paw cross the boy's angular features. "Here." He reached into a leather pouch at his own waist and withdrew a piece of cured meat. "You must be hungry. You've no more flesh on you than a rabbit."

The boy did not approach, so Rannac tossed the morsel to the ground at his feet. "Eat." He made his meaning clear by raising another piece of flesh to his mouth, tearing off a bite.

He was starving. Rannac could almost hear the shrunken stomach growl. The stubborn set to the boy's face wavered and Rannac saw his throat close with need. He gave in. Without taking his eyes off Rannac, he stooped and snatched the offered morsel from the ground. He sniffed at it, wrinkled his nose, then took a tentative bite.

His expression when the meat touched his tongue drew a chuckle from Rannac's throat. "First taste of flesh, eh? You'll soon get used to that."

Sooner than Rannac thought, hunger overcame distaste, and the scrap was gone within moments. The pinched face turned towards him, all suspicion evaporating in the wake of his need as a scrawny arm extended in a silent plea. "Eat?" The boy repeated the word back to him.

"A fast learner, too." Rannac removed the whole pouch from his hip and placed all of his rations in the waiting hand. He could easily catch another few rabbits on the journey home. Rannac preferred fresh meat in any case.

The boy sank to the ground, tore open the neck of the pouch and descended on the offering, seeming to forget about Rannac in his need. Rannac fought the urge to jab him in the side, scold him for taking his eyes off an enemy. There could be no need great enough for that. But he stilled his twitching fingers. There would be time to teach the boy. The most important thing now was gaining this lost boy's trust and, ultimately, his loyalty to the clan before Eldrax snapped both their necks.

It appeared Rannac had already earned some of that trust, or at least, the boy now saw him as the lesser of two evils. He leapt behind Rannac as the hides in the temporary shelter parted and Eldrax reappeared for the third time to check on his unexpected prize.

The Chief grunted. "We're breaking camp. The scouts can find no more of the witches hiding in the trees." He scowled at the boy lurking behind Rannac. "I hope the walking skeleton is strong enough to make the journey."

Rannac glanced at the slender figure, seeing the green fire blazing in the depths of his eyes. His lips tugged. "I'd say so."

"Then bring him." The Red Bear disappeared. With his departure, the boy appeared to diminish. The pain, fear and exhaustion that he was unwilling to show in front of his enemy sapped the will from his limbs.

"None of that," Rannac slapped him sharply on the back, straightening him. "Never let your fire die, you hear me, boy?"

The youngster glared at him for the blow.

"That's right, be furious at me if you need to be. Now here." Rannac removed the fur cloak swathed around his neck and slung it around the boy's bare shoulders. "The wind across the Plains is unforgiving. I'll have Halima fashion you proper coverings when we make it back to camp." He glanced down at the boy's bare feet and sucked his teeth. "You'll know about those before journey's end."

The boy flinched under the fur, his skin appearing to recognise an unfamiliar touch, even if his mind did not.

"It won't bite." Rannac grabbed his upper arm and propelled him from the shelter. "Not anymore."

The rest of the hunters were already collapsing the temporary dwellings. Eldrax stalked between them, barking orders, never still, impatient to be on the move. His reasoning was clear. A group of five elf-witch women crouched, huddled together amid the chaos. Already their light red-gold skin appeared sallow in the naked light of day. Terror bulged in their large eyes as their attention tore between their captors and the open sky above.

Rannac shook his head. They would be dead before Nanna grew fat in the night sky. The thought of Eldrax's giant form siring a witch-child on one of these scraps of women was laughable. Whatever secret Juran had found in keeping this boy's mother alive had gone to the Great Hunting Grounds of the Sky with him.

"Lorhir. Galahir." Rannac barked. At his summons, two adolescents broke away from the rest of the group and came towards him. Opposites they were. Galahir was pale and yellow-haired, with eyes like the sky. Just entering manhood, he was already filling out the broad frame his Thal mother had gifted him. He would never be as tall as Eldrax. No Deni blood ran in his veins, but he would come close in bulk.

Lorhir, dark-skinned and dark eyed, stalked in Galahir's shadow. He was pure Cro and almost as willowy as the lost boy standing at Rannac's side. Surviving a snake bite as a youngster, the ordeal had taken its toll on his body.

Rannac often had misgivings over Lorhir's strength, pondering whether the boy would have been better left as a regular hunter. Physically, it appeared he would never survive the rigorous test all boys joining the ranks of the raknari had to pass. But the boy had one of the fiercest wills Rannac had ever known, and Lorhir's speed and suppleness made up for whatever he lacked in might. Against all odds, Lorhir had survived and become the best of the young men currently under Rannac's wing.

"Who is this?" Lorhir jabbed a finger at Juran's son. Green met brown as both boys sized each other up. Galahir simply tilted his head, regarding the newcomer with his usual slow, considering manner.

"I'm not sure yet," Rannac said. "But the Chief wants him and he is now under my protection until he learns our ways. I am done here." He indicated the shelter behind him. The two adolescents obeyed without question. But Rannac did not miss Lorhir's eyes lingering suspiciously upon the half-elf boy. Adoption into a clan for males was rare. Lorhir was no doubt wondering what was special enough about this boy to stop the Red Bear from killing him on sight. Rannac sighed. Lorhir never could get past his insecurities. It was a severe flaw.

His two proteges soon dismantled the shelter, and they were ready to depart. Eldrax moved to the head of the group, the great bear skull already in place upon his head concealing his features. Not that a mask of bone would hide his identity from any who saw him.

The elf women cried out, struggling ineffectually as they were picked up and borne away from their forest.

"Come, boy." Rannac kept his hand firm on the lost boy's arm, pulling him along as the raiding group moved forward. The boy dug his heels in, resisting Rannac's grip, a look of pure desperation on his face as he turned back towards the trees they were leaving behind. The crushed look in his eyes tugged upon even Rannac's calloused heart, but there was no time for sympathy, no time for want. Such things were a weakness, and this boy needed to be strong. That lesson began now. Rannac pushed him on, forcing him to turn to the beckoning horizon. "Whatever life you had there is lost now, boy." He said gruffly. "Better to forget. A new life awaits."

***

CHAPTER 5

FORETOLD

Eldrax prowled through the dark. Night had fallen. His company slumbered, heedless of his restless feet, as he paced between them. More than once, his eyes flickered restlessly to the boy seated on the ground next to Rannac. The oversized cloak about his shoulders made him appear even more pathetic than he had looked wrapped in elf leaves. Eldrax could see the need to sleep pulling on the raw-boned body, but those green eyes refused to close. The boy was toying with the green pouch tied at his hip, a frown slashing his brow. Now and then he tugged at the tied neck, but the knots would not give way to him, and so the boy gave up. He appeared reluctant to tear the pouch to get to the contents inside.

Eldrax snorted and resumed his pacing. It could not be him. The son of his most hated enemy could not be the one. *Answer me,* Eldrax hissed into the recesses of his mind. But the voices he had heard so long ago remained silent. They had not spoken to him since the day he had let himself be outsmarted by an elf-witch. The day Eldrax had felt his own mortality threatening to reach out and steal the fight from his body. He stole more glances at the stripling. *Not him. Not him. It has to be one of* mine.

Eldrax crouched with his hands on his knees, recalling the vision he had witnessed. Through hardship, blood and storm, he had pursued that witch. Their dance had ended on a crumbling cliff edge. With the thrill of triumph singing through his veins, Eldrax had held her at bay. And as he threatened to crush the skull of Juran's infant spawn in his hand, he had almost had her on her knees. Everything he ever wanted, all that he had risked the loyalty of his men for; killed his own mother for, kneeling before him and willing to submit.

But Juran's mate had surprised him with her will to save her newborn infant and escape. Eldrax gritted his teeth at the memory of how he had let his rage get the better of him, how he had let the witch goad him into following her on to that crumbling pinnacle. Even now, a cold sweat would break out on Eldrax's brow when he remembered the rocks disintegrating beneath his feet and the gut-wrenching fall into the abyss.

He should have died that day. The rocks had beaten and broken his body, burying him alive at the bottom of the ravine, but he had not died. Fate had spared his life. It was not done with him yet. Eldrax closed his eyes, seeking the answers that tormented him with their absence.

The rocks rumbled into stillness. They pressed down on his body, threatening to drive the last of the breath from his lungs. Eldrax cried out in rage and agony, feeling his broken bones shift. Outwitted by a witch! Eldrax howled again.

He pushed at the rocks holding him prisoner with his good right hand. His left lay mangled and broken at his chest. The stones shifted and grumbled, refusing to budge. Eldrax fought harder, the first stirrings of panic cracking through his blood fury. He was Chief of the Hunting Bear Clan! With the death of his rival, Juran of the Black Wolf, he was now the most powerful man on the Plains. He would not die under a pile of rocks.

His struggles loosened a stone above his head. Falling, it cracked against his skull, turning the world black.

Eldrax did not know how long he lay there, hazing in and out of consciousness. All the light was extinguished. I'll be joining you soon, mother, *he thought to the dark, feeling her dried blood crack on his hands.*

Eldrax.

He started at the sound of his name being whispered. He strained his eyes into the darkness, seeking the speaker, but he was alone.

Eldrax. *The voice hazed across his ear like a breath of a lover. But there was no warm stirring of the stagnant air against his flesh. Instead, ghostly fingers brushed across the inside of his skull. He balked, shaking his head, but the fingers sank in, drawing a snarl of pain from his parched lips.*

Saviour. *The voice whispered inside his mind.* Saviour of Mankind.

And with those words, the fevered madness inside Eldrax's centre soothed and the raging river of his soul grew calm. He saw everything then with startling clarity. He saw the giant monsters that had chased him from the site of the Black Wolf's demise issuing from the black forest. They rushed forth to meet a gathering of men on a bloody Plain, he, Eldrax, at their head. As the battle turned, a flash of light blinded all, and a being with golden skin came down to earth.

Enlil... *the voice whispered,* Nunamnir. Stirring. Killed his Nephilim. Bring end to all. Man must stand together. Find Ninmah's Forbidden children, Eldrax, Child of Enki.

And green eyes, a colour he had never seen, flashed in the darkness of Eldrax's mind. Indigo and green bound together.

Ninmah. Ninmah. *The name echoed through his skull.* Ninmah. *Recognition sparked. It was a name that elf-witch who had found and healed his wounds as a boy had uttered. He had spoken it with the reverence of a deity.* Ninmah's Forbidden children.

His *children. Clarity of purpose and vindication gripped Eldrax's heart. He had been right! He had been right all along to seek the witches. This vision inside his head was telling him so. He had just failed to see the need for them went deeper than a trifling ability to heal. He was destined to defeat the gods themselves! Eldrax's heart sang. The boy whose mother abandoned him. The boy whose father beat and humiliated him would become the saviour of Mankind. A man to be loved and feared wherever the light of Utu touched. And his witch children would help him to such greatness.*

Eldrax awoke. He was still alone and buried in the blackness. The voice had fallen silent, but the meaning of the vision and the certainty of his path remained as a smouldering fire within his heart. He had a destiny, and that meant he was not *going to die here. Renewed strength flowed to his limbs as he kicked loose the stones that trapped him. Broken and twisted, but filled with purpose, Eldrax roared free of the avalanche into the light of a new day.*

That voice. That voice. Eldrax opened his eyes. That voice had saved his life and returned him triumphant to his clan. He had worked hard in the seasons since to make the Hunting Bear the strongest Cro clan on the Plains. Feared. Untouchable. His clan might not love him, but Eldrax did not seek love. Love was a weakness. Fear and respect were all he needed to sleep easily.

Only one accomplishment still eluded him. Siring a witch child. He had captured many elf-witches in the turning of seasons since being denied Juran's feisty mate, but none had shown her strength or courage. All had died. *Find Ninmah's Forbidden children.* The vision of green eyes flashed through Eldrax's memory again, calling his attention back to the scrawny boy at Rannac's side.

No, not him. Eldrax snarled to himself. *But I will enjoy using your son, Juran. If he is useless, then I will spill his blood. If he is what Rannac suspects, then he will serve my purpose as I please. But when I have taken every part of him, and fully bent him to my whim, I vow to you, he will die by my hand. As you should have done.*

Muffled whimpers in the dark drew Eldrax around. The five witches he had captured were clinging together, huddled in fear. *Ninmah, Ninmah.* He heard them cry out in plea. Weak, so very weak. He should not wait for them to fade. Juran's witch had borne him a living child. Perhaps that was the secret. If he put his seed in their bellies right now, perhaps they would strive to live in order to spare the life of their unborn Forbidden children. Ninmah's Forbidden children.

That elf-witch of Juran's would have done anything to preserve her child. Even submitted to him. What a pity he hadn't found her in the forest instead of her spawn. But she must have perished. She would not have allowed her son to fall into his hands had she lived. Eldrax felt the bitter tang of the final denial of that witch flow across his tongue before moving on. He would find another. Eldrax rose, selecting the strongest looking witch as he approached the huddled group. Dark hair and indigo eyes. Just like her.

Perfect.

***

"Nyri Nyri Nyriaana."

"Juaan, please, I need you. Come back... come back."

The screams woke the boy from the doze he had fallen into. He bolted back upright, eyes flying around the camp. A firm hand clamped down on his shoulder, steadying him. The boy lifted his face to the man seated at his side. The grey eyes set in the wolfish, weathered face held his steadily.

Another scream. The boy whipped his head around, his heart pounding as the sound ripped through him, making the hairs on his body prickle. He made to bolt to his feet, but the hand on his shoulder held him in place. The grey-eyed man beside him grunted a few sounds and shook his head slightly. There was a tightness to the skin at the corners of the man's eyes, a sour twist to his mouth. Whatever was happening, this grizzled warrior did not approve.

"Oo, du mu," the man beckoned, trying to guide him to the ground. "Oo."

The boy stared at him, askance. How could he rest? The screams went on and on, tearing against his nerves. Who was being hurt? Why was no one stopping it? The rest of the men were rolled up in their furs. It was obvious the screams of agony had woken most of them, but none were perturbed. A couple even threw their arms over their heads to muffle the sounds and closed their eyes again.

The boy tried once more to get to his feet. If no one else would do something, then he would!

"Naruk, du mu!" The warrior's fingers bit into his bones this time as he restrained him and a stream of sounds flew out in a low warning. The man cut his hand across his own throat and then pointed at the boy. His meaning was obvious. *Move and you will be killed.*

Hot tears prickled in the boy's eyes. Choked by anger and fear, he sagged to the ground and put his hands over his ears, trying to block out the ceaseless sounds of pain and distress. As one set of screams broke off into despairing sobs, the boy relaxed his hands, praying that he had heard the last. But his prayers went unanswered. As the glowing silver crescent in the glittering black sky above sank towards the far horizon, another scream would lift to the heavens.

It was with raw eyes that the boy watched the great shining orb rise over the horizon at dawn, stirring the sleeping men around him. Throwing back their furs, they gathered together their supplies with practiced ease. Morsels were produced and quickly devoured, washed down with liquid from skins at their hips.

A hand nudged his shoulder. The grey-eyed warrior was holding out a dried morsel to him with the remaining fingers of his left hand. The boy's stomach growled. He did not want to accept anything from these strangers, but once again, his need overcame his pride and he snatched the offering from the man's maimed hand.

The rich taste filled his mouth. Something told him the flavour was wrong, strange, and the dry texture stole the moisture from his tongue. But as he swallowed, the easing of his stomach was a sweet relief. The man beside him chuckled and extended another morsel before offering a skin.

"Rannac." The man jerked a thumb at his own chest. "Rannac." He patted with more vehemence when the boy frowned in confusion, forgetting the morsel that was halfway to his lips. Was he supposed to do something? "Rannac, du mu," the warrior insisted again. Comprehension dawned. He was telling the boy his name.

"Rannac." He tested the word on his tongue.

The man's grey eyes crinkled at the sides as he dipped his chin in approval. He then pointed at the boy, a hope flickering across his features as he cocked his head.

Panic clamped a clammy hand around the boy's throat. Nothingness yawned behind him, denying an answer. Who was he? "I don't know," he whispered.

The warrior's hands closed about his upper arms. This time, the hold was not in restraint. Calm and strong, the calloused hands held him steady until he breathed through the terrible sense of disorientation. When at last he was in control, he lifted a resolute face to the warrior. The grey eyes glowed with approval. He patted the boy on the shoulder, murmuring soft words. *Never mind,* the boy read his meaning.

The boy cocked his head. Why was this stranger taking such care of him? The rest appeared indifferent to his presence. All except... No sooner had he thought of him, the hulking red-haired leader strode into view from wherever he had spent the night. The shrewd black eyes made the boy's skin crawl as they swept over him, a lazy smirk curling over the pale lips.

Behind the brute, the boy spied a small group of women. They were of the same species as the dead man back in the forest. Diminutive, with red-gold skin, tapered ears, and dressed in leaves and moss. Their indigo eyes were staring. The boy's throat tightened at the look in them. Their despair, anguish, and hopelessness echoed his own. The boy swallowed. The women's coverings were tattered and torn. Bruises bloomed across patches of exposed skin. He knew he had discovered the source of the screams from the night. He took a hesitant step towards them, drawn by some pull. Perhaps these women had the answers to the darkness in his mind.

A hand closed around his arm. This one was much larger and stronger than Rannac's. "I would not, boy." The red-haired giant growled down at him in the boy's own tongue. "Elf-witches not take kindly to you. Kill you if you go near. Almost killed you before. You lucky they only stole your memories. You Forbidden, like me. I know cruelty to ones such as us. I told you I saved you from their hate. Do not waste my effort."

"I owe you nothing!" the boy spat back. "Monster."

The pale hand cut across his face before he could draw another breath. His ribs screamed as he contacted the hard ground, drawing a cry from his lips. The giant was in his face before he could blink, catching him around the jaw.

"Owe me life again. Could have snapped your worthless neck for that, but I merciful man. You will come to see the truth of my words, boy. And you will be grateful I found you when I did." He released the boy's jaw with a rough shove and strode away.

Sniffing back the burning tears that wanted to break loose, the boy pushed himself back to his feet, his arm winding protectively around his ribs.

Rannac was staring after his departing leader. The boy caught him in an unguarded moment, seeing a flash of concern cross the older man's face before it was smoothed beneath the usual mask of calm. It cracked into a scowl when he looked at the boy, a hiss of disapproval sliding between his teeth. The boy set his jaw. What did he care what this half-handed man thought of him?

He began to limp towards the huddled women again, but Rannac caught him around the scruff and marched him to the centre of the group that was preparing to move out. The pain in his side was too great for the boy to put up much of a fight.

"Lorhir. Galahir." Rannac bit out as the boy found himself deposited in front of the other adolescents he had seen the previous day. They appeared to be a couple of Furies older than he. The big one with startling blue eyes ducked his shaggy head shyly, but the shrewd dark one held the boy's gaze, assessing, just as he had the day before. This lanky youngster was not much bigger than him. The boy felt a familiar wave of dislike as he held the haughty, dark gaze. This boy reminded him of someone, but the answer danced tauntingly out of reach. He strained against the darkness, to no avail. He dropped his head into his hand to rub his aching brow. The swelling behind his ear throbbed, stealing his concentration.

Rannac pushed him forward, forcing him to move along with the column of men, all filing behind the giant man at their head. The boy shuffled along, feeling a peculiar sensation of his heart tearing further in two with each step he took away from the forest, now left far behind. He had to get back there somehow. He had to return. He vowed he would not rest until he had found a way to do so.

The great orb in the sky crept slowly overhead as the journey went on. How far were they to travel? The boy's ribs ached fiercely as he stumbled along, struggling to keep up with the fur clad hunter ranging along ahead of him.

"Du mu." Rannac nudged his shoulder, slipping the boy another morsel of food.

Du mu? Rannac had uttered these sounds whenever he had needed to draw his attention. Was that his name now? Du mu? The boy considered it. It felt wrong, but it was the closest call sign he had had since waking in the forest. Du Mu.

The food lent him strength, but exhaustion tugged on every step. He had not slept since waking in the forest and the lack of rest was taking its toll. But whenever he slowed or faltered, Rannac would jab an unforgiving finger into his back, jolting him back to wakefulness, pressing him along. The older warrior might have been the kindest to him, but it was clear he would suffer no weakness.

The boy, Du Mu, distracted himself by studying the passing land-scape. If he were to return to the forest and find what he had lost, it would be wise to know the return path. The surrounding land was vast, open and rolling, covered in gently waving grasses and rocks of multiple hues. In the distance, huge grey pinnacles rose, cutting a high jagged line on the horizon ahead as they reached for the sky itself.

It was a barren landscape compared to the forest he had left behind. But despite the unnervingly revealing nakedness, Du Mu could not help but feel a vibration in his blood that sang in response to the freedom the vastness offered. The wind brushed across his face, dancing through the waving grass, and Du Mu sucked in its cold, clean fragrance, letting it fuel his fatigued muscles.

He could not guess how these men were finding their way. All the grasses and rocks looked much the same. He wondered where they were taking him, but his exhaustion robbed him of the ability to worry too much. All that mattered was staying on his feet.

When the great orb was high overhead, the hated leader at last raised a fist. The boy muffled a sob of relief when the men immediately sank onto their haunches, unslinging their loads, and shared out rations. Du Mu collapsed to the ground, and this time Rannac let him, pressing another morsel into Du Mu's trembling hands.

But as Du Mu raised the offering to his lips, a flash of red caught his eye. A cluster of bright berries had tumbled from a sling and onto the ground. The boy's throat closed, his mouth watering as an explosion of half images flickered in the recesses of his mind; whispers, a flash of warm indigo, laughter. The sight of them made him both yearn and grieve.

Forgetting Rannac's now unappetising dried morsel, the boy lurched to his burning feet and staggered towards the shining fruit, aching for a taste...

A dark hand flashed out, snatching the berries from the ground before Du Mu could reach them. Letting out a cry of dismay, he whirled towards the one who had stolen the fruit. Lorhir stood there, a smirk playing around his mouth as he bounced the berries in his hand.

A red mist of fury descended over Du Mu's eyes as all the pent-up emotions from the past days boiled to the surface. Du Mu lunged for the older boy, but Lorhir just laughed. Quick as a snake, he kicked out with his leg, cutting Du Mu's feet from beneath him. Du Mu choked, spitting blood as his face hit the ground. Lorhir laughed louder, calling something towards the watching men, who chortled in response over their own meals.

Ignoring his screaming ribs, Du Mu threw himself to his feet and swung at Lorhir with his fist. He did not even get close. His intended blow met empty air. Something hard struck him across the cheekbone, stunning him, and he tasted dirt for a second time. Another blow struck him in the ribs opposite his previous injury, stealing his breath. Then Rannac's voice cut across the air and Du Mu felt Lorhir's looming presence melt away from his side.

A movement in his periphery caught Du Mu's attention as he blinked his eyes open. Galahir was stepping towards him. Du Mu bared his teeth, letting loose a threatening snarl, while simultaneously bracing for whatever this hulking boy might plan to do to him. But Galahir only stiffened, hurt curling across his broad features before he backed away, leaving Du Mu bruised and humiliated in the dirt.

Gritting his teeth, Du Mu sat up, wiping at his bleeding lip until the sound of a snivel cracked through his simmering shame and anger. Lifting his eyes, he saw he had come to rest near the huddled elf-witches. Forgetting the berries and the vile Lorhir, Du Mu staggered back to his feet, drawn once more towards his fellow captives. He did not know if they had eaten. No one appeared to be offering them anything. He spied the uneaten dried morsel Rannac had given him lying on the ground where he had dropped it during his beating. He scooped it up and held out the dried offering as he approached the women.

"Get away, you Forbidden piece of filth!" the nearest snarled in his face. The boy reared back. The vicious expression twisting the fine features hit him harder than the blows he had received from Lorhir. "Half spawn of Ninsiku! This is all your fault. Aardn should have planted that rock on your infant head when she had the chance. Sefaan be damned!"

"I-I..." the boy stammered, shocked to the core. All he had done was try to bring food.

A laugh brought Du Mu around. Eldrax stood there, triumph gleaming in his eyes. "I warned you. You are Forbidden. You do not belong. You belong nowhere, I am your only salvation."

No. No. No. The boy twisted internally, fighting the blank walls inside his mind. It was not true. *Where are you? Where are you?* He thought desperately. *Where's who?* A small inner voice responded. *Who are you looking for?* A sob broke from the boy's throat. He turned his back on Eldrax to face the women. They knew. They knew him. He could see it in their cold regard. Du Mu set his jaw. They were just frightened and in shock. He would prove to them he meant them no harm, that it was not his fault they were here. He was as much a prisoner as they were. Determination strengthened his spine. He would gain their trust, he would know again who he had been, and then he would free himself and them from this monster's grip.

When he faced Eldrax again, his gaze was undaunted and resolute. Du Mu had the satisfaction of seeing a flicker of uncertainty flare to life in the cruel black depths.

***

Chapter 6

LOST BOY

The first of the elf witches died before they reached the foothills of the Mountains. She had stolen a blade from one of her guards and driven it into her own chest. That guard's body now lay beside that of the witch, his throat ripped open to the air.

Rannac kept the trembling boy's face turned away as the first of the vultures swooped down behind them to take the first pick. "Keep moving," he ordered, not letting the youngster focus on the violence he had just witnessed. But he could not shield him from the gore dripping from Eldrax's hands as he stalked at the head of his band. Nor did Rannac want to. This was the boy's new life now. He needed to harden to it fast. "You're not going to vomit again, are you?"

The glare he received belied the greenish cast of the boy's skin.

"Good. Here, drink." Rannac thrust a water skin at him. "I'll not have you waste rations again."

Lorhir had found the boy's weakness in the face of the execution amusing. He was up ahead now, regaling the older hunters with the story, throwing glances over his shoulder at the scowling object of their amusement.

Rannac sucked his teeth. Lorhir's behaviour was unbecoming of a raknari warrior, a clear betrayal of his own fears and weaknesses. As leader of the clan's raknari fighters, it was Rannac's duty to stamp out such flaws.

But an insecure adolescent was the least of his concerns at present. His eyes returned to the Red Bear's back, a frown creasing his brow. Jana had been a skilled hunter. A father to three babes. Now his blood needlessly soaked the Plains.

Rannac had witnessed Eldrax grow out of the dangerous rages that had plagued his adolescent seasons. Ever since the Red Bear had dragged himself back to camp, broken and half dead, a cold, hard purpose had tempered the fevered burning in his eyes. Shedding all the boyish tantrums, the Red Bear had set about making the Hunting Bear the strongest clan on the known ranges. Rannac's fears for Eldrax's rule following the death of his father, Murzuk, had been laid to rest. He had helped his new Chief become the leader the clan had sorely needed.

Only Eldrax's destructive need to possess elf-witches for himself had remained. Over the seasons, he had caught many, and it was their losses that still had the power to stoke the old blood rage within. Rannac had never understood the obsession. Undersized women with underwhelming skills. They did not match the fantastical beings of the Dugnamtar's fireside stories. As the seasons turned, however, sightings of the elf-witches had grown fewer and fewer, until they had almost ceased entirely. Rannac had believed his Chief saved from his madness.

That was until Tanag had brought news from the shin'ar forests. A last stronghold of elves had been found.

Now Jana lay dead. Rannac wondered how many more would suffer before these four remaining witches succumbed to the inevitable. His hand flexed upon his arshu staff. He hoped the sore-footed boy limping ahead of him possessed the skills needed to appease the Chief, allowing him peace.

The Light Bringer, Utu, passed through the sky as they followed Eldrax on the return path to the main Hunting Bear camp. The foothills reached out to embrace them as they left the Southern Plains, then wove and climbed through the twisting valleys and peaks. Eldrax drove a merciless pace, impatient now to return home. Perhaps fearing the loss of another witch, this time to exposure.

Rannac himself kept a close watch on Juran's boy. The fleeting rests and gruelling travel were taking a heavy toll on the untried youngster. His bare feet bled as the unforgiving rocks cut at his skin. He stumbled often, but each time forced himself back upright before Rannac could give him a customary jab in the back. Lines of agony carved into the young face, but he refused to fold.

Pride stirred in Rannac's heart for this boy of his own blood. He fortified himself against it. He owed it to his brother to keep his son alive by teaching him to survive, but that was as far as he could allow himself to go. Rannac could not let himself grow fond of the boy. Such sentiment had no place in his life. The life of a hunter was unforgiving. The life of a raknari was even more so.

Nevertheless, he did not enjoy watching the boy suffer. It was a relief when they began to descend from the foothills on the fifth day of travel, the sight of the Northern Plains opening out below them. Utu's golden rays sparkled off the river that snaked through the vast grasslands and there, tucked into a wide curve of the watercourse, stood the Hunting Bear camp. The smoke from several cooking fires billowed up from the mass of shelters.

Beyond the camp, the Plains continued rushing away north until they ended against a black forest and the soaring Mountains beyond. The Mountains of the Nine Gods.

Rannac shivered despite himself. He had never understood why Eldrax had insisted on founding their main camp upon the site where the Black Wolf, Rannac's birth clan, had met their grizzly end. The memory of what they had found that day would forever haunt Rannac. The day when Eldrax's father, Murzuk, had led a hunting group to poach on Black Bear territory. As a warrior, Rannac was no stranger to the sight of death. But the violence of the Black Wolf's demise was a sight he never wished to witness again. Flesh and bone torn apart, guts and blood strewn; sprayed over the churned winter snows. And then there had been the footprints of the ones who had wrought the destruction. Human footprints. Footprints the length of a man's arm.

Eldrax, young and foolish as he had been, had followed the giant tracks, ignoring the commands of his father and Chief, and entered the distant black forest. And there they had met with the bane of the Black Wolf.

Monstrous giants awaited in the murk. The flash of fear had been clear in even the Red Bear's flinty eyes. They could not fight. The Black Wolf had tried and failed. Rannac had fled for his life along with his Hunting Bear brothers with the monsters in pursuit. Had he not stumbled upon the underground passage and dragged his Chief Murzuk down into it, Rannac knew he would have met the same fate as his brother. Memory of the glowing blue eyes shining out of the blackness still had the power to wake Rannac from his sleep in a cold sweat.

Their stories spoke of such creatures. Watchers, the tales named them. In lifetimes past, they had gifted sacrifices to the forest and the Mountains to appease the gods and return joy to their lives. Rannac's eyes strayed to the soaring peaks ahead. The Sky Gods. The creators of Humankind. It was said they still dwelt in those ranges, after abandoning Man to die. Before that fateful day, Rannac had never known if he accepted the tales passed down from his ancestors as true. But seeing the beasts of the black forest with his own eyes, Rannac could now believe them. What other being would need such guardians if not the gods themselves? And then there had been the underground passage itself. Rannac recalled the smooth, perfectly round stone walls. No man nor beast had made such a passageway.

As much as he had dared, Rannac had argued with Eldrax not to build their home on this threshold to the gods. Their presence so close to the black forest was a dangerous invitation. But Eldrax had not listened to counsel on the matter. Like the child he had not long grown from being, he wanted to possess what had once belonged to his rival: the old power on the Plains. Juran. Eldrax would not be second to any man. Dead or alive. And so here the camp had been founded.

It had taken many seasons for Rannac to rest well. But the monsters of the forest had never so much as blinked a burning blue eye in their direction, much less emerged to slaughter the Hunting Bear. And the rewards of their new home had quickly overshadowed any unseen threat. The camp abutted a bountiful game trail, readily feeding the rapidly growing clan. Eventually, even Rannac had taken one eye off the brooding tree line.

The faint sound of drums rolling across the Plain pulled Rannac back to the present. The outer sentries had sighted the returning column of hunters and the beats pulsed across the air to welcome their return. Spirits lifted, and many of the men increased their pace; the promise of warm campfires, cooked meat, and the embrace of a lover calling them home.

"Take them to Halima," Eldrax barked at the men bearing the remaining elf-witches as soon as the first of the shelters reached out to surround them. "I want them well taken care of." The Red Bear turned to Rannac, hesitated for a moment, then said: "Him, too."

Rannac glanced down at the boy at his side. His green eyes were sweeping the camp, but what the boy made of the sight before him, Rannac could not guess. He wasn't even sure he could take that much in. The child's gaze was bleary with exhaustion as he swayed on his abused feet. The fur cloak Rannac had wrapped around him was sliding off one slender shoulder. He did not have the strength to hold it in place any longer.

"Come, boy," he said, taking him by the arm and propelling him forward.

"To be taken care of by the women, too?" Lorhir sneered from close by.

"Close your mouth, pup," Rannac said. "Otherwise, this one will not be the only one needing care." He swung his arshu staff in the adolescent's direction to drive his point home, the antler tips whistling close by Lorhir's face.

Lorhir scowled and fell silent. Rannac wasted no more time with him. He guided Juran's boy between the shelters, heading for the inner circle and the Dwelling of the UnClaimed. Stares followed him, or rather, they followed his young charge. Hushed whispers brushed against his ears as some craned their heads to get a better look at the strange adolescent that had come among them. Only half conscious, the boy did not meet the curious gazes with the hot defiance he would have given them days just before. Rannac hoped some rest would be enough to return his fire.

Halima's domain was easily twice the size of the other dwellings within the camp. A shelter for the UnClaimed girls who had come of age, and old crones whose mates had since passed on to the Great Hunting Grounds.

"Halima," Rannac called out as he pushed through the billowing entrance.

The matriarch of the Hunting Bear clan was already directing the hunters who had borne the elf women inside. "Hold them," she barked as the witches balked when placed upon a pile of soft furs, behaving as though the skins had leaped up and bitten them.

Rannac felt the familiar tightening of his stomach as the tall, handsome woman straightened to face him. "What can I do for you, Old Wolf?" she asked, the tense lines in the rich skin around her eyes betraying her stress. "Not another one."

"Not quite," he said, pushing his new charge forward into Halima's line of sight.

"A male?" she snorted. "What does Eldrax want with him?" But then the matriarch truly beheld the boy before her, and her dark eyes widened. "Ea above! Is he?"

"A witch-child. Yes. Half Cro, half elf-witch."

"But, how?" The matriarch breathed.

Rannac shrugged a shoulder and said nothing. Eldrax did not want the boy knowing the truth of his parentage. The fewer people who knew of his origins, the better.

"I'm guessing the witch was the mother," Halima circled the boy. "I cannot see a witch male sullying himself with a non-witch female." Her full lips twisted. "Your mother must be an extraordinary witch for you to have survived this long, boy," she said.

She was, Rannac lamented silently.

The boy lifted his gaze to the woman standing before him and Rannac heard Halima's intake of breath. "Such eyes!"

"Hmm. Green is not a colour I have ever encountered. But then, we've never had a half-elf witch in our midst, either."

"What's your name...oh!"

Rannac was in time to catch the scrawny body just before the boy hit the ground. "Easy there, boy, I've got you." The child's eyes fluttered but did not fully open.

"Bring him, Rannac." Halima directed, choosing a pile of furs as far away from the female witches as she could. Wise as ever. "He's exhausted."

Rannac grunted. "He hasn't let himself sleep since we took him from the forest. I'm surprised he's made it this far."

Halima grunted. "Indeed. He looks as if he wouldn't last a day. What do those witches eat? I've yet to see one that is well fed." Halima made a quick study of the boy. She clucked her tongue at the state of the boy's bare feet. "How was he even standing?"

"He's a fighter." Rannac let his maimed hand linger on the boy's as he folded it across the narrow chest.

"You're fond of him."

Rannac drew back immediately, ready to deny it, but Halima arched a knowing eyebrow at him, and, as usual, she scrambled his thoughts for a moment. *She's the Chief's Claimed mate*, he told himself sternly.

"Yes, I can see it." The matriarch's brow pinned together. "There is something about this one. Be careful, Old Wolf. It would not do to get too attached."

"I'm not a fool," he grumbled.

She let out a laugh. "Oh, how well I know that." Halima sobered. "So. Eldrax finally has a witch-child. What does the Chief plan to do with him?"

"I do not know." Rannac folded his arms. "It remains to be seen if he inherited any of the witch magic."

"I hope for his sake that he did. The chief will not suffer the burden of a worthless male."

Rannac grunted. "I have to ensure he vows loyalty to Eldrax and becomes a sworn member of the clan before the seasons turn. If he refuses…" Rannac shook his head, trying to banish the sliver of doubt as he recalled the hatred and fear in the boy's eyes whenever he beheld the Chief. Whether he remembered or not, it would not be easy to convince him to trust the Red Bear.

"What's his name?"

"He doesn't know. He can't remember anything."

"What do you mean, he can't remember?"

"Just that. He can't remember anything before being found by Eldrax. I suspect this had something to do with it." Rannac pointed to the back of the boy's head and the bloody lump protruding there.

"Eldrax?"

Rannac dipped his chin in affirmation. "His past appears to be gone from him."

"*Muntacha khalvir chi.*"

"Excuse me?"

"'Poor lost child' in the tongue of my mother's People." The matriarch's eyes roved over the boy. "And that wasn't the only strike, I see," Halima reproved, studying the bruises blooming over the boy's face.

"As I said, he's a fighter."

"Then he'd better learn to temper himself if he wants to keep his head on his shoulders. Nameeda!" Halima barked, and a young girl came scurrying from the shadows at the back of the shelter. "Fetch water. I want you to wash and bind this boy's wounds."

"Who is he?" The girl's bright grey eyes swept over the prone form. Rannac could understand her burning curiosity. The boy would be the first male Nameeda had not known from birth.

"Enough time for questions later. Do as I say."

The girl scrambled away.

"I suppose we will have to place a name on him," Halima mused. "We can't keep calling him 'boy'."

Rannac cocked his head, recalling the desolate look in the boy's eyes as they had reached camp. "What did you call him just now? Lost boy?"

"*Khalvir chi.*"

"Khalvir." Rannac tested the word on his lips. "Good as any. You named Galahir and Lorhir. May as well keep the custom."

Nameeda returned at that moment with water and hide strips.

"Send word to me when he awakens," Rannac said, turning to leave. "Take care of him."

"Of course." Halima's warm fingers reached out to press his in assurance.

Rannac grunted and swept from her domain, flexing his tingling hand as he went.

***

Chapter 7

FRIENDS AND FOES

"*It's gone.*" *A cold sweat broke out over Juaan's body as he looked down at his empty hip.*

"What?" Nyriaana's indigo eyes swept the deep undergrowth and the twisted boughs above. Attuned to his emotions as always, an anxious frown slashed across her red-gold brows.

"My mother's pouch," Juaan snapped in his desperation. "It's gone." Tears started in his eyes as he looked back in the direction from which they had travelled.

Keep it with you and remember. Remember the people who have loved you and sacrificed themselves for you. *His mother's words moments before her death rang through Juaan's mind. He had sworn over that tied leaf and the objects contained within that he would remember and survive for his mother. Nyri did not know it, but he had also extended that promise to her; adding the most significant gifts she had given him over their seasons together to the contents of the pouch. The most treasured of all being the green pebble she had so sweetly given him upon their first meeting. The day she had given him back his hope.*

Now it was gone. How was he to find it, camouflaged as it would be among the tangle of leaves that lay behind them? The light was fading fast, the ceaseless forest chorus shifting to the voices of the night. They had been wandering all day foraging for food for the tribe. Juaan did not know when he had last seen the pouch. He bowed his head, overcome by the sense of loss. He felt like he had lost a part of his mother all over again.

A small hand slipped inside his. "Don't be sad, Juaan," she said.

He tried to pull his hand away. "You don't understand. You cannot imagine what it meant to me."

She pulled him around and Juaan felt a faint flash of indignance and hurt. "I lost my mama, too," she said. "I do understand."

Through his devastation, chagrin wormed its way through Juaan's chest. "I'm sorry, Nyriaana."

She was silent for a moment and Juaan knew she was struggling to regain her own composure before she raised her wide indigo eyes to him. "I will help you find your mother's gift," she said. "Don't be sad."

"How?" Juaan waved a hand at the forest before them before letting his arm fall back against his thigh with a slap of finality.

Juaan felt a spike of smug satisfaction. Nyri's emotions were easier for him to read than any other being. He did not feel so blind when he was with her. He watched as her fine features contorted with the effort of deep concentration. "Nyri, what are you—?"

"Shhh!" she interrupted him.

Juaan closed his mouth. For a long moment, nothing happened. Nyri's jaw flexed as she clenched her teeth. He grew worried that she would hurt herself as her face flushed. "Nyriaana."

A soft chirrup overhead brought Juaan's face up. A monyet was sitting in the branches above, its large eyes blinking down at him out of its almost humanlike features. Long fingers grasped the tree as the long, dark tail trailed down towards them. A whole troop of his brethren soon joined him. Juaan blinked at the host of creatures above when a low growl drew his eyes back down. A forest wolf pack shouldered out of the undergrowth and sat patiently before the girl at his side.

Nyri opened her eyes, and they were bright in her triumph.

"I-I didn't know you could do this," Juaan stammered.

"Sefaan has taught me."

Juaan cast his eyes to the ground. He did not say the tribe Kamaali had also been teaching him the art of Ninmah's Gift, and he had still to master the most basic skills. He did not need to speak. The truth lay awkwardly in the air between them.

"They can see," Nyri gestured to the waiting monyets above, moving quickly forward and not allowing Juaan to dwell on his failures as a part of her tribe. "They can smell." She pointed at the wolves. Nyri closed her eyes again.

"What are you doing now?"

"Showing them what we're looking for. Hold still."

The wolves rose to their paws and padded forward as she spoke. Each one approached Juaan, sniffing at his skin and coverings, before turning away and disappearing back into the undergrowth. The monyets chittered, and then they too bounded away.

Juaan opened his mouth to speak, but held his tongue when Nyri did not reopen her eyes, the effort of concentration creasing her brow once again. She was tracking her hunters. Juaan could not help being in awe of the tiny girl beside him. He knew most adult Ninkuraaja would find it challenging to spread their awareness between so many of the Great Spirit's Children at once. Nyri had barely seen out her seventh Fury.

He had always known she was special. He flexed the hand still held in hers.

The ambience of the forest had taken on a half-light before Nyri's head lifted and she turned her face towards the faint sounds of a babbling brook. She opened her eyes. "There." She pointed

Relief swept through Juaan like cool air filling starved lungs. In a rush, he swept Nyri into his arms and swung her around. "Thank you, Nyri, Nyri Nyriaana." He beamed as he set her back on the ground.

She giggled. "Come on!" And she set off at a run, towing him along by the hand, weaving her way unerringly through the web of trees and thick undergrowth.

A wolf waited by the side of the running water. Before his great paws lay Juaan's leaf-leather pouch.

Juaan let out a soft cry and bounded forward. The tears streamed down his face as he prepared to seize his lost treasure from the ground. He would never lose it again.

A green and red-gold form darted out from the undergrowth before him, snatching the pouch from the ground before Juaan could close the distance. His cry of relief turned to one of fury.

"Daajir!" Nyri shouted as the Ninkuraaja boy came to a halt before them, his mother's last gift held firmly in his hand. "What are you doing? That belongs to Juaan. Give it back."

Daajir ignored her. He weighed the pouch in his hand. "I have always been curious why you treasure this so, Forbidden," he drawled. "What could be so important to a mindless monster like you?"

Juaan's hands balled into fists. "Give it back. Now." His voice shook with barely controlled rage.

Daarjir's large indigo eyes, so similar to Nyri's but lacking any of her warmth, slid down to Juaan's coiled hands. Juaan thought he saw a vestigial smile ghosting across Daajir's impassive face. "Come and take it, then, Forbidden, see if you can before I..." He left the threat hanging as he took the pouch between both of his hands and pulled.

"No!" Juaan roared and leaped forward. But before he could lay so much as a finger on the hated boy, a snarling mass of fur knocked Daajir hard to the ground. The forest wolf pinned the Ninkuraaja boy with two paws upon his chest as the fangs gaped a mere hand's breadth from his vulnerable face.

"Let it go, Daajir."

Juaan's head snapped around. It was Nyri who had spoken, but he had barely recognised her voice. Her cold tone held an echo of the wolf she still guided.

Daajir flexed his jaw and tightened his grip. He didn't believe Nyri meant her threat. His own brow creased as he tried to exert his own influence over the Child of the Great Spirit. But Juaan saw a fire he had never before witnessed flaring in Nyri's eyes, and the hairs on the back of his neck lifted. Gone was the innocent girl. In her place stood a force Juaan would not want to tangle with. The wolf snarled and snapped its jaws, his teeth grazing the tip of Daajir's nose.

"Let it go," Nyri commanded. Daajir's fingers opened, and the pouch dropped to the ground. "Juaan."

Juaan swept forward and grabbed his mother's gift from the leaf mould. He was comforted by the sensation of his father's symbolic spear-head and Nyri's pebble sliding together under the leathery material between his fingers as he clutched the pouch to his chest.

"Now leave," Nyri growled, as the wolf stepped away from Daajir.

The Ninkuraaja boy scrambled to his feet and spat in Nyri's direction. "Heretic Forbidden lover," he accused as both Juaan and the wolf snarled in unison. "One day soon, you're going to have to pick a side. Him or us. Choose wisely." Swiping the leaf mould from his dark hair, Daajir swirled and stalked away.

Juaan took a few deep breaths to calm his temper and the fear Daajir's parting words had stirred in him before he turned to Nyri. "Why did you do that?"

She shrugged. "You could not attack him, Juaan. The Elders will do terrible things to you. I know." She stared up at him, her face naked in its understanding. "They'll be angry at me, but not as much as you."

Juaan swallowed around the lump that had formed in his throat. Reaching out, he wrapped an arm around her slight shoulders. "I don't know what I did to be blessed with you in my life, my Nyri Nyri Nyriaana." With her at his side, the foes he faced no longer seemed so dark. He looked down at the leaf-leather pouch. The tie had frayed and snapped. He would have to replace it with something much stronger. Something that would not break so easily. That would have to wait until the morning. Darkness had truly fallen and Nyri was shivering faintly in the chill, whether from cold or exhaustion, he could not tell. He tightened his arm. "Let's go home."

Cool water splashed over his lips. Choking, Du Mu awoke. He scrambled backwards before his eyes were even fully open. "Get away!"

There was a startled gasp and Du Mu focused. A girl was sitting on a pile of furs beside his feet. She was slender in form and brown-skinned, like the majority of these fur clad strangers he had fallen among. The girl's clear grey eyes widened as they fixed upon his face. She scooted closer, speaking in an eager torrent as she extended one finger towards his eyes.

The boy grabbed her wrist, twisting it away hard. "Don't," he hissed.

The girl stiffened, her dark skin paling as she let out a yelp. But her cry of alarm had barely passed her full lips when something cold and sharp pressed hard against the boy's throat.

"Ni gytha ba!"

Du Mu lifted his gaze to meet the dark, stony glare of the woman holding the piercing object to his pulse. He did not understand her words, but she made her meaning clear as the object in her hand dug deeper into his flesh. The boy opened his fingers, releasing the girl.

"Lata cha khalvir." The adult female barked at him, her glare unrelenting. "Nameeda, tuc ba Rannac."

The girl fled. Du Mu locked eyes with the fierce woman above him. Now that the girl was gone, she lifted the small knife in her hand away from his throat and sank back on her haunches. But the point of the blade did not waver as she kept the tip trained upon him.

Without taking an eye off the weapon, Du Mu took in the surroundings in his periphery. He was still trapped within the great structure covered with animal skins Rannac had brought him to. Strange faces lurked here and there in the shadows, female faces, all staring right at him. The only familiar figures were the four remaining women who had come with him from the forest. They sat huddled in the middle of the shelter, staring hopelessly into the empty air.

The sight of their faces brought the boy's own sense of helplessness crushing back down on him. He wrapped his arms around his aching chest, the deeper pain of loss outmatching the ache of his cracked ribs. He sniffed, a few tears breaking loose in this dark place.

The tip of the knife wavered. "Chi chi khalvir."

A sudden gust of wind ruffled his hair, bringing Du Mu's head around. Rannac was striding across the space towards him, and the boy's fear receded enough for him to dry his tears. But the thought that this hard-bitten figure was the only comforting sight he had to cling to did nothing to lift his sadness. The girl he had grabbed hurried along in the warrior's wake, struggling to keep up.

The older man's eyes pierced the boy as sharply as any blade as he came to stand before him. He jabbed a gnarled finger at the girl's reddened wrist. The boy dropped his eyes, shamefaced. "I'm sorry," he muttered into his knees. He noticed his sore feet were bound. Had the girl done that while he slept?

"Kaba." The adult woman dropped a pile of furs at his side.

When he stared at them stupidly, Rannac let out an impatient sigh and dragged him to his feet. The boy winced as the sores and the cuts on his soles burned under his weight. Rannac paid little attention to his discomfort. He yanked the swathe of fur wrapped around Du Mu's shoulders, leaving him standing naked and shivering but for the leathery pouch bound around his waist.

Flushing, he tried to turn away from the woman and the girl, but Rannac just rolled his eyes and kept him in place. Picking through the furs and skins on the ground, the older man began to dress him. He pulled soft coverings over his legs before binding thick furs around his abused feet and calves. He then wrapped leathery skins around his midsection. Rannac finished by swathing a mantle of grey fur around Du Mu's shoulders. The boy wrinkled his nose at the musty smell. It brought no flicker of recognition to mind.

His task complete, the older man crooked a finger at Du Mu, then strode from the shelter, leaving him to follow as he would. What choice did he have? Hanging his head, the boy limped gingerly along in Rannac's wake and out into the world beyond. A fresh breeze filled his lungs as he stepped from the heavy air of the shelter. The world outside was a whirl of activity assaulting his senses from all sides; sights, smells, and sounds. The animal skin shelters pressed in all around him as men, women and children wove around them, busy with unfamiliar tasks.

Before Du Mu could hope to make sense of anything, a man bounded up to Rannac. His dark face was tense as he spoke to the older man in a rush, gesturing sharply. Du Mu felt Rannac's wiry muscles coil. His grey eyes slid to the boy and then away in the direction the man had indicated. He hissed between his teeth, appearing torn.

A soft voice broke in at the boy's elbow. It was only now he realised the grey-eyed girl had followed them from the shelter. She babbled, pointing at the boy and then at herself before waving the older man away. The boy could not understand her words, but he got the gist: *go, leave him with me.*

Rannac's brow pinched together, but the other man was urging him again. Blowing out a breath of defeat, he relented before piercing the boy with a warning look. Once again, the meaning was clear. *Behave.*

Du Mu gritted his teeth. The girl had startled him before, but he would never hurt her deliberately. He wasn't a blood-thirsty monster like *him*. Unbidden, the image of Eldrax ripping out the throat of the hunter on the journey to this place broke through his careful control. Bile rose in his throat, and he swallowed it down with an effort.

Rannac continued to glower for a moment, brows bristling as he drove his point home. Then he turned and bounded off through the shelters with the man who had summoned him on his heels.

An awkward silence fell in his wake. Du Mu could feel the girl standing at his elbow, but he didn't turn his head to meet her waiting gaze until a soft, insistent hand tugged on his arm. He rounded on her impatiently. Why couldn't he be alone? He needed to speak with the women inside the shelter. He needed to find his answers, but he didn't know how he was to get to them if he was continually followed.

Du Mu was now surrounded by the people who had taken him and the women prisoner; and the red-headed leader had made it clear he did not want Du Mu to go near his fellow prisoners. Why was that? Du Mu did not believe the monster's words. That he wanted him to stay away for his own safety. No. Something told him Eldrax did not want Du Mu to learn of his past. Du Mu tightened his jaw in determination.

The raw frustration and anguish he was feeling must have been strong enough to break through onto his face, for the girl pressed her lips together sympathetically. She dared to reach out to take his hand. Du Mu tensed. Her touch was far from comforting. It was wrong, unnatural. It only served to increase the size of the aching hole inside his chest. She smiled hopefully at him. There was something about these people that seemed overly expressive to Du Mu. When he did not return her gesture, she sobered and dropped her hand, rolling her eyes with a sigh.

"Nameeda." She patted her chest. "Nameeda."

The boy nodded, acknowledging that he understood. "Nameeda," he repeated, then braced for the inevitable query to follow. She pointed at him and raised an eyebrow.

He shrugged. "Du Mu?"

Her grey eyes danced with sudden amusement, souring his mood further. He had obviously misunderstood the meaning behind 'du mu'. "Naruk." She shook her head, lips still twitching with mirth. She pointed at his chest again. "Khalvir. Khalvir."

Khalvir? He tilted his head, but Nameeda had already turned away and was beckoning for him to follow. Du Mu hesitated for a moment. He did not want company, but he was at a loss to know where else to put himself. Rannac had gone. It was either follow the girl or return to the shelter and the company of the frightening sharp-eyed woman. Knowing he wasn't about to get close to his fellow prisoners with her keeping guard, he chose the former. Perhaps he would learn something that would aid their eventual escape.

It wasn't as terrible as he imagined. Nameeda chattered as he walked by her side. Du Mu couldn't understand what she was telling him, but the sound of her bright explanations almost made him forget his fear.

Almost.

Wherever they travelled, men and women stopped dead in their tracks to stare at him, their gazes bugging at his eyes and ears. Embarrassed, the boy brought his hands up to cover the subtle, tapering points.

"Naruk." The girl's hand was on his arm again, tugging his own away from his ear. She smiled and shook her head. Too startled by her sudden proximity to move, Du Mu let her reach up and brush the edge of one ear before her fingers lighted under an eye. Nameeda then pulled back, her smile breaking into a grin. She liked and accepted what she saw, he realised. The moment tugged at something deep inside. A peculiar feeling that this had happened once before swept through Du Mu, but no image came to give the sensation meaning. It was both a torture and a balm. One side of his mouth lifted, mimicking her smile, which broadened in response.

"Nameeda!" a voice called out. Du Mu tensed again, the smile dropping from his face as another boy, roughly the same age as he was, bounded from between two shelters. He was tall with dark skin. Intense brown eyes burned out over high cheekbones. His waving hair fell down his back in a braid. He slewed to a halt when he beheld Du Mu standing next to Nameeda. An array of emotions shifted over his face. Surprise, confusion, curiosity, but Du Mu did not miss the final tightening of his eyes as his gaze flicked between himself and the girl. He instinctively took one step away from his companion.

"Tamuk!" Nameeda rushed to the boy, grabbing his hands in joyous greeting. A flush of pleasure crept over the newcomer's face as she did this, dispelling his suspicious expression. He then allowed himself to be towed back to where Du Mu was standing.

A long stream of sounds came from the girl's mouth as she gestured excitedly. She finished with the word *khalvir* again, pointing at him. She was addressing him. Khalvir? He shook his head. No. No. That wasn't right. The sound of it rankled.

The pair paid him no mind. The girl was talking to the other boy again. Tamuk, had she called him? Tamuk listened silently to her story, his eyes widening with surprise as they flitted to Du Mu's face, as though only just seeing him for the first time. Du Mu felt the urge to cover his ears again.

When the girl was done, Tamuk came forward and clapped Du Mu on the shoulder. He was strong, and Du Mu felt the warning mingled with the greeting in this one overly forceful gesture. "*Hata ji,* Khalvir. "

Not knowing how else to respond, Du Mu dipped his head. He assumed it was a welcome. *Khalvir. Khalvir.* The name sat ill at ease upon his shoulders.

The wind shifted, carrying with it a warm scent along with the sound of crackling. Du Mu's stomach rumbled audibly. Tamuk's eyebrows rose before he barked a laugh. He poked a finger into Du Mu's arm, tutting, then beckoned as both he and Nameeda set off toward the crackling sound. Once again left with no choice, the boy trailed after them.

The conflagration seared across Du Mu's eyes as he rounded the last shelter. Hot orange tongues of fire blazed amid a circle of dwellings. The sight and sound seized the boy's heart with a sudden panic. Images teased in the corners of his mind: fear, flight, searing heat against his skin... He shook his head, scrambling away.

"Khalvir." The girl called after him.

No, no, that's not it. He screwed his eyes shut, his head shaking faster as he chased the flickering ghosts in his mind.

"Khalvir." Her hand was warm on his then, calm, reassuring, steadying the shivers in his own hand. The ghosts fled. The boy opened his eyes to find the girl looking kindly at him. She beckoned again. Du Mu shifted his gaze to the centre of the space ahead. The dancing, spitting tongues still dredged a mortal fear from his deepest centre, but then his gaze strayed to Tamuk waiting nearby. A smug smile was tugging at the corners of the other boy's mouth. Gritting his teeth and forcing his panic aside, Du Mu stood straight. He would not show weakness. Taking one step, then another, he approached the small inferno with the girl's hand still firmly on his. The warm scent of something delicious carried him the rest of the way.

An elder woman was tending to an object spitted over the consuming tongues. Nameeda approached, hands held out before her in supplication. The elder graced the girl with a smile and drew a knife, carving pieces from whatever was burning over the hungry orange tongues. Wrapping the steaming objects into pieces of hide, the greying woman handed them to the waiting girl, who dipped her head in thanks.

Nameeda then returned to the boys' sides, holding out a piece of the steaming portions to each. Du Mu hesitated, unsure, but Nameeda extended her offering until he had no choice but to accept. Scalding juices slid down his fingers, making Du Mu flinch and almost drop the offering. He looked across at Tamuk and saw with surprise that the other boy was gleefully licking the fluids from his fingers. He then sank his teeth into the browned lump contained within the hide.

Nameeda was watching Du Mu expectantly. Shifting on his feet, he took a tentative sniff, then bit into the offering. *Oh.* His eyes rolled closed as the delicious juices flooded his mouth. This food faded the dried morsels Rannac had offered into insignificance. Within two bites, the offering was gone, and Du Mu found himself licking and sucking his own fingers clean, savouring every drop.

Nameeda's face split into a faint grin. Du Mu flushed, ducking his head as the warmth of the food radiated out from his stomach. It made him feel better. Comforted. If only a little.

It was with more interest now that he followed his two new companions around the cluster of shelters. He did his best to discern the meaning of their chatter as he took in the sights. He looked for anything that might aid him when the opportunity arose to escape.

The shelters seemed to go on forever, faces, faces everywhere. The boy knew it would be a long time before he recognised them all, before he learned all the routes through the tangled web of shelters. *Do I have that time?* Uncertainty shivered through him. What did the red-haired beast want from him? And if he couldn't give it, what then? The memory of the man having his throat ripped open flared through Du Mu's mind again, sending panic shooting to his fingertips.

The inability to communicate only increased his sense of helplessness and division. He wanted to talk to someone; he wanted answers, any answers. Du Mu wanted to understand this vast world he had woken to. He felt like he was drowning.

A crack split the air, ripping the boy's thoughts back to the present. It was quickly followed by another. It sounded like wood being smacked together. Soft grunts and pants of exertion accompanied the loud clashes. Wary now, he followed his two guides towards the sounds. Rounding a rack of drying meat, the shelters suddenly gave way to a large circular space. At the centre, a group of boys had gathered in a loose ring. Two other boys, locked in combat, struggled in their midst. Long staffs crowned with sharpened antler prongs at both ends struck and parried. Muffled yelps of pain punctuated each successful strike. The wicked prongs tore fur and raked flesh. Du Mu's eyes widened at the savage sight. Shouldn't someone be stopping the fight? Both combatants were bathed in sweat and blood.

But nobody stepped forward to intervene. Instead, the surrounding boys appeared to be shouting encouragement. Du Mu flinched when the larger of the two boys scored another strike and Tamuk let out a loud whooping noise close to his ear. "*Kisnido ekundir*!" he cried, pumping his fist in the air.

Du Mu and his two companions were close enough now for him to recognise the smaller combatant as the slender boy called Lorhir. It was clear Lorhir's larger opponent had the strength, but Lorhir had the speed. His sharp, dark face was set in fierce lines as he swung his weapon, twisting, dancing, as if the long, double-ended pole was an extension of his body.

Du Mu watched, becoming strangely entranced by the display of skill. Lorhir wasn't only fast. He was also cunning. For a moment, he appeared to be losing, falling back before his enemy. The bigger boy rushed forward to take advantage, scenting blood.

It was a mistake.

In the flicker of an eye, Lorhir reversed the fortunes of the fight, whipping his staff out and catching his larger foe unawares. He cut his opponent's feet out from under him and landed him on his back. Du Mu heard the air rush from his lungs.

Tamuk groaned as Lorhir strode around his fallen victim, holding his weapon aloft, seemingly unaware of his own wounds in the heat of his victory.

"Tamuk!" One of the young men in the observing ring spied Du Mu's second companion and waved him over, brandishing two more of the fighting staffs. Shocked, Du Mu watched as Tamuk grinned and rushed to take one of the offered poles. A new circle formed as the two fresh combatants circled each other, testing with small feints and dodges. The boy could not help but notice that Tamuk's eyes flicked to Nameeda whenever the opportunity arose.

"*Uzu!*" The call demanded attention and Du Mu turned his head just in time to see Lorhir bearing down upon him, two blood-soaked staffs in his hand. An unpleasant light flared in his eyes. He flung one weapon at Du Mu. Shocked into stillness, Du Mu failed to snatch the weapon from the air, and it clattered to the ground at his side. He blinked down at it dumbly.

"Lorhir, *naruk!*" Nameeda was suddenly at his side, furiously trying to halt Lorhir's advance. He twisted around her, continuing to bear down on Du Mu, the malicious glint in his eye turning to a small smile when Du Mu could not keep the panic from his face. The remaining weapon in Lorhir's hands swung around, whistling towards Du Mu's head. For his own life, he couldn't have moved. There was no time to feel afraid or even to close his eyes as he watched death approach.

A resounding crack split the air. Du Mu flinched. The sharpened prongs of the oncoming weapon had halted a mere breath from his wide-open eyes, blocked by the haft of another.

Tamuk twisted Lorhir's staff aside with his own, then planted himself before Du Mu. Lorhir glared, letting loose a string of furious sounds, but Tamuk did not budge. Du Mu felt the presence of two others come to stand at his back, combining with Tamuk against Lorhir. He had no time to see who these other supporters were, for Nameeda was tugging on his arm, babbling at him, gesturing that they should leave. *Yes*, he agreed silently as he continued to gaze at the weapon that had landed at his feet. His heart raced against his ribs. In his mind's eye, Du Mu kept seeing the razor sharp prongs rushing towards his face.

A cold sweat broke out over his body. This encounter had only heightened the sense of danger he was in. One misstep and his life would end in a fountain of blood. If he was to have any hope of surviving long enough to escape, Du Mu needed to learn who was friend and who was foe, and learn fast. Lifting his gaze from the weapon at last, Du Mu levelled Lorhir's dark stare with his own. He was grateful for this frightening lesson. He had already learned that this wily snake was most definitely an enemy.

***

Chapter 8

First Hunt

"Did you see that?" Tamuk said as he followed Nameeda and the new boy they had named Khalvir away from the proving circle. "He didn't close his eyes once." He cuffed the other boy on the shoulder. Khalvir started badly. The new boy whipped around, a warning blazing in his strange eyes as his lip lifted away from his teeth. Tamuk raised his hands. "Ea above! I didn't mean any harm."

"He's just frightened," Nameeda interjected.

Jealousy flashed at Nameeda's defensive tone, but Tamuk tempered it. She had a soft spot for helpless things. He knew that well. It was one of the many reasons Tamuk loved her. This... Khalvir, however, was far from helpless. He was new and exciting, a rare rogue male, a unique half-witch. His features were fierce and straight, his body promising suppleness and strength. Women would want him, they would want to bear children who would carry his strength and elf-witch blood. Tamuk knew, and it sent a shiver of fear through him as he looked at Nameeda.

He would have to find a way to sour Nameeda's regard of this newcomer before it could grow, but he would need to do so subtly. Nameeda had taken the rogue under her wing, and Tamuk was wise enough to know he would only damage his own pursuit if he acted against anything under her care. And so it was, for her sake alone, he had defended this Khalvir from Lorhir. But he would bide his time and make sure Nameeda saw who was the best man to take care of her and the children she would raise. No outsider was going to steal her affections.

"He doesn't understand us," Nameeda continued.

"I don't think that will be a problem for long." Khalvir was watching them intently. His eyes narrowed in concentration as he studied their interaction and the movement of their mouths. "I can see why you said Rannac likes him." Another stab of resentment. Tamuk and the rest of his peers worked hard to gain their spear master's approval, and this boy arrived and took what many never gained.

Nameeda's next words drove the knife in further. "Yes. I've never seen the Old Wolf look at a boy the way he looked at Khalvir here. He was almost... protective of him."

"Strange," Tamuk bit out from between his teeth. Rannac was a hard man. Not in the sometimes violent way of the Chief, but he was an unforgiving teacher. Tamuk had always understood the need for a lack of mercy. He even welcomed it. Rannac was teaching them to become warriors, not infants. Raknari warriors, whose lives would be given to defend the clan against any threat. Caring too much was a not a luxury a warrior could enjoy when lives ended oft times on the point of an enemy's spear, or upon the horns of an ox.

It was unthinkable that Rannac should feel any kind of affection for this scrawny stray, but Tamuk trusted Nameeda's instincts too much to doubt her perception. He wondered what was so special about this boy. He eyed him again critically. For Nameeda's ears, he said, "Well, whatever it is Rannac likes, it has got under Lorhir's skin, and anyone who can annoy the Jackal, is a friend of mine. I'll watch out for you, Khalvir."

It was worth choking out the words when Nameeda beamed up at him. His stomach interrupted the moment by rumbling loudly. "I wonder if Tiki has any of that antelope left?" Tamuk struck out back towards the cooking fire. "Khalvir here looks like he needs to eat a whole antelope to himself." The new boy's furs hung limply from his lean frame. "Did the witches not feed him?"

"It's a miracle they didn't kill him. Halima told me the witches hate half-breeds. Even more so than even the Thals or the Deni."

"Then how did he, er... even come to exist?"

Nameeda rolled her eyes and gave him a pitying stare. "It won't have been by choice." She pointed towards the Dwelling of the UnClaimed where three elf-witch females were being herded along before a stern Halima. "Another man must have succeeded where our Chief has failed."

"Shhh!" Tamuk's heart leaped. "He might hear you."

"The Red Bear is in his tent. Occupied. He brought *four* elf-witches back from the shin'ar forest." But despite her bold words, Nameeda's head sank into her shoulders and she glanced about nervously.

"That can't have pleased him," Tamuk whispered. His Chief was a proud man. Failure was not something he ever accepted. Particularly when another might possess something he lacked. "He must doubt he'll ever sire a witch-child himself." His words were a mere breath.

"Why do you say that?"

"Because if he had any confidence at all, Khalvir would not be standing there."

Nameeda paled, and Tamuk was instantly sorry for upsetting her. She had too soft a heart for the reality of the world. "Come on, let's eat." He grabbed her hand and towed her the last few strides towards the fire.

Tiki was still tending the flames and readily handed the little group more portions from the spit. Tamuk thanked Ea that she was in charge of preparing the meat. Others were not so generous. Tamuk settled near the fire and Nameeda pulled Khalvir down beside them. He came willingly enough. He did not seem to find her touch so much of a threat as Tamuk's.

"Meat." Tamuk held a dripping portion out to Khalvir and repeated. "Meat."

"Meat?" The boy took the offering, studying it. "Meat." He tested the word again.

Nameeda's eyes brightened. She pulled a pebble from the ground beside her and handed it to Khalvir. "Stone."

The most peculiar expression passed over the boy's face as the small rock was placed into his palm. The reddish-brown skin of his brows pinched together beneath his tangled hair. His body tensed as his eyes flickered. It looked to Tamuk as though he was searching for an answer deep within. But then his shoulders slumped and Tamuk could have sworn there was a gleam of tears in the green eyes before Khalvir blinked them away. "Stone," he repeated dully after Nameeda.

"Yes." Nameeda quickly moved on to a stick. If Tamuk had noticed the brief reaction the pebble had brought about, then Nameeda would certainly have picked up on it.

The game continued as they ate. Tamuk and Nameeda gathering as many objects as they could find and naming them all. Khalvir was a quick study. Tamuk would give him that. They tested him often, presenting him with items they had already named to see if he remembered. He rarely made a mistake. But the strange incident with the pebble had had a lasting effect. The boy had not been exactly happy before, but now a shroud of gloom appeared to have settled over him. His strange green eyes were distant. It was as though someone had died. It was depressing.

"How about we do something else?" Tamuk had been growing bored with the naming game, anyway. He could see an exhausted slump stealing over Khalvir's shoulders, along with the gloom.

"Like what?" Nameeda eyed him.

"How long has it been since we tasted eggs?"

Nameeda scowled. She had caught up with the direction of his thoughts. "No."

"Yes. Galahir saw the tracks. C'mon, Nameeda. It'll be fun. It'll certainly take his mind off whatever is making him so miserable."

"You'll get him killed! He's done nothing like that before."

"Then he'd better learn. I'll expect he's quite fast." To demonstrate, Tamuk picked up another rock and shot it towards the rogue boy's face. "Khalvir, catch."

The boy's hand flashed out, catching the rock just before it hit his forehead. He pinned Tamuk with a glare. Tamuk got the impression Khalvir was still making his mind up about him.

"See!" Tamuk pointed. "He'll live. I'll show him what to do." *And prove who is the best.*

Nameeda still appeared unhappy.

"What do you think Rannac or Eldrax will have him do first?" Tamuk pressed. "They won't be forgiving. Better the first hunt be against a bird and not a bull ox!"

"A hatchet bird," Nameeda pointed out.

"I'm aware of that," Tamuk grinned. "Why do you think it'll be so much fun?"

Nameeda rolled her eyes. "Males," she said under her breath. But Tamuk could see she was relenting. She knew as well as he that he hadn't exaggerated over what the Chief would throw at the new boy. For the men of the clan, they proved useful, or they had no place. There was no middle ground. "Just promise me you'll be careful," she said reluctantly.

"I'm always careful." Tamuk gave her the rakish grin that never failed to draw a smile. Her lips twitched in response. "Khalvir," he turned to the new boy. "Ready for some excitement?"

He blinked. "Excitement?"

"Yes. You look like you could do with some." He caught hold of one scrawny arm. Ignoring the flinch, he pulled Khalvir to his feet and towed him towards the edge of the camp.

"Hey!" Tamuk called, spying Ekundir and Galahir squatting next to a shelter. The latter was binding Ekundir's wounds. The more hunters in a group, the greater the odds of a reward. "Feeling strong enough to outrun a hatchet bird, Ekundir, or are you just going to sit there lamenting getting your backside landed in the mud? Again."

Ekundir's chin came up. "Next time we spar, Tamuk, we will see who gets landed in the mud."

Tamuk's lips curled. "Perhaps. But how about some eggs first?"

Ekundir barked a laugh, the annoyance fading from his face at the prospect of a delicacy. "Coming, Galahir?" he cuffed the other boy roughly around the head as he rose.

The large, sandy-haired boy took the blow without complaint and nodded. Galahir was never one of many words. Tamuk was often unsure how much of Galahir's silence was because of timidness or being the half-wit Lorhir claimed. Whatever the reason, Galahir had surprised everyone by surviving this long into the life of a raknari. To say Rannac's decision to add him to the warrior ranks had shocked Tamuk was an understatement. Only Galahir's great strength imparted to him by his part Thal parentage lent him any advantage. Strength was not a skill needed in the upcoming hunt. Still, Galahir would prove useful as a lure.

"Is the half-witch rogue coming too?" Ekundir eyed the new boy with a curl of his lip.

"I thought it was a good first test for him."

Ekundir snorted. "I'd say we could at least use him to distract the bird, but there is so little meat on him, he wouldn't occupy the pile of feathers long enough for the rest of us to get away."

"Ekundir," Nameeda reproved.

Tamuk was careful to hide his smile at Ekundir's barb. "Let's go." He snatched up a couple of long poles that rested against the side of a shelter.

Galahir took point as he led them to where he had seen the tracks east of the river. Nameeda trailed in the wake of Tamuk's hunting group. She didn't seem to want to let them out of her sight. Tamuk rolled his eyes but did not protest. Whatever made her feel better.

They crossed the river at the ford. Once on the other side, Tamuk crouched to the ground. The tracks of a hatchet bird were plain to see. There was no mistaking them, even for Galahir. Satisfied with the identity of their quarry, Tamuk studied the surrounding area. Tamuk had yet to beat Lorhir in a fight, but no one could surpass him in tracking. "This way."

The Plains were still as hard as rock, so close after the passing of winter, and they did not give up their secrets easily, but Tamuk soon had the clues he needed. A scratch here, a rumpled clump of grass there. He travelled in a crouch at the point of the group, moving faster as the trail became more recent.

"There!" He pointed in triumph at last. He could just make out the dark brown hump in an area of tall grasses, the feathers waving gently in the breeze. The giant bird itself was of no worth. The meat of a hatchet bird was lean, tough, and tasted like a hog's backside. Its eggs, on the other hand, were a valued delicacy. If one could possess them.

Tamuk scanned the area. The hatchet bird had chosen a site on flat, open ground, giving itself the advantage of speed, but to the west of it was a small copse of closely packed trees. Perfect.

Tamuk took a pole from Ekundir's hand and thrust it at Galahir. "Here. You bait it. The rest of us will hide in the trees until the bird is clear."

Galahir's lips turned down at the corners, but he did not argue as he took the pole from Tamuk's hand. Leaving him crouched in the tall grasses, Tamuk led the rest into the cover of the trees. They would make their play from here. As soon as Khalvir, Nameeda and Ekundir were safely concealed, Tamuk let out a shrill whistle, signalling for Galahir to begin.

Tamuk watched as Galahir stalked forward, pole extended until he was the length of the wood away from the sleeping bird. The sandy-haired boy hesitated for only a moment before giving the giant creature a sharp jab with the tip.

It all happened in a heartbeat. An angry rattle throbbed through the air as the hatchet bird reared up onto its clawed feet. The hooked beak gaped as its sharp red eyes fixed upon the intruder. Galahir wasted no time. He was already racing away, running for his life.

"Now!" Tamuk cried to Ekundir as the bird gave chase, flaring its flightless wings. Tamuk burst from the trees, Ekundir at his side. The other boy let out a shrill whistle as he peeled away from Tamuk. "Hey! Over here! Over here, feather face!" He threw stones, distracting the bird from disembowelling a tiring Galahir. The fierce head swivelled, and upon seeing a closer threat to its nest, the bird pivoted to give chase to Ekundir.

Tamuk stayed low, breathing in the scent of the tall grass, feeling the thrill of his racing heart as he rushed towards the nest. Five enormous globes were nestled amid a carefully arranged pile of sticks, feathers and grass. Keeping one half of his mind on the deadly bird racing between Galahir and Ekundir, Tamuk seized one of the pale blue eggs.

Wasting no time, he tucked it inside his furs and fled. Sprinting back towards the cover of the copse, he whistled his success to his two darting companions.

He unveiled his prize to Nameeda and Khalvir as Galahir and Ekundir threw themselves through the tree line. A moment later, there was a heavy thud and a violent shiver of branches as the hatchet bird collided with the closely packed trunks. Its body was too large to fit between the spaces, but in its fury, the bird continued to lash out with its clawed feet. It gouged great clods of earth from the ground, but even the hatchet bird's legs weren't long enough to reach the triumphant young hunters within.

Tamuk stole a glance at Khalvir's face. He was pale as he watched the attacking tower of feathered fury. Tamuk hid a smile. *Not so special after all, if that's all it takes to rattle you.* His plan of proving his superiority to Nameeda was proceeding well.

Eventually, the call of its remaining eggs overcame the bird's anger, and it ceased its efforts to reach the group in the trees, returning to its nest.

"Your turn," Tamuk clapped Khalvir on the shoulder as soon as he and the others had regained their breath, thrusting the second pole at him. If possible, the alarming green eyes became even wider as the boy divined his meaning. His throat flashed in a nervous swallow.

"Tamuk." Nameeda took a protective hold of Khalvir's arms, sending a renewed flash of jealousy through Tamuk's stomach. "It's too soon. Give him more time."

"If he is going to be one of us, he needs to prove himself able," Tamuk said with a little more vehemence than he intended. He had just proven that he could provide. Let Nameeda see what this scrawny rogue could do. "Ready, Khalvir?"

The half-witch glanced around at the expectant eyes surrounding him. An icy fire flickered to life within his own green depths and he gripped the pole as he lifted his chin, accepting their challenge.

"That's the spirit." Tamuk pushed Khalvir towards the edge of the trees and thrust him into the open. "Go on."

The rogue boy glanced back once, then faced his formidable feathered enemy. Tamuk watched as he crept forward, mimicking what Galahir had done. But there was no need to get close enough to prod the bird this time. Already roused, it sensed Khalvir's approach. Hissing, it rose to its full height, swelling dangerously as its feathers lifted. Tamuk thought he heard what sounded like a curse loose from the boy's mouth before he fled, running for his life through the grass as the deadly bird gave chase.

Ekundir let out a low whistle. "He's fast."

"What did I tell you?" Tamuk smiled at Nameeda.

She kicked Ekundir in the shins. "Don't just stand here watching! Go out and help him!"

Rolling his eyes, Ekundir hefted the second pole and ran from the trees. Hollering out to the pursuing bird, he turned its attention from the fleeing Khalvir, confusing it.

Time for another egg. Tamuk swept through the grasses on silent feet. Grabbing another egg from the nest, he grinned and turned to make his escape. But, drunk on his own success, Tamuk had not nearly been watchful enough. Half way back to the safety of the trees, a pounding of clawed feet was his only warning as the hatchet bird's mate burst from the undergrowth. "Ea above!" Tamuk cried, the egg flying from his grasp as he threw his hands up to defend himself. There was no time to run, no time to put up a better fight. He was defenceless. Terror lanced through him as he braced for the first impact of ripping claws.

It never came.

A second body barrelled out of the grass, knocking Tamuk clear of the vengeful bird. There was a brief hiss of pain, and Tamuk and his rescuer crashed to the ground.

"Khalvir!"

Without a word, the half-witch boy grabbed his arm and, together, they fled. Ekundir and Galahir rushed into their rescue, throwing stones and sticks, distracting the birds long enough for Tamuk and Khalvir to reach the trees.

Tamuk collapsed, panting, as the safety of the copse reached out to shield them.

"Tamuk!" Nameeda was there in a blur of grey furs, throwing her arms around him. "Oh, Tamuk, I thought..." she trailed off.

"I'm alive, girl," Tamuk said gruffly, though on the inside his heart was hammering like a herd of stampeding oxen. Nevertheless, he glowed in the face of her concern. She had run to him first. Appeased, Tamuk felt generous enough to lift his gaze to the boy who had saved his life as Galahir and Ekundir bolted back into the trees, panting hard. A sharp tang of sweat and nerves mixed with the leaf mould. "Thank you," Tamuk said to Khalvir as he caught his breath. "I owe you my life."

The boy regarded him steadily, but the skin around his eyes was taut.

"Nicely done, Tamuk," Ekundir's voice dripped with sarcasm. "You almost get yourself killed and you lose the egg. We've run our feet for nothing!"

Tamuk flushed, keenly aware of Nameeda's hands on him. But before he could bite out a retort, Khalvir gave a small cough and pulled a large round globe from behind his back.

"You got it?" Tamuk's mouth fell open.

A smile twitched about the solemn face.

Ekundir barked out a laugh. "Perhaps the rogue will make a true Hunting Bear man after all."

"You're faster than even I thought, Khalvir," Tamuk lamented. "If Rannac decides it is the raknari for you, Lorhir might meet his match." Despite himself, Tamuk savoured the thought.

"I'd give an egg to see that," Ekundir agreed.

Tamuk pulled himself to his feet, keeping Nameeda's warm hand in his. He would not admit that his brush with death had left him shaken.

"Let's get back to camp," she urged. "Halima will have my hide if I am not returned before dark."

Tamuk glanced out of the trees towards the nest and its remaining contents. Two eggs were a poor show for a hunt, but Rannac had taught him the wisdom of knowing when one was beaten. Two hatchet birds now guarded the nest, their sharp, red eyes on alert for another attempt. They would have to satisfy themselves with the catch they had and live to hunt another day. "Let's go back," he agreed

Tamuk had turned to lead his group from the trees, when there came a muffled thud and a rush of dry leaves.

"Oh!" Nameeda exclaimed.

Khalvir had collapsed. He tried to rise again, but his left leg gave out, refusing to support his weight. He let out another hiss of pain, the skin around his eyes tightening further.

That was when Tamuk saw the tide of red soaking through the furs on the boy's lower leg. "Ea above," Tamuk cursed. "He got slashed."

***

CHAPTER 9

ACCEPTANCE

"Bind it!" Nameeda snapped when her companions stood staring uselessly at Khalvir. Inwardly, she seethed. This foolish hunt had almost cost her the life of her dearest friend, and now Khalvir was wounded. It remained to be seen how badly.

She pulled the furs from around her shoulders and fell to her knees at the rogue boy's side. "Hold still." Whether or not he understood her words, he appeared to know what was best for him. He remained immobile while she bound the fur tightly around the seeping red, fists clenched and breathing in uneven gasps through his nose. "There. Galahir, you carry him. We need to get him to Johaquin. Now. It's alright," she soothed as Khalvir tensed when Galahir stooped to lift him.

"It's safe," Ekundir said, peering out of the tree line. "The birds are on their nest. They've lost interest."

"Stay low," Tamuk hissed, and led them out of the trees and back across the open ground. A stream of red waved out behind Galahir as he forded the river. *The gods,* Nameeda thought as she stayed close to the large boy's side. Khalvir was still bleeding heavily through her binding.

"Do you need Ekundir to take over?" Nameeda asked Galahir as they made the far bank, eyeing the distance they still had to travel.

"No." The half-Thal ducked his head. "He weighs no more than a spear-cat cub."

Nameeda was almost certain, even skinny as he was, Khalvir weighed more than that, especially now his furs were saturated with river water. But she didn't argue. Galahir prided himself on his strength and she did not intend to take that away from him. It did not stop her from watching closely for signs that Galahir's arms might give way and topple his already tortured load to the ground. But he strode along tirelessly, his arms as steady as they had been from the moment he had first lifted Khalvir from the ground. The blood continued to drip.

It was a relief when the first shelters reached out to envelop them. Nameeda rushed ahead.

"Johaquin!" she called out as she thrust aside the draping hides, admitting herself entry to the dwelling of the clan's *ashipu*.

There was a rustling in the shadows as the wise woman shuffled from the rear of her domain, pushing past dangling talismans and faintly smoking herbs. Nameeda wrinkled her nose. She hated the *ashipu* shelter. Johaquin made the hairs on the back of her neck stand on end.

"What's this?" The *ashipu* croaked, pointing a long-nailed finger at the boy in Galahir's arms. "I do not know him."

"He's a rogue, respected *ashipu*," Nameeda said, trying her best not to stare at that one milky eye. "Our Chief returned with him from the raid on the shin'ar forests."

Johaquin grunted. Unimpressed. "A witch. Why does this boy need me? What of their legendary healing ability that our revered Chief covets so much?" There was a peevish edge to the old crone's voice.

"He's a half-witch." Nameeda resisted screaming at her. "Please, wise *ashipu*, he needs your help. He got slashed by a hatchet bird. He's bleeding." She wrung her hands before the healer in supplication. Khalvir's light, reddish-brown skin had already paled several shades.

Her pleading paid off. Johaquin swelled importantly as she pointed to a pile of furs. "Put him there, boy," she directed Galahir.

Galahir did as he was told, then backpedalled away from the old crone.

"Take the furs off, witch," Johaquin snapped her fingers at Khalvir.

"He doesn't understand," Nameeda interjected.

"Huh. Take. Your. Furs. Off. Boy." Johaquin enunciated each word.

"He doesn't speak our tongue. Doesn't mean he's deaf," Tamuk muttered under his breath. Ekundir elbowed him sharply in the ribs, cutting him off.

"Oh, here!" Nameeda said and ripped the furs from Khalvir's wounded leg herself. There was a collective sucking of teeth from the young men behind her as the extent of the damage was revealed. Khalvir balled his fists as he gazed down upon the two gaping gashes in his calf and the blood sliding down his ripped skin.

"What happened here?" A stern voice broke the stillness. Nameeda turned to see Rannac had returned. In that moment, Nameeda pitied Tamuk as the older warrior took in the bloody scene, his jaw working furiously. He rounded on the three adolescents waiting behind him. "Start talking."

To his credit, Tamuk squared his shoulders and stepped forward. "We found a hatchet bird nest. We hunted the eggs. I failed to see the bird's mate return. Khalvir saved my life, but he got injured."

"And you thought it would be a good idea to take a boy who has never seen a hatchet bird before on this hunt of yours?" Rannac growled.

Tamuk lifted his chin. "I thought it would be a good first test of skill."

"That was not for you to decide, boy!" Rannac snapped, the colour rising under his skin.

"It's nothing the rest of us haven't faced." Tamuk muttered mulishly.

"This is different," Rannac hissed. "You had better hope he survives your misguided actions, Tamuk, or it will be you the Chief comes after if this half-witch dies."

Tamuk blanched. "Th-the Red Bear?"

"Yes. This boy is not to be put at risk unless the Chief or I deem it necessary. Understand?"

"Y-yes, Rannac," Tamuk stuttered.

Rannac dismissed him. "Johaquin, don't just stand there like a toothless old she-wolf! Mend the boy. Quickly."

The old healer woman drew herself up, affronted, but something on Rannac's face made even the old crone hold her tongue and she shuffled away.

Nameeda flinched as a small, red-headed child darted from the shadows, wads of fur clutched in two pale hands. The little girl threw herself to her knees at Khalvir's side and pressed the furs hard to the wounds. Selima. The Chief's unwanted daughter.

"Out of the way, you useless child!" Johaquin returned and aimed a kick at Selima, who scowled at her as she scurried back. Nameeda spared a moment to feel sorry for the motherless girl. Eldrax had dumped her into the callous care of the *ashipu* when her Thal mother died in childbirth. Nameeda thanked the gods she had not shared the same fate.

Khalvir's eyes widened, and a sheen of sweat broke out over his skin as the old healer woman approached him with a thin bone needle and strand of gut. He let out an unintelligible protest and tried to rise.

"Galahir, Ekundir, hold him down," Rannac ordered. The two boys rushed to obey their raknari leader as they had been conditioned to do. Each of them seized an arm, pinning the wounded boy to the furs. Khalvir cried out as he struggled in vain. Anger and panic brightened the green eyes. Nameeda had the most peculiar experience, then. It was as though the air in the shelter had taken on the still, heavy prickling before the explosion of a thunderstorm. It made the hairs on the back of her neck stand on end.

"It's alright, Khalvir," she tried to soothe. "Johaquin is trying to help." She wanted to tell him it would not hurt, but it would have been a lie.

Rannac yanked a piece of firewood from the ground and thrust it between the boy's teeth. "Bite on this," he ordered as Johaquin bent over his leg.

Nameeda slipped her hand around Khalvir's. His eyes turned to her. She saw the pupils contract as his fingers clenched painfully upon hers, a keening cry breaking loose from between his teeth. Johaquin had made the first piercing.

"Shh, shh," Nameeda brushed back the sweat-damp hair from Khalvir's brow as the muffled wails went on and on. His head fell back, his eyes focusing and unfocusing. She did not know if he was aware of her presence, but somehow, in that moment, she was keenly aware of Tamuk's attention upon her.

At last, it was over. Khalvir was only semi-conscious when Johaquin pulled back to reveal the ugly stitches holding the boy's rent flesh together.

"There," the healer said, satisfied. She reached up, pulling a bunch of dried leaves dangling from the beams above, before thrusting them into the fire crackling at the centre of her dwelling. She then waved the smoking herbs over the boy's leg. The already overpowering scent of the *ashipu* dwelling grew unbearable as Johaquin chanted, clutching a rat skull talisman in her free hand. "If the gods favour him," the old crone said, "that should keep the curses at bay. I have done all that can be done for him." Her grizzled head came up, and she waved her hands. "Now get out. The boy needs rest. Get out."

"Can't I stay with him?" Nameeda ventured.

"Why?" Johaquin barked. "What can you do for him that I cannot? You think yourself a greater healer than me?"

"N-no," Nameeda stammered.

"Let's go, Nameeda." Tamuk gripped her shoulders and pulled her away. Khalvir twitched as her hand left his, but he made no other movement. His eyes were closed. Nameeda bit her lip as Tamuk propelled her from the shelter and into the open air.

"I hope he'll be alright," she murmured.

"Would you look at me like that if I was injured?" There was a peculiar tone in Tamuk's voice as he released her shoulders. Nameeda turned to face him. His eyes were guarded, his shoulders stiff.

"What are you so worried about?"

"Would you?"

"Oh, Tamuk, you know I would." She reached out to grasp his hands. "You know I have."

He was not mollified. "You like him."

Nameeda blinked. "I don't know him."

"You're concerned enough for him to want to stay in the *ashipu* tent at his side." There was a definite accusation in Tamuk's tone now.

Nameeda's mouth dropped open. "I want to make sure he recovers for *you*, you idiot." She shoved Tamuk in the chest. "Thanks to your little stunt, I fear what the Chief will do to you if Khalvir doesn't recover."

Tamuk's face softened minutely before his features tensed again. "You were getting close enough to him before he got kicked."

Nameeda sighed. "Tamuk. I couldn't just ignore him when he looked so... lost. His entire life has been ripped away. He needed someone. But now he's lying injured, and you are in danger." Tears started in her eyes and she dropped her gaze to the ground, suddenly angry with herself. This wasn't the first time caring too much had got her in trouble. "I should have just left him with Halima. Then none of it would have happened."

Tamuk's arms were suddenly around her, pulling her close. "No, no I am sorry, Nameeda. It was my fault. You were just trying to help, like you always do. And I," He broke off and shook his head. "I was being foolish. Can you forgive me?"

Lifting herself onto her toes, Nameeda planted a kiss on Tamuk's chin. "You *were* foolish. You'll always be the most important to me. Nothing will ever change that."

A smile tugged at his lips, dispelling some of the gloom that had settled over his face. "Not even a mysterious half-witch from the shin'ar forests?"

"Ha!" Nameeda barked a laugh. "It would take more than that to win me. But if he is to survive, he will need more guidance than what Rannac can give him. The Old Wolf is often away."

Tamuk's chest rose under her cheek before he blew out a breath. "Well, he did just save my life after I risked his."

She smiled. "Then will you help him, Tamuk?"

"Yes."

Nameeda kissed his chin again. "Thank you."

"But for his sake, and mine," Tamuk's muscles tensed once more, "we had better hope Johaquin's herbs work.

They did not.

The next day, Nameeda dared to re-enter the *ashipu* dwelling. She froze in the entranceway when she saw the towering figure of the Chief himself looming over the furs where she had left Khalvir the day before. The pale visage beneath the wild mane of red hair was grim.

"I don't understand," Johaquin was prattling. Fragrant smoke curled in the air above her, catching the light glowing through the stretched hides of the shelter walls.

Nameeda's heart sank to her stomach as she crept up behind them and gasped. Khalvir still lay upon the furs. Sweat ran in rivulets down his face. His eyes were closed, his breath coming fast and shallow. The wounds on his leg were now angry and swollen. Forgetting her innate fear of the Chief, Nameeda rushed past him and Johaquin to kneel at the boy's side. Khalvir was gravely ill, and it was all her fault. All Tamuk's fault.

"Khalvir," she called. "Khalvir?" He did not respond. His head moved back and forth slowly.

"He cannot hear you, girl," Johaquin said. "The curses have seized him."

"Nyri, Nyri, Nyriaana." The words tumbled from the boy's lips. "Nyri!" He began to thrash.

"He's run mad!" Johaquin stepped back.

"He's calling for something," Nameeda snapped. She did not understand the words Khalvir spoke, but the need in them was plain.

"Not something," Eldrax grunted.

Nameeda's eyes shot to the harsh face. A faint smile was playing around the wide lips. It was apparent the Chief knew what the boy was saying, but he was no more forthcoming than that. His black gaze was locked on the stricken figure. "We both lost, boy," he muttered so softly that Nameeda had to strain to hear him. The faint smile vanished. "Your loss is punishment for mine, but I will see to it that it is not the last. You will not die so easily. Not yet. You owe me a life for your defiance, and I intend to take what I am due."

The hairs on the back of Nameeda's neck stood on end as she heard the dark promise in the Chief's low growl. She did not know what Khalvir had done to offend, but the cold fury burning in the black depths of the Chief's eyes was very real.

She pretended not to have heard and stroked the sweat-slicked hair from Khalvir's brow. He had to survive, for Tamuk's sake. "Shhh," she soothed. "Khalvir." She placed her free hand in his and squeezed. The heat of his skin alarmed her. "Shhh."

"Nyri." The sigh passed through the boy's lips as he returned Nameeda's grip, and he quieted under her touch.

Eldrax shifted, and Nameeda felt him appraising her. "You will stay with him, girl," he commanded. "He is your responsibility."

"But—" panic shot through Nameeda as Johaquin interjected.

"I will mend the boy!" she snapped. "I am the healer here."

"Healer?" Scorn dripped from Eldrax's voice. "You cannot contemplate the meaning of the word. You stand here on my favour, Johaquin, only for the lack of a true healer. This boy will die only when I deem it fit, and I have a lot more to take for what he did to me yet.

He is responding to this girl. She stays or I will burn your wretched shelter to the ground with you in it, do you hear me?"

Johaquin blanched as her head sank into her shoulders. "Yes, my Chief. Yes."

Eldrax turned away from her, casting his eyes once more over the feverish boy and Nameeda sitting beside him. "Do not move from his side." With that, he stalked towards the entrance, as dangerous as the bear he was named for.

"Father!" Selima's young voice called out. The little girl leaped from the shadows and rushed after him, but the Chief only snarled at her, sending her scurrying back. Her black eyes filled with tears as she bowed her head, her wild red hair shielding her face. Selima's sniffles were the only break in the silence that had fallen over the shelter in the wake of the Chief's visit. Nameeda shifted uncomfortably.

Johaquin moved first. She bared her teeth at the still billowing entranceway through which Eldrax had disappeared, then rounded on Nameeda. Her face twisted in disgust. "Do not get in my way," she snarled. "I already have one unwanted brat forced upon me." She jerked a thumb at the still-crying Selima before bustling off into the shadows, muttering angrily.

Nameeda blew out a breath, inwardly wincing at the position she had now put herself in. Tamuk had not been mistaken when he had once told her her caring would get her into trouble one day.

"Oh, Khalvir," she murmured to the unconscious boy. "You have caused me nothing but trouble." He remained unresponsive, but at least he was now quiescent, his face relaxed with her hand in his. It was the most peaceful Nameeda had seen him since first laying eyes on him. And so she did as she had been ordered and remained where she was, one hand wrapped around the long, slack fingers.

"How is he?" A soft voice called her attention around.

"Tamuk!" Nameeda gasped. "What happened?"

Bruises marred his face, one dark eye was swollen shut, tracks of blood streamed from his nose. He held one arm close against his ribs.

Tamuk tried to grin, but it ended in a wince as he hobbled forward. "Rannac was right," he rasped as he sank gingerly down beside her. "The Chief was most displeased. He gathered us all together. No one is to harm the half-witch on the pain of death. You should have seen Lorhir's face."

"Oh, Tamuk." She reached for him, wiping the blood from his face as gently as she could. She had been prepared to be furious with him. They were here because of his foolish jealousy. He had admitted it himself. But she could not be angry with him now. He had received punishment enough. And, jealousy aside, Tamuk was right. They had thrown younger boys than Khalvir into more dangerous situations than hunting hatchet bird eggs. Young men learned to feed and defend the clan, or life weeded them out. The Hunting Bear had the strongest of men. They didn't get to be that way by being shielded from danger.

Her concern appeared to make Tamuk forget the pain of his wounds. Indeed, he now seemed almost glad of them as he leaned into her hand. Her assurances from the previous day had cured him of his fears. His gaze was utterly benign now as he gazed down at Khalvir. "Tell me what I can do," he said.

"Are you strong enough to fetch water?" Nameeda felt again the searing heat of Khalvir's body. The slightly parted lips were cracked. "I bet he's thirsty."

Tamuk winced again as he staggered back to his feet, though Nameeda now suspected he was exaggerating the discomfort just a bit. She rolled her eyes internally. He planted a kiss on her brow as he limped away to find a skin.

***

Juaan gritted his teeth and concentrated as Sefaan had directed him.

"Do you feel it, boy?" the elderly Kamaali asked. She was the voice of the Great Spirit of KI. The most powerful of the tribe.

Juaan did. The power was there at his centre, coiling and burning. He could feel the Great Spirit of KI flowing through the land beneath his feet. But he could not influence the energy. At least, not when he was trying. The connection between his consciousness and Ninmah's Gift stuttered and started evading his grasp. No matter how Sefaan tried to guide him, he could not be a Ninkuraaja.

"It's no use!" he cried, opening his eyes. Leaping to his feet, he grabbed a stone, and, in temper and frustration, flung it at the nearest tree.

It was a mistake.

The stag he had been trying to influence startled. Faster than anyone could react, the Child of KI bolted blindly in its panic.

"Nyri!" She was sitting directly in the stag's path and he knocked her to the ground, his hooves trampling the girl beneath him. Her cries of pain tore through Juaan's heart. "No!" Juaan lurched towards the crumpled heap that was the centre of his world. "Nyri? Nyriaana?"

"Juaan," she whimpered.

"I'm sorry, I'm so sorry. Nyri?"

Sefaan was at his side. A bony hand reached out, the fingertips spreading over Nyri's paled forehead. It was the longest moment of Juaan's life. "She is not in danger," Sefaan said at last, opening her lavender eyes and Juaan breathed again. "A broken leg. Get her to Baarias. He will heal her."

Juaan swallowed. He actively avoided the tribe's healer as much as Baarias avoided him. But their loathing of each other did not matter now. All that mattered was Nyri. Scooping her as gently as he could into his arms, Juaan lifted her from the ground. She gasped and let out a low cry, her small hand curling around his neck.

"Shhh," Juaan soothed. "I'll get you to Baarias and then it won't hurt anymore. I promise." He set off at a swift walk, trying to keep his gait as smooth as possible so as not to jostle her.

Stares and harsh whispers followed Juaan as he made his way through the eshaara grove. The tribe was thinking the worst. That Nyriaana had met the inevitable doom they had all foreseen for keeping company with a monster. He gritted his teeth.

"Baarias!" he called out as he ducked through the entrance to the healer's tree.

The akaab himself straightened from where he had crouched at the sound of Juaan's voice. Stiff-backed, he turned, then his lilac eyes widened, and he darted forward. "What happened?" he demanded. "What have you done to her?" His voice held all the dark expectations of the tribe outside.

Anger and hurt sliced through Juaan's chest, but he could not deny it. This had been his fault. He had caused Nyri this pain, all because he could not control himself. "She's got a broken leg," he forced the words from between his teeth.

"Give her to me." The healer came forward to take Nyriaana from Juaan's grip.

"No," Nyri clung to his neck all the tighter. Juaan knew she was remembering all the times in the past when the Elders had tried to separate them.

"It's alright, Nyri," he murmured. "Didn't I promise to always stay with you?"

"T-to the end," she said weakly.

Juaan thought he heard a hiss emit from between Baarias' teeth. It was so hard to look at him. To see a face so akin to his mother's glaring at him with the utmost mistrust and dislike.

"Bring her here," Baarias directed, pointing to a pile of leaves and moss.

Juaan lowered Nyri gently upon the soft nest, prying her fingers from around his neck. She caught his hand in hers before he could step back, keeping him close. Baarias' eyes narrowed, but he said nothing as he crouched over Nyri's broken leg, placing his hands upon her and closing his eyes.

Through his contact with Nyri, Juaan felt a swell of power and Nyri's hitching breaths steadied. The pain he had felt faintly through his connection with her was gone. Baarias had eased her discomfort.

"Hold still now, dear one," the healer said. His voice filled with a gentle tenderness he reserved for everyone but Juaan. The power swelled again, tingling against Juaan's fingertips where he held Nyri's hand. All Ninkuraaja had an innate ability to heal their own wounds and sicknesses, but it took a powerful connection to the Great Spirit to heal another.

Baarias' face was smooth and controlled, assured in his skill as he healed Nyri's leg with the energy of the earth. Envy chased through Juaan's gut as he witnessed in his mind's eye the exceptional ability of Baarias. He wished with all his might he could have been the one to ease Nyri's pain and restore her to health. But he couldn't even hold the slightest influence over one of the Great Spirit's Children.

At last, it was done. "There," Baarias said, opening his eyes and pulling back. Reaching for some thick leaves and long strips of bark, he bound Nyri's leg tightly. "It will take a few rises of Ninmah to heal fully, dear one. Go steadily."

Nyri looked down at her leg and beamed. "Thank you, Baarias. I wish I could heal others like you can," she echoed Juaan's desire.

The healer smiled and cocked his head. "I need someone to take my place when I am gone," he said. "You have the strength within you, Nyri. One day, I will teach you."

"Did you hear that, Juaan!" she said excitedly. "I'm going to be an akaab."

Juaan smiled back, but on the inside, he was numb. His Nyriaana was already finding her place in a world he would never be a part of. He and Baarias locked eyes, a terrible knowledge passing between them. This was but another step towards the time when Juaan would be forced to break his promise and leave Nyri forever.

The boy drifted. Half-formed visions twisted through his drowsing mind. Often he was running through a forest, giant trees dwarfing him on either side. He was chasing someone, but the figure was ill-defined, twisting on the edge of his vision like smoke. He could not see the face, but knew instinctively that the figure he chased was a girl. Sometimes she ran along the ground, other times she took to the trees overhead, graceful as a bird. He yearned to catch up, but she remained out of reach, no matter how much he strived.

Other times, when he burned, a voice called to him, speaking constantly, whispering in his ear. Sometimes, another, more distant voice joined with the first, encouraging, pulling him through the fire that consumed his body. He had to fight. He had made a promise. Promise? His thoughts spun. He could not remember the words, but he knew there had been a promise. And so the boy pushed back against the fire, meeting it with his own, for at his centre, another flame burned. This flame was much more powerful than the inferno that sought to destroy him. He did not need to think. His own body took over, searing away the hurt and mending the pain. The flames died, leaving him cool.

A gasp sounded close to his ear and there was a stream of sounds, but he could not make them out. It did not matter; he had won. He could feel his awareness of the world returning. Du Mu fluttered his eyelids open, a smile already forming on his face to greet the one whom he knew would be waiting.

Grey eyes filled his view.

The smile died on his lips. The half-formed visions shattered.

"Khalvir?" the voice asked. It was the same voice that had been calling to him. Not a ghost of his past, but a very real and present girl. "Khalvir?"

It was all wrong.

Du Mu rolled his eyes closed again, reaching for the memory of the face that he had instinctively expected. But he could not see it.

"Khalvir?"

No. Not me. He opened his eyes again. Someone had taken the furs from his body, leaving him naked. But furs were not the only things that had been taken. Panic shot through Du Mu when he saw the pouch had disappeared from around his waist. He groped at his sides, but it was gone. Just like his visions and the centre of his soul. A cry slipped past his lips.

The girl's voice, urgent and reassuring, spoke in his ear. A heartbeat later, she thrust the pouch into his questing hand.

Du Mu seized it and clutched it to his chest. He glared up accusingly at the girl, furious that she would dare to touch it.

A young male voice cut in then, and Du Mu's gaze shifted past the girl into the bruised face of Tamuk. The other boy glowered back at him reprovingly. Nameeda appeared hurt. Du Mu experienced a shiver of guilt, but did not apologise. They would not understand him anyway, and he did not want them. Neither was who he sought.

The energy he had spent searching for the pouch had drained him. Du Mu sank back into the soft furs beneath him and closed out this unwanted reality.

Sleep was quick to take him back into its embrace. He tried to return to the memory, to the figure he had chased. But she was gone. He wept. *Where are you?* His heart cried again, but his call went unanswered.

Light and dark passed. Irritatingly, Nameeda did not leave his side. Tamuk was also an almost constant presence. Du Mu wished they would leave him alone. "Take me back to the trees," he begged more than once, unable to bear the hole gaping at his centre. If he could just return to the forest, then he would understand. But they did not heed him.

He ate what they offered, drank when they lifted the waterskin to his tortured lips. Weak as he was, he almost did not have the will, but something inside would not let him simply give up. This was not over. With nothing else to do, he listened to his companions' chatter as he lay upon the furs, still working to piece together their strange tongue. Du Mu found that if he let his mind drift, let the rhythm of their conversations roll over him, he fancied he could almost understand what they were saying. The sounds may be different, but the way they were spoken remained the same.

And, if he thought about it, the words themselves were not altogether unlike the ones he understood. It was as though the familiar sounds had been deliberately distorted, creating a barrier between whatever he was and these people he had woken to. Du Mu continued to listen, fascinated now, as he slowly pieced together what he knew with the words he had yet to learn.

He would not admit it, but the voices of his two companions became a comfort. A reassuring constant in this strange place.

When the light dawned on the third day of his recuperation, an unwelcome visitor loomed over the furs upon which he lay. Nameeda was still sleeping close by as Du Mu looked up into the pale face of the Chief. The black eyes were shadowed but, somehow, deep inside, Du Mu could sense a reluctant excitement flaring to life inside the hulking man. Rannac was at the red-headed leader's back. The older warrior's face was impassive but, with the same strange sense with which he perceived Eldrax's pleasure, Du Mu knew that Rannac was pleased. Even relieved.

Du Mu drew back from the Chief, his heart picking up speed as Eldrax sank into a squat beside him. But for the first time, the fierce visage was not scowling. His ferocious temper, which always before seemed to threaten at the edges like the black clouds of a thunderstorm, was quiet. Du Mu guessed the Chief was attempting to arrange his coarse features into a kindly expression.

"I glad to see you well, boy," he said haltingly in Du Mu's tongue. The black eyes slid to the sealed flesh on his lower leg, still marred by the frightening old woman's stitches. Excitement burned brighter in the black depths. "How you do it?"

"D-do what?" the boy stammered.

"Heal yourself?"

Du Mu frowned. He had done nothing. He saw impatience flash across Eldrax's hard features at his lack of an answer, and his heart thudded faster in response.

Eldrax drew a long breath through his nose and the annoyance melted away. "You healed flesh fast. No one heal that fast. How do it?"

Du Mu's mouth went dry. He could not answer. "I don't know," he said, and braced himself for the blow that was sure to come.

It never came. Rannac was murmuring in his leader's ear, and the red-headed beast was listening. He gave a curt nod when Rannac finished.

"What did you... feel when you recover?" The giant leader thumped his chest.

Relieved that he wasn't going to be beaten, Du Mu considered the question. He faintly recalled the fierce heat at his centre, burning hotter than his physical body. He touched his chest. "It was like a fire inside here."

Eldrax reared up, letting out a bark of exclamation. He slammed a gnarled hand on Rannac's back, causing the older warrior to wince. "That good, boy. Bring me great joy. Here."

Du Mu flinched away as a pale meaty hand shot towards him. But it did not come in attack. It came in offering. A large leg of cold meat was clutched in Eldrax's fist. "From my own hunt," Eldrax said. "For you. I treated you roughly before, boy, but need to learn. Obedience to Chief makes clan strong. Do as I say, and I look after you. Forbidden like us need to protect each other." And he reached out to pat Du Mu gently on the shoulder.

Du Mu's eyes widened in surprise as he accepted the Chief's gift.

"Once you on feet, you learn become part of proud Hunting Bear clan. Rannac here will teach you how to feed and look after clan while you seek to control power. I check on you again soon, boy." And with a last squeeze of his shoulder, the Chief left. Du Mu let out a silent breath of relief. Rannac took the red-haired man's place at his side, muttering and indicating that Du Mu should eat the Chief's offering. Du Mu was suddenly too hungry to argue.

As he chewed, he mulled over the Chief's words. He did not know what he had meant by learning to control his power, but he dismissed it. He had also said that Rannac would teach him how to feed the clan. Du Mu had already ventured from the camp with Tamuk and Nameeda. If that experience was anything to go by, feeding the clan was a risky and chaotic business.

Risky and chaotic.

Du Mu's heart jumped. This was it. The opportunity he had waited for. Already, a plan was forming in his mind. If he learned well from Rannac, let them think he was becoming one of them, then he would be allowed to venture beyond the confines of the camp again. Once out, all he had to do was wait until the birds had distracted his companions again, and then he would flee. He would be gone before they realised he was missing. He had been a fool to stay and save Tamuk's life that first time.

He would not miss a second opportunity.

Hold on, he thought to the unknown presence lurking deep within. *I am coming home. I am coming* home.

***

Chapter 10

THE GODS

"Where are we going, my Chief?"

Tanag's voice broke into Eldrax's thoughts. There was a quaver to the other man's voice as he followed closely on Eldrax's heels. He understood his loyal warrior's fear as the Forest of the Nine Gods loomed above them; a swathe of cursed woodland blanketing the feet of the Mountains themselves.

He understood Tanag's fear, but that did not mean he was going to heed it. Ignoring the shiver of unease that had no place in his heart, Eldrax strode on, approaching the first of the trees as though this forest were the same as any other. "I mean to enter, Tanag," he said. "And you are coming with me."

"My Chief." Now the note of doubt in Tanag's voice was clear.

He does not trust you... The voice he could never rid himself of taunted from the inside of his mind. Even in death, he could not escape her.

"Be gone, mother," Eldrax snarled at the filmed black eyes glinting accusingly at him out of the shadows.

"Wh-who are you talking to?" Tanag's eyes followed his own but remained unfocused. He did not see the dead Thal woman standing there. Eldrax was alone in that torment.

He forced his mind back to the present. "No one. Now be silent if you want to keep your skin."

Tanag's step faltered on the tree line. "The Watchers?"

Eldrax turned to see Tanag's dark face pale. He caught him by the furs, dragging the other man level with his eyeline. "If a raknari warrior of the Hunting Bear lacks the courage to follow his Chief into any danger, then you need not fear the gods' creatures, Tanag, for I will kill you myself," Eldrax snarled softly into his face.

Tanag swallowed. "I do not fear for myself, my Chief," he said. "I fear for you. If we lost the mighty Red Bear, it would leave our clan vulnerable to the torment of our rivals. We need you."

Eldrax grunted, allowing the flattery of the other man's words to assuage his ire. He lowered Tanag back to the ground. "This is not the day I die, Tanag," he said. "Fate has a different destiny for me. Juran's spawn. He is the beginning of it. The path unfolds, and it is time I became what I was born to be. The saviour of Mankind itself."

Tanag stared at him, but said nothing. The other man did not see. But he would, soon they all would see. He just had to find a way to convince them. Eldrax faced the warped and twisted trees again and stepped inside.

Black mud squelched under his fur-wrapped feet. The putrid stench of rotting flesh assaulted his senses, casting him back to the first time he had so brashly entered the domain of the Watchers. His heart thudded in response, his limbs thrilled in preparation for flight. Eldrax hissed against his body's reaction. He was no longer a wild, unwise boy. He was a man. The most powerful Chief under Utu. The creatures of the gods would not strike fear into his heart and break his childhood vow a second time.

Eldrax took a long breath through his nose, familiarising himself with his enemy's scent. "I vowed to kill you one day," he muttered. "Your doom is upon you."

Or is it your doom you hear, my precious son?

Eldrax snarled at the voice in his mind and thrust his hands into the black mud at his feet. Bringing up fistfuls of the stinking mire, Eldrax smeared his face, concealing his pale flesh. The web of leaves and twigs he had woven into his black furs rustled softly as he stalked forward, keeping his head low.

Nothing moved as he made his way through the mangled trees. All Eldrax could hear was the measured rhythm of his own breath and Tanag's softly sucking steps. No birds sang. No small, helpless rodents scurried for cover to save their worthless hides.

In this forest, death was the master of all. The black trees frowned down upon those who dared to breathe under their rigid boughs.

Eldrax shrugged off the eyeless stares and continued. He would walk where he pleased. He did not know where he was to find what he sought, nor even if it existed. But if he could locate it, it would make the coming days, perhaps even several of the coming seasons, if that was what it took, pass much more smoothly. And perhaps with a lot less bloodshed. It would not do to waste life when he needed all the strength he could muster. And so Eldrax turned his soaked feet deeper into the forest. The evidence he sought, if it existed, was most likely nearer the Mountains of the Nine Gods themselves.

"Eldrax," Tanag's voice was only a breath. "We should not be here. This place is not for man."

"Not for man?" Eldrax arched an eyebrow. "Not for man? You have heard our stories, Tanag. The accursed gods created us on this land.

We share our blood with it. We are bound to it. And we have earned our right to everything upon it. It is ours to rule. Mine to rule. It is *they* who do not belong, and so I will tread where I please. If they wish to descend from their Mountains to punish me for it, let them come!" Eldrax roared the last words to the silent forest, his blood singing with fiery purpose.

"My Chief!" Tanag hissed, freezing in place where he stood.

Eldrax ignored him. The silence did not break. The Watchers did not fall upon him. Instead, he fancied the forest was watching him, appraising him. He lifted his head high, threw back his flaming mane of red hair and strode on into the murk.

The stench grew stronger the farther they travelled. Tanag gagged and wrapped his furs over his nose and mouth. The ground rose beneath Eldrax's feet, and his mouth twisted into a smile. The Mountains were close. He could almost scent his ultimate foes.

"We will rest here," he commanded. The dim light had not changed, but his stomach had begun to whisper of its need. Eldrax loathed being hungry. It often made him do things he regretted. Without looking at Tanag, he sank to his haunches and began digging through the bag of supplies he carried on his shoulder.

Tanag hesitated, his pale eyes darting around the shadowed trees.

"Sit down, Tanag," Eldrax growled. "It stinks enough in here without having to smell your nervous sweat as well." Ever obedient, Tanag sank down into the mire beside Eldrax, though he didn't take his attention off the trees long enough to slake his hunger. Eldrax shrugged. That was the fool's own choice. "And since you have the eyes of a hunted buck, you take first watch." Swallowing the last of his cured meat, Eldrax rolled himself in his furs with his back against the nearest tree and closed his eyes. With the practiced ease of a warrior, he was asleep within moments.

The lifting of his hairs woke Eldrax from his slumber. Experience told him to remain completely still as he opened his eyes to take the first look at his surroundings. The immediate area was empty but for him. The forest remained unchanged, the deafening silence still reigned, but now there was an anticipation to it, like the holding of a breath before the storm.

Tanag was gone.

Eldrax cursed and threw himself to his feet. There was no sign of a struggle. Tanag had wandered off on his own. Eldrax snarled softly, tempted to leave the man behind and continue on alone. But the weak part of himself that he had never fully succeeded in banishing held him in place. Tanag had been his shadow since his first days as Chief. Totally loyal men were rare. It would not do to waste one. Even if Tanag was a fool.

Keeping low, Eldrax trailed Tanag's footprints through the mud. The sudden snapping of branches ahead brought his head up. Something was moving. And it was not the man he sought. Too big. Eldrax threw caution to the wind and rushed forward on silent feet.

The trees parted, revealing Tanag. The warrior stood frozen in place, head turned towards the sound of tormented branches. His dark hand trembled upon the haft of his arshu staff. The thud of heavy feet and breaking of boughs grew louder. Eldrax's heart leaped as a pair of glowing blue eyes high above the ground blinked into existence. Looming through the dark, their gaze swept ever closer towards the man seized by fear in the creature's tracks.

"Tanag!" Eldrax hissed. But it was no good. Tanag did not hear him. Cursing, Eldrax leaped the rest of the distance. He threw himself on top of Tanag, bearing them both to the ground as the gaze of the Watcher fell upon the place where Tanag had stood. Eldrax held still, the twigs and leaves woven into his black furs camouflaging him perfectly with the ground. The ground vibrated beneath his cheek as the Watcher drew closer and the sound of its breath rattling through its throat shivered through the dead air.

Tanag panicked, fighting to get free. Eldrax clamped him in a grip as strong as a bear's bite, pinning him in place as a giant foot thudded to the ground, a hand's breadth from his own face. The smell of the bluish skin wrapped in rotting animal hides made Eldrax's eyes water. He felt the wind of the creature's other foot buffet the furs on his back as it passed over him, before the ground vibrated with another thud. The foot beside his face lifted away.

Eldrax kept his grip upon Tanag until the sounds of the Watcher's passage faded into the trees ahead of them. Only then did Eldrax lift his head from the stinking mud. The impression of the beast's foot beside him was as long as his arm. Eldrax's hand flexed upon his weapon. What he wouldn't give to kill one of those beasts. A feat worthy of a warrior such as himself. He thrust himself back to his feet, denying the urge to run into the trees on the heels of the beast.

Not now, not now, he told himself. His younger self would have rushed ahead, but he was not that man any longer. He had to think of the greater goal. Freeing mankind from the threat of the gods once and for all.

Tanag had just put all of that in jeopardy.

"You fool!" He backhanded the smaller man back to the ground as Tanag tried to rise. "I should have let that creature spike your innards from the nearest tree! Now get up."

He saw Tanag flush in shame before he staggered back to his feet, wiping the blood from his mouth.

"Follow me." Eldrax spun on his heel. "I want to get out of this cursed forest before it becomes impossible to rid myself of its stink."

The land grew steep as Eldrax forged on into the unknown, his every sense straining for the slightest whiff of an ambush. More than once, he and Tanag were forced to climb on all fours, grasping the tangled tree roots to haul themselves up the now-brutal incline. It was in one such instant that Eldrax's hand recoiled. His fingers had instinctively expected the touch of another rough tree root. Instead, his flesh came up against something cool and smooth. A rock. In any other environment, such an encounter would not have caused alarm. But Eldrax had not encountered stone since entering the Forest of the Nine Gods.

And this was no ordinary rock. He ran his fingers over the surface. Smooth as water. Eldrax's pulse quickened. The shape of this rock was unlike any he had ever encountered. It was not rounded, but flat, with sharp edges and corners jutting out of the mud. Excitement flared through him. He had begun to fear he had set out on a fool's errand.

"We're getting close." With renewed energy, Eldrax climbed on. As he went, the way became increasingly cluttered with the strange stones. Panting from the exertion, Eldrax climbed faster and faster, ignoring the burn in his legs until he stumbled out onto a large, flat expanse.

The sight took his breath. The ground beneath his feet was solid stone, but not natural rock. Stretching before him was a broad pathway formed by countless flat, seamlessly interlocking stones.

"The gods," Tanag breathed. "Eldrax, we should leave."

"Not until I get what I came for." The Red Bear stepped along the pathway. A wall rose, interrupting the flat expanse on the far side of the clearing. Close beside it was a long mound of carefully placed rocks. The same stone as the pathway formed the wall, the blocks fitting together so tightly that Eldrax would not have been able to pass a leaf through the cracks. The individual stones of the wall were larger than those in the path. And they were not entirely smooth. Eldrax moved forward until he could make sense of the ridges and hollows carved into the surface of the wall.

He blinked, taking a few moments to absorb what he was seeing.

"By Ea!" Tanag's eyes were wide as he beheld the carvings before him. In that moment, Eldrax could not help but share the other man's awe. It was one thing to hear the stories of how the gods had created and abused man. It was another to be confronted with the physical truth of it.

Eldrax's lips lifted back off his teeth as his eyes followed the story unfolding in the stones; the gods themselves descending from the heavens and their creation of humankind. There were many reliefs of men bowed before the giant, elongated beings, toiling for their pleasure. The hackles on the back of Eldrax's neck rose as he beheld the subsequent betrayal of their creators drawn out in cold, hard stone. He reached out to touch the tortured image of his ancestors cast from the protection of their so-called deities and left to die in a merciless world. Men, women and children alike.

"They will suffer for this," Eldrax snarled. "I will put an end to all the torment they have caused." It was by decree of the gods that half-breeds like himself should not exist.

That was the reason I abandoned you, his mother's voice whispered in his ear. *I could not bear the shame of a Forbidden child. It is their fault you murdered me, my son.*

The red mist of fury teased around the edges of Eldrax's vision. Crying out, he seized a loose stone from the edge of the wall and smashed it repeatedly into the relief depicting an elongated being beating a cowering human. Splinters flew from the wall, cutting his face and hands, but Eldrax did not stop until the stone came away from the whole. The forest reverberated with the crack as it struck the path below. Eldrax thought Tanag would climb out of his own skin. Indifferent to the disturbance, Eldrax stooped to lift the carving.

"Why did you do that?" Tanag dared to question.

"Because I intend to make war upon the gods and bring an end to their tyranny," Eldrax finally spoke his plans aloud. "It is my destiny."

Tanag recoiled. "War? But, my Chief, no one has seen the gods since before the Great Winter of Sorrow. They do not exist anymore," he said. "If they ever did."

"Oh, they existed." Eldrax stepped over to the mound of stacked rocks. He could not know for certain what lay under the carefully arranged mound, but his gut told him his suspicions were right. He heaved one block away from the pile, revealing a dark, musty interior. His instincts had not let him down. Eldrax thrust an arm into the hole he had made and pried loose the object of his desire.

Triumphant, he held the elongated skull before Tanag's ashen face. The surface of the bone gleamed faintly in the dim light.

"B-but what need is there to fight?" Tanag rasped, staring at the giant skull. "They do not affect us."

"Don't they? Then why do the Thals, the elf-witches, and the rest still live in fear? Why would they rather die than break the lores laid down by the traitors who gave them life? The Cro are strong because the Great Winter of Sorrow taught us the wisdom it failed to impart on our foolish cousins. Our ancestors defied the gods' plans for us to perish during those dark times by turning their backs on the traitors."

"Those times are over." The raknari warrior was still trying to avoid the inevitable.

Eldrax barked a disgusted laugh. "You are a fool if you believe the gods are done with us. Don't you see? The long winters are returning. With each turn of the seasons, the herds return later, forcing us to scrape a living off rodents. Weakening us. Heed me, Tanag. The gods intend to come for us again, and when they do, I will be ready for them."

Tanag was still staring at the skull. "How do we fight a god?"

Eldrax tightened his fingers on the bone. "Not with the Hunting Bear alone." The admission left a sour taste in his mouth. "I intend to bring the other clans under my rule."

Tanag hissed. "The other Chiefs will never submit to that."

"If they do not see the reason I put before them, then they will die," Eldrax said. "What are a few blind fools against the freedom of Mankind?"

Tanag fell silent. His eyes strayed towards the damning carvings and the giant creatures leering over their slaves. His mouth arranged itself into a determined line.

"And not just Cro," Eldrax went on. "The witches. They hold the power we need. I now have Juran's brat. He has inherited his cursed mother's gifts. It is a sign to begin. The boy will serve me in this fight before I take his life from him."

"Does Rannac know of your plans, my Chief? As leader of the raknari, he must prepare the men."

Eldrax shook his head. "No. The Old Wolf defied me once. I may have forgiven him, but I have not forgotten. What I must do now goes against the ancient lore of the Plains. Rannac is an inflexible fool. I cannot be certain he will stand by my side unless given good reason."

"Then why not just kill him?" Tanag growled.

Eldrax gripped his weapon. He should do just that. He should. But that weak part of himself that refused to die rose to strangle the thought. He could not yet bear the idea of destroying his old mentor. Rannac was the one man Eldrax had ever come close to thinking of as a father. Unless Rannac challenged him openly, he could not kill him.

He would not admit this vulnerability to Tanag. He could let no one bear witness to his weakness. "It is not so simple," he said instead. "Rannac has taught most of the raknari since boyhood. If I killed him, it could divide the Hunting Bear's warriors. I need them all focused on the common enemy if we are to win. We must ensure Rannac sees the necessity of what must be done and falls in line. I have had your loyalty since the days before I became Chief. Never once have you questioned my orders. Do I have your loyalty now, Tanag?"

Eldrax's words worked as he had hoped, and pride straightened the other man's shoulders, driving out any doubts he might have had. "I would give my life for you, my Chief," he said.

Eldrax gripped his shoulder. "Then let us begin."

***

CHAPTER 11

NO MERCY

"No, no, like this." Rannac repositioned the boy's hand on the haft of the hunting spear.

Khalvir studied the new grip, flexing his long, slender fingers around the wood. "This?"

Rannac jerked his chin and then pointed at the stump across the proving circle. "Throw."

Drawing back his arm, the boy let fly the spear. His form was solid, natural, but he still lacked the strength, and the weapon fell short of its intended target. A snicker drew Rannac's attention to the outer edge of the circle. Lorhir was sitting with a group of the other adolescents, watching Khalvir's first efforts.

Tamuk snorted on Rannac's other side. "Ignore him."

"No," Rannac shook his head as Khalvir limped off after his spear. "He needs to face it. If he does not earn a place in the clan, then the other men will turn on him. Eldrax will not protect him forever. And nor should he." Rannac quashed the small quaver he experienced at the thought. The boy might be of his blood, but leniency would not help him.

Nevertheless, he was finding it increasingly difficult to keep his liking of the boy at bay. Rannac twitched a smile when Khalvir lifted his chin haughtily in Lorhir's direction and returned to where Rannac waited. *So like you, Juran.*

The humour faded when he looked down at the boy's leg. He limped, but in truth, Rannac knew Khalvir should not even be walking after the injury he had suffered. When Rannac had first discovered what had happened, he had despaired. The blow the hatchet bird had dealt had cut deep into the muscle. He had been certain the injury had sentenced the boy to death, or worse, to live his life as a cripple and most likely be put to death.

Neither fate had come to pass. After just three short passes of Utu, Rannac had entered the *ashipu* dwelling to find the boy alert, with nothing to show of his injury but two angry lines in his skin. It had been uncanny, and, Rannac would willingly admit, the sight had lifted the hairs on the back of his neck.

This was the first evidence of the fabled witch power Rannac had ever experienced with his own eyes. All this time, he had secretly believed that Eldrax's obsession with possessing the witches was a mad folly. A misguided desire left over from a delirious childhood dream.

Perhaps it had not been such a dream. With that kind of magic on their side, how many lives could be saved? How many women would be spared the loss of children and men to the brutality of the world if wounds and sickness could be healed with a mere thought?

Eldrax had later translated the boy's words spoken in the *ashipu* shelter. Khalvir held the power of the elf-witches within, but he was not aware of how he had used it to heal himself. For once, Eldrax had tempered his impatience, his mood lifted by the knowledge that he might finally possess what he had sought his entire life. He was determined now to win the boy's love and loyalty.

Before leaving on a hunt to celebrate his turn in fortunes, he had ordered Rannac to teach him how to hunt and let the boy settle into his new life. Once he had gained more strength, once he was a sworn member of the Hunting Bear, bound to his Chief until the end of his days, then Eldrax would demand more of him. Rannac prayed the boy would find a way to master this mysterious ability of his. Rannac could not help him and patience was not a virtue he had ever managed to impart to the Chief.

Rannac tilted his head as he watched the boy. Khalvir had taken an extraordinary leap in understanding the Clan tongue, but Rannac doubted he had gained enough mastery to be questioned on the matter of his powers. Nevertheless, he had them, and that eased Rannac's heart. Now the boy's place was assured. Unless, of course, the Red Bear managed to get his own witch child.

Rannac comforted himself with the knowledge that such a feat was impossible. Even if he hadn't been a fool to believe in the elf-witch's power after all; the Chief was indeed mad to believe such delicate women could survive carrying any offspring of his to term. Surely, it was not physically possible. Juran's witch mate had succeeded in bearing his child. The evidence of that was standing plainly before him. But Eldrax, with both Thal and Deni blood flowing through his veins, was half again the size of Rannac's deceased brother.

No. This boy was Eldrax's only chance of possessing a witch child. And that all-but ensured his safety. Rannac would get to teach his brother's son and raise him to manhood. The knowledge lifted his heart.

"Ah, so this is the witch-child I have heard so much about."

Rannac turned and smiled. A large young man was making his way towards him across the circle. Rannac raised a hand in greeting and the young man mirrored his action, gripping Rannac's hand as they met. "Akor."

Rannac had not seen his old protégé since before leaving to raid the shin'ar forest. Eldrax had sent him on a long patrol of the Hunting Bear's vast borders. Akor's rugged face was leaner than Rannac remembered. Pickings on the trail had evidently been slim. The young man's red hair, however, was as vibrant as ever. A mark his father appeared to stamp on all of his offspring. But, unlike his younger half-brother, Mahasu, Akor had also inherited his father's terrifying stature.

Eldrax had fathered the young man on an UnClaimed female a winter or two before he became Chief and took Halima as his matriarch.The Red Bear often lamented that he had got Akor on a woman he had never Claimed.

Akor's physical appearance was where the similarities to his father stopped, however. His face held a good humour that had been stolen from the Red Bear long ago. He was a formidable warrior that no one would cross lightly, but he was more considering than Eldrax had ever been. And keenly intelligent. Akor was one of the few boys Rannac had allowed himself a particular fondness for. He often reminded Rannac of Eldrax's mother.

"My father was practically purring when I returned home. Now I understand why." Akor's dark eyes were on Khalvir.

"Eldrax has waited for one of his kind for a very long time," Rannac acknowledged.

"That was better," Tamuk approved. Khalvir had attempted to hit his target with the spear again. This time, the flint had pierced the ground at the very foot of the stump.

"Again," Rannac barked. He might not have the ability to help the boy in the matter of his witch power, but a man he would make him.

A man who could survive the very worst of trials. And the boy would most likely hate him for it, but Rannac could live with that. Being fond of one another was not important.

"How well I remember that pain," Akor lamented.

Rannac snorted. "You were raised with a spear in your hand. He was not. He's going to have to work harder than you ever did." And if it broke him, so be it. If Khalvir could not keep up, he was dead anyway. Rannac's eyes flashed to Lorhir and his small group of companions again. Rannac would not always be watching him. Any sign of weakness would mean death. It was the way of things.

It was Akor's turn to snort. "Poor child. Let me know if you need any help in his teaching." Eldrax's son flexed his shoulders. "I have little else to do now that I have returned."

Rannac grunted his acknowledgement as Akor wandered away, no doubt to find food. He kept Khalvir throwing the spear until the boy's dominant arm trembled with exhaustion.

"I think he's done, Rannac," Tamuk ventured, as the boy swept the sweat from his brow, his face drawn with fatigue.

Rannac shook his head. "He has another arm."

"Rannac—"

Rannac quelled Tamuk with a glare. "Other arm." He pointed to Khalvir's opposite hand to make his meaning clear. There was a brief flicker of consternation on the young face before Khalvir turned to face his target again, shifting the spear into his left hand. His first throw went wide.

"You just lost the clan food. If you can't feed your people, you have no place. Again."

"Again."

The spear barely made it three strides from the exhausted boy's feet. Utu was setting in the west and Rannac knew he had finally pushed Khalvir to the limit as the boy stooped to retrieve it.

"Alright, enough." He lifted the spear from the bleeding fingers. Khalvir had not once hit the target. The strength he needed for that range was still beyond the boy. But he had not backed away from Rannac's merciless drive, even when his blisters burst and the skin of his fingers grew raw. It was a good sign.

The boy lifted his cool, bleary gaze to Rannac's face, and he knew Khalvir was questioning whether he was an ally or an enemy in that moment. The pride he felt in the boy's determination cracked through his control, and Rannac let a smile slip onto his face as he cuffed Khalvir's jaw gently. "Good work, boy. I will make a fine hunter of you."

The look of reproach faded, and understanding kindled in the depths of his eyes as Khalvir gazed down at his sore hands, flexing them.

"Come," Rannac took the boy by the shoulder. "Halima can bathe those hands."

Tamuk trailed in their wake. The other boy appeared to have taken to Khalvir since their little misadventure. He and the girl, Nameeda. Rannac was glad of their burgeoning friendship. The boy would have plenty of enemies. It was essential he had allies of his own to guide him when Rannac could not. He would learn that much faster.

"Halima," Rannac called as he shrugged through the entrance to the Dwelling of the UnClaimed.

She turned at the sound of her name, rising from where she had been crouched over a prone form. He caught a flash of anxiety pinching across her proud features before she shuttered it away. "Rannac," she acknowledged. Her gaze flickered over his shoulder to Khalvir and Tamuk. "Boys sleep in the hunter's dwelling. You know that."

Rannac dipped his chin. "Do you have a skin of water?"

"Why?"

He cut off further questioning by lifting one of Khalvir's hands. To her credit, Halima did not flinch at the sight of his raw flesh. She simply turned away and retrieved the required skin. "Hold out your hands."

Khalvir hesitated. The matriarch tutted impatiently and grabbed his wrists, sluicing icy river water over the tortured flesh. The boy flinched, but held still. After a few moments, Rannac saw his shoulders relax as the liquid numbed the pain.

"You could have taken him to the *ashipu* dwelling, Old Wolf," Halima grumbled.

And miss an excuse to be in your presence? The errant thought crossed Rannac's mind, never to find the light. "He's had a hard day. I thought I'd spare him Johaquin's attentions," he said instead.

This pulled a smile from one corner of Halima's full mouth. "There, boy," she said as the skin ran dry. "I have some leather I can wrap those in."

"Do it," Rannac said. "I want him with the spear in his hands again tomorrow."

Halima's eyes went over the weary face before her. "Don't you think he needs more time to recover from his injuries? As you said, the boy has probably had enough of Johaquin. You might send him straight back to her if you push him too hard."

Rannac arched an eyebrow at her as she collected the strips of leather and bound the boy's hands. "I do not meddle in your domain, Halima. I'd be grateful if you did not meddle in mine."

Halima blinked, then shrugged. "As you wish," she said, tying off the leathers with a firm yank, drawing a bitten-off cry from Khalvir. "That'll hold."

Rannac inspected the bindings and grunted his approval. "Tamuk, take him with you to the hunter's dwelling. Eat and rest. Have him in the proving circle again before dawn."

"Yes, Rannac," Tamuk dipped his chin. "Come on, Khalvir."

"You have my gratitude, Halima," Rannac said, dipping his chin to the matriarch as his charges departed.

The low moan pulled Halima around before she could respond and the matriarch rushed back to the pile of furs she had crouched beside when Rannac had arrived.

"Mahasu," he breathed when he beheld the only surviving son of Halima and the Chief lying upon the furs. The child's skin was pale and slicked with sweat. "What's wrong?" Rannac was at Halima's side in one stride, unable to help himself.

"Nothing," Halima attempted to brush him off. "Go back to Eldrax, Rannac."

"He should be with Johaquin. He has a curse."

"I can care for my son better than that old vulture!" Halima snapped. "She never did the rest any good." There was an underlying quaver to this last, so faint Rannac would have missed it if he hadn't known her so well. "Leave, Rannac," she tried to push him away from the sight of the frail boy. "This is my business. There is no need to trouble the Chief. Mahasu will be well again."

This was why she didn't want him to witness, Rannac realised. She feared the Chief hearing that all might not be well with their only surviving offspring.

"Halima?" Rannac placed a hand on her shoulder. "You know me better than that. I will not be the one to tell Eldrax if you do not wish it."

The strong shoulders sagged, and she reached up to place her hand on his. "No, I know you wouldn't, but Tanag will the moment he catches wind. M-Mahasu is my last hope, Rannac. I can't lose him. I can't. No matter how many times the Chief visits me, his seed does not quicken. I-I am failing him and I know he will soon seek another chief mate if I cannot give him what he needs. I will betray the women in my care." Pain twisted her features before she could control herself.

Rannac refrained from telling Halima his own thoughts on her son. He had begun to teach the child the ways of the spear, and from what he had witnessed thus far, the boy's chances of survival were slim at best. Unlike Akor, he was a far cry from his mighty father. "Easy," Rannac soothed instead. "If the boy is supposed to live, then it will be. No one can do more than you, Halima."

Halima sniffed and, to Rannac's surprise, she leaned into him. "Tell that to Eldrax," she whispered.

Rannac's arm went around her, and she sighed, curling further into his embrace as though hungry for someone to cling to. If Eldrax caught him in such a position with his chief mate, it would cost Rannac more than a broken leg, but he could not draw back. Halima was the only woman who had ever made him forget himself. "Courage, my matriarch. Your strength is what Eldrax values most. Do not let it fail," he murmured into her hair.

Halima let herself be held for a few heartbeats more before pulling herself away, standing erect, sniffing. "Forgive me, Old Wolf."

Rannac stepped back, returning the appropriate distance between them. Sorrow and fear still haunted the depths of Halima's dark eyes, but her gaze was now steady as she stood over her sickly son. "Is that all you'll be needing from me, Old Wolf?"

"Yes. I thank you, my matriarch." Rannac matched her cool tone, bowed his head, then swept from the shelter.

He almost collided with Eldrax on the other side of the hides. The Red Bear was encrusted with the grime of travel, his furs soaked red. The Chief's hunt had clearly been a successful one. He gripped a large skin in one hand. Whatever was contained within strained at the leather with its weight.

"You visit Halima?" The dark eyes glittered down at Rannac and Rannac was sure the dread Chief caught the flash of guilt on his face before he mastered himself.

"Yes. The witch-child needed injuries attending to. His hands are not hardened to the haft of a spear."

The hint of menace lifted from Eldrax's pale face. A glow kindled in his eyes. "He walks and hunts just days after a crippling injury. Did you ever doubt me, my dear Rannac?"

Rannac knew better than to lie to his Chief. "I admit I believed the stories of the witches' power to be just that. But, I cannot deny, the way his wound healed... that was no work of Johaquin's."

Eldrax barked a laugh. "Is any healing?" He swiped a bloody hand across his mouth. Rannac could almost feel the Red Bear's muscles twitch. "Where is the boy?"

"He is sleeping, my Chief," Rannac said quickly, reading the Chief's desire to march straight to the dwelling where the boy rested and demand a task from him. "Leave him to me."

Eldrax raised an eyebrow at him.

"He is still wary of you, Eldrax. Being pushed too soon could damage any chance you have of gaining his trust. I beg your patience.

If I witness him achieve anything else out of the ordinary, I will come to you immediately."

Under other circumstances, Rannac would never have risked contradicting any desire of his Chief's. He gambled his neck on Eldrax's current good humour for the boy's sake.

"Very well, Old Wolf. I will leave the boy alone, for now." Eldrax took a step closer, however, letting Rannac feel the weight of his proximity. "But you know I am not a patient man. Ensure his survival and get from him what I need, Rannac, or I will seek it for myself. There is much to be done."

"My Chief?" Rannac frowned.

Eldrax's eyes flickered to the Mountains in the distance, then clapped Rannac hard on the shoulder, causing him to wince inwardly. "At dawn, you will come to my shelter. I have much to show you. But for now, I have ensured my clan will not go hungry for many turns of Nanna. The boy's healing is a sign. Tonight the Hunting Bear will celebrate! Join me, Old Wolf."

Before he could dwell on what Eldrax was planning, his Chief threw an arm around his shoulders. Together they made their way towards the centre circle as the fires roared to life.

***

Chapter 12

Warning

Utu had barely risen above the far horizon when Rannac approached the Chief's shelter at the centre of the camp. Eldrax was already waiting, squatted outside his home as he knapped the edge of a fresh cutting flint. He had all the appearance of a coiled predator. Invulnerable and dangerous.

Rannac allowed himself to feel a swell of pride for the man before him. He had overseen the raising of Eldrax since he was a boy. In the art of wielding a spear, he had no equal. And not just with a spear. Put any weapon into those mighty hands, and Rannac knew no man could ever stand against him. Under the Red Bear's watch, the clan women knew safety; the children were well fed on the bounty of rich territories no other Chief dared to challenge for.

Rannac might disagree with the violence Eldrax might display at times, but he hadn't made the Hunting Bear the strongest clan under Utu by being soft-hearted. Power and fear were the language between the clans. Juran had committed his own number of atrocities in the Black Wolf clan's rise to power. It was an unfortunate consequence of protecting one's own.

And Eldrax protected them well. Yes, Rannac was proud of the hand he had played in his making.

"Rannac," Eldrax stood as he saw him approach.

"My Chief, what is it you wished of me?"

"Your company on a hunt, my old friend."

Rannac frowned. "Didn't your hunting group just return with an ox?" Rannac saw Eldrax draw a quick breath to temper his patience and thought better of saying any more.

"Can I not just wish for your company, Old Wolf, to hunt together as we once did? It has been far too long."

"Not since you became Chief," Rannac recalled.

Eldrax cocked his head. "Not since I broke your leg?"

"No." Rannac ignored the sudden ache he felt from the old injury. An injury that symbolised the breaking of their old relationship. It gladdened his heart that Eldrax finally wanted to return to that. No matter how mighty Eldrax had become, he still needed guidance, and if their previous bond was reaffirmed, Rannac would be in a better position to do just that. "But what about the boy?" he asked. "You asked me to teach him to hunt." Rannac was also afraid to leave him unguarded. He did not know what mischief Lorhir may try to cause if he left camp now. Adolescents were disobedient, volatile, and not entirely in control of their emotions. No matter Eldrax's ruling, if the wrong word was spoken, Rannac knew he may return to bloodshed. He did not speak this fear to Eldrax, however. To do so would risk the Red Bear ripping Lorhir's throat out as an example to those who might consider harming his new prize. He had already bloodied Tamuk for getting Khalvir injured. "He has seasons' worth of experience to catch up on."

"Then another day will not hurt him." Eldrax flung a spear in Rannac's direction, which he caught. "But if you do not stop talking, it will be two."

Rannac's lips twitched as his Chief turned on his heel and led them from the camp. He followed as Eldrax struck out north towards the Mountains before turning west further out into the open Plains.

The wind combed through Rannac's hair, bringing with it the scent of damp earth and rock, and of Utu above. He breathed it in, letting it focus his mind on the task at hand, taking in everything the breeze told him of what came from afar. A shift of direction and the word on the wind changed. Now it told of musky fur, warm dung and the scent of trampled grass.

A wicked smile broke out across Eldrax's face, and he signalled to Rannac. Rannac jerked his chin, tempering his own excitement for the hunt to follow, and fell in on Eldrax's left flank as they stalked forward. A herd of antelope came into sight. Their tan hides blended with the yellowing grasses as they grazed. Rannac was quick to pick out a couple of sickly looking animals which would make easy kills, and just as swiftly dismissed them. They were not the quarry Eldrax would want. Instead, he shifted his gaze to a large buck grazing near the edge of the group, its deadly horns curving impressively towards his back. He made a quick signal to Eldrax, who flexed his fingers upon the haft of his hunting spear and grinned.

"You know me too well, Old Wolf."

It might have been many turns of the seasons since Rannac and Eldrax had hunted together, but Rannac was still in tune with his old protégé. He knew how to move without having to share a word or a hand signal. He stalked around the herd, careful to keep his scent downwind of the herd's lookout. Keeping low, he crept to within striking distance of the target animal. But Rannac did not strike. With a cry, he leaped out of concealment, startling the buck.

Swift and graceful, it reared up, sounding the alarm to the rest of the herd as it bounded away from Rannac.

In the sudden panic and confusion, it did not see the larger man lying in wait directly in its path until it was too late. Eldrax did not bother with his spear. Roaring out, face alive with excitement, the Red Bear burst forth, catching the large antelope by its horns, attempting to drag it down with his bare hands.

The beast was strong. It put up a valiant struggle, dragging Eldrax this way and that as it fought to be free. Rannac held his breath, fearing it would gore his Chief. But Eldrax only laughed louder as he threw his great bulk on his victim's back, buckling the willowy legs. In one move, Eldrax twisted his mighty hands. There was a resounding crack, and the hunt came to its end, hunter and prey tumbling to earth in a heap.

Rannac watched as Eldrax disentangled himself from his kill, still laughing from the thrill of the hunt. He was unharmed, save from perhaps a few bruises. Rannac let out a breath. "I'm getting too old for this," he muttered. "Would it really be too much to use a spear?"

The Chief grinned. "Where is the fun in that?"

"It would put my mind at ease."

"Bah, you worry too much, Old Wolf."

Rannac shrugged. "What do you think has kept me alive all these years?"

"Certainly not common sense."

A barb of shock went through Rannac at the veiled jab. Reminding him that, however proud he was of Eldrax, however close they became, there were teeth behind that smile, and only a fool would forget it. Rannac certainly never would.

He sank down beside the Red Bear as they cleaned the carcass. Peace reigned as the breeze sighed through the grass and the shadows cast from the clouds above danced across the land. The amount of flesh the buck yielded warmed Rannac's heart. The sight banished the thought and memory of starving mothers and deprived children from winters past.

"How is Juran's boy progressing?" Eldrax asked, as his knife sliced through muscle. "I hear he has been given a name."

"Khalvir. Halima gave it to him. It means 'lost' among her mother's People."

Eldrax grunted, waiting.

"He possesses great potential. Fierce, determined. Only his physical weakness holds him back."

"Cursed fruit eaters," Eldrax growled of the witches. "No wonder they waste away so easily. Yet another curse the gods need to answer for."

"The gods?"

"Who else would have had the power to influence a People so strongly that they would rather starve than slaughter an animal to survive?"

Rannac was not sure how to answer, and so he remained silent.

"See that he is fed well, Old Wolf."

"He cannot be seen to be favoured above the others," Rannac warned. "Winter approaches and he is already resented for being an outsider. To provoke further hard feeling would be... unwise."

Eldrax skewered with a glare. "Feed him."

"As you wish, my Chief. As soon as he is fit, I will send him on his first hunt. He is nearing manhood. He must provide for the clan. That might assuage any hard feelings towards his extra rations. I have been overly hard on him, but he has yet to break."

"Good. I need that boy strong, Rannac. He must be if he is to suit my purposes."

Rannac failed to see how becoming an accomplished hunter would aid the boy in learning the healing powers Eldrax coveted, but he said nothing. "I promise you, my Chief, Khalvir will not let you down."

The grin that spread across Eldrax's face showed all of his teeth as he clapped Rannac on the back. "I will hold you to that, Old Wolf."

They divided the meat and all usable parts of the animal before spreading the load between them. The rest they left to the scavengers, who were no doubt already closing in. Time to leave. Even if it were not for the risk of tangling with a spear cat, Rannac admitted to himself that he was eager to return to camp, eager to resume Khalvir's training. The boy was a joy to work with, studious and dedicated, and his every success made Rannac's old heart sing.

A shriek split the air, stopping Rannac in his tracks. The panic and terror conveyed in that one long sound froze his blood. "What was that?"

Eldrax's head whipped around. "Human," he concluded. His pale face was tense, a frown lowering over his heavy brows as he pointed with his spear. "That way."

"But why would anyone be near the Forest?" Rannac hissed, staring towards the threatening tree line.

Another scream of denial and suddenly Rannac was standing alone. Impulsive as ever, Eldrax had not waited to ask questions. The great Chief cast aside his load and bounded away towards the sound of distress, hunting spear held poised in his hand.

"Eldrax!" Rannac hollered after him. The memory of the last time he had seen his Chief racing towards that black line assaulted his mind. His muscles threatened to lock down at the memory of the creatures that dwelt there, but he was the leader of his Chief's raknari warriors.

His place was fighting at his leader's side, and to die for him if he must. Rannac threw down his own load and sprinted on Eldrax's heels.

It was fortunate that he was the swifter of the two, and he caught his Chief a spear-throw's distance from the first of the twisting trees. The breeze blew the stench of mould and death towards him and Rannac gripped his hunting spear, wishing it were his fighting staff. He had never thought to be so close to this accursed forest again.

"No!" a woman's voice shrieked. "No!"

The snapping of twigs and the loud rasp of a slow breath raised the hairs on Rannac's neck. It was coming from around a bend in the tree line. Eldrax met Rannac's eyes. The Chief's black gaze was devoid of emotion, focused, as only a warrior could be. He lifted a pale hand and motioned to Rannac to guard his flank before stealing forward.

The sight that met Rannac's eyes as they rounded the bend in the trees almost made him falter. It was the Black Wolf all over again. His brother. His birth clan. Mangled body parts lay strewn across the ground, leaving a bloody trail of guts in the grasses leading straight into the forest itself.

"By Ea!" Rannac swore.

Deep inside the trees, out of sight, the woman screamed again, pleading for salvation. But before Rannac could twitch a finger, her cries ended in a wet gurgle. Only the eerie sound of the wind filled the sudden silence, rustling over the dismembered corpses in the grass.

"The Watchers," Eldrax snarled, fury radiating from his coiled body.

Rannac's knuckles were white on his spear as he stared down at the bloodbath. The Watchers had ventured from their forest. He thanked whatever power was out there that it was not Hunting Bear bodies littering the ground. If it had been, it would have been his fault. He had let himself get complacent. He had let his guard down, the uneventful seasons softening his judgment.

Eldrax stepped out, threading his way through the remains. "Rogues," he said. "There is no totem."

Rannac shook his head. It made no sense. "Why are they here? These are not lean times. Why risk trespassing on Hunting Bear territory, risk the Forest of the Nine Gods?"

"Rannac," Eldrax hissed, "here."

Rannac turned his head. His Chief was standing beside a torso. One arm remained attached to it. The cold, rigid fingers clutched a large, strangely shaped stone along with a long black feather.

"A warning," Eldrax said, plucking the feather from the dead grip.

Rannac lifted the stone. "The gods," he swore. The stone was water smooth against his fingertips, its sides flat and straight. He swallowed. Just like the tunnel he had discovered in his escape from the Watchers all those long seasons ago, this rock did not belong. It was not water that had polished the rich yellow surfaces smooth. He turned the stone over and nearly dropped it.

On the opposite side was a carving, more intricate and detailed than anything he had seen in his lifetime. Not even the most skilled Thal *ummani* could match the subtle intricacies marking this stone. Silently, Rannac absorbed the story that the carving told. Fear seized his heart as he beheld the tall, elongated being standing above the cowering men at its feet, raining death and destruction down upon them.

"A warning," Eldrax repeated. "The gods are stirring." And the Chief lifted the object he had plucked from the ground beside a second body. Twice the size of a man's head, long and glinting, the empty eye sockets of a god's skull stared, knifing deep into Rannac's soul.

***

CHAPTER 13

FOREBODING

The spear in Du Mu's hand felt in turns both natural and repulsive as he squared off against Rannac. The flesh of his palms and fingers burned beneath the wrappings. His body shook with exhaustion. But Rannac would not let him rest. The glowing circle in the sky rose and set, rose and set, and each day followed the same pattern. Rannac would gather him at dawn and bring him to the circle at the very centre of the camp. Once there, the grizzled warrior would order Du Mu to throw the spear at a stump of wood until he could throw no more. Other times, like today, he would have him mock fight with either himself or Tamuk or the one named Galahir.

"Ah!" Du Mu landed on the hard-packed dirt as Rannac caught his arm and flipped him into the air.

"Enough." Rannac called out as he staggered back to his feet.

Another man had appeared at Rannac's side. Du Mu had seen him before, often recoiling for a moment, mistaking him for Eldrax, but he was far younger than the formidable Chief. Now that he saw him up close, Du Mu guessed, despite his size, the newcomer was only a couple of seasons older than himself. Du Mu's eyes flickered to Rannac, questioning the man's presence now.

"This is Akor," the older warrior waved a hand at the man beside him. "I thought it useful for you to learn how to battle a man bigger and stronger than yourself."

Akor grinned and Du Mu could not help but take a step back as the tower of muscle saluted him with the spear he carried.

"Not raknari, but you still might need to fight." Rannac motioned Akor forward.

The words Du Mu had grasped grazed past his ears as he forced his quaking body to stand erect. Nameeda's teaching of the Cro tongue had been as relentless as Rannac's spear training, and Du Mu slept like a dead man each night; mentally and physically exhausted. For this he was grateful, for then he did not dream. If he did not dream, then it was easier to focus on the task at hand and the reality currently filling his senses; the cool air blowing over his sweat-coated face, the scent of wood smoke and charred meat, the flap of a hide in the wind, and the red-haired man approaching him.

The weapon in Du Mu's hand felt as heavy as stone as he raised it once more into the defensive posture that Rannac had taught him. Akor came straight on, whirling his own spear. Du Mu no longer froze in the face of the attack. His eyes tracked the warrior's motion, the shift of his large hands upon his weapon. He got his own weapon up just in time and the impact of wood on wood ricocheted up his aching arms. Du Mu gasped as the power of the blow sent him to his knees.

"Do not meet him head on!" Rannac's voice cracked over the air. "And do not hold back, Akor. Use everything you have."

That had not been the other man's full strength? Du Mu swallowed as he moved, circling away from Akor.

"Use your speed, let his blows slide by, then look for an opening."

Du Mu listened hard to Rannac, knowing his life and the bones in his arms depended on it. Again and again, Akor came for him, bruising and battering Du Mu upon each of his failures.

"No, move that way," Akor breathed, too low for Rannac to hear his help. "Angle the haft."

Du Mu barked a triumphant laugh as this time he caught Akor's blow and sent it wide with a flick of his wrist and smacked his own haft into the young giant's ribs. He had done it. But in his triumph, he failed to see the man's fur-wrapped foot scythe out to cut his own from under him.

Du Mu landed in another painful heap. Laughter shivered across the air from the other side of the circle. Lorhir and a couple of others were there yet again to watch him fail. Du Mu leaped to his feet and his triumph evaporated in a blaze of heat. The spear in his hand burned. Snarling in his exhaustion, pain, and frustration, Du Mu turned and let the weapon fly with all his might.

A heavy thud reverberated through the air, cutting off the taunting sniggers. *The gods.* He had not looked before throwing the weapon. Du Mu brought his head around, dreading the sight of Akor impaled upon his spear, and stared. Not Akor, though the other man stood close by, his eyes wide with shock. The haft of his weapon shivered, the razor-sharp tip embedded deep into the centre of the scarred tree stump. He had hit it. Hit it dead centre. He stared down at his abused hands, and then again at the weapon, blinking.

A hand clapped down on Du Mu's shoulder and he looked up into Rannac's face. The older man's lips did not twitch, but the grey eyes had warmed. The expression dispelled the pall of gloom that appeared to have clung to him in the past days since he had returned from his hunt with the Chief. Du Mu's responding smile cracked the layer of sweat drying on his skin. He couldn't help it. He had struck the target at last. He was one step closer to achieving his aim. To escape the camp.

If only he could get to the elf-witch women before he made his move, he might figure out a way to take them with him. But someone always appeared to be watching them. Or him. Any attempt to approach was deftly blocked.

A subtle shift in the gleam of Rannac's eyes was Du Mu's only warning. The warrior's spear caught Du Mu around the back of the knees, and his pride in hitting the target was smashed in a swirl of dust. He choked as he looked up at Rannac, askance.

Rannac said nothing, simply pointed at his own eyes, then at himself, before making a cutting motion with his hand. *Never take your eyes off your opponent!* Du Mu read.

The bruises forming down his back throbbed and the many abrasions stung his skin. The last thing Du Mu wanted was to rise to his feet again. *But if you don't, you might never find what you seek. You have to go back to the forests.* Du Mu screwed his eyes shut and shook his head. The moment he thought about the forest, the yearning in his heart was almost a torment, though it was not as strong as it had once been. With each day that passed, it seemed to fade. That frightened him. He did not want to lose himself. He had to get out of here, and soon, before his past was lost to him forever.

Akor did not seem to expect Du Mu to rise again. He lounged, leaning upon his spear. But if he thought Du Mu was going to give in, he was going to disappoint him.

Disappointment was the farthest emotion from Rannac's face when Du Mu once again pushed himself to his feet, using his spear to support his aching body. He staggered slightly before righting himself and levelled his gaze at Akor, who let out a delighted laugh. "I can see why you like him," he said to Rannac, then saluted Du Mu with his spear, ending the bout. "I like you, too, boy. Rannac," he dipped his head to the older warrior, and then turned and disappeared between the surrounding shelters.

Rannac's grey eyes glowed as he stepped to Du Mu's side, surprising him by ruffling his hair. "Good. Enough for now." Rannac was keeping his words simple, and Du Mu was grateful. He was too tired to concentrate. "Go. Rest. Eat."

With that, Rannac walked on past him, leaving him alone as the troubled expression once more deepened the lines of his face. Du Mu wanted to ask him what was wrong, but the warrior was gone before he could gather the words.

Du Mu stood for a moment, shifting from foot to foot. He had lost count of the days he had lived inside this camp now. Even so, he still did not feel comfortable enough to return to the shelter where he slept with the other boys and young men and take food without Rannac or Tamuk present. He was not blind to the resentful stares he drew from the others, the outright scowls when Rannac handed him a larger ration than the rest of them.

A low cry drew Du Mu's attention to the opposite side of the circle. Galahir was on the ground. Lorhir and several of the other boys were circling around him, taunting, daring him to get back up. It was not a fair fight. Anger flared inside Du Mu. Like Nameeda, Galahir had been nothing but kind to him since he arrived in camp. Without a thought, he ran across the circle and pushed himself between Lorhir and the downed boy.

Lorhir rocked back in surprise, then his dark eyes narrowed. "Stay out of this," he snarled. "Greedy rogue." Lorhir swung the fighting staff in his hand threateningly. "Leave, before I put you in your rightful place."

Du Mu was suddenly keenly aware of the weapon in his own hand, and he levelled the spear at the other boy. He had had enough of this one's taunts.

Lorhir's lip curled, and he beckoned Du Mu forwards. One of his companions caught his arm, hissing what sounded like a warning in his ear, but Lorhir shook him off. "Come on, then, rogue."

Du Mu coiled.

"Khalvir!" Nameeda's voice broke the standoff. Du Mu turned to find the girl striding towards them. She threw a dark look at Lorhir before speaking to Du Mu. "Saw," she pointed to her eye. "Rannac. Came to find you." She finished her hand signals by pointing to him. She then caught him by the furs and dragged him away from the open ground. "Get up, Galahir. Let's go." The sandy-haired boy got back to his feet and trailed after them, shamefaced, before he disappeared off on his own path.

Du Mu's own cheeks flamed, seething on the inside as Lorhir's jeers followed them. He wanted nothing more than to turn back and wipe the smug smile off the scrawny boy's face. But Nameeda's grip was firm. He would hurt her if he fought free of her grip and so he allowed himself to be towed back into the tangle of shelters, leaving the other boys behind.

Nameeda suddenly halted, spun and surprised Du Mu by slapping him on the chest.

"Ow! What for?"

"Don't fight with Lorhir." She jabbed a finger, enunciating each word. "He'll put you down hard."

Du Mu raised his chin.

"Yes, he would. The other boys, they're born holding spears. You are only learning. Don't be..." she uttered a word Du Mu did not catch, but she smacked the side of her head in the same instant and so he got the gist.

Du Mu's stomach chose that moment to grumble. Nameeda rolled her eyes and produced a few strips of dried meat from a deep pouch at her side. The one corner of Du Mu's mouth lifted.

"Ah, a smile," Nameeda teased. "I am..."

He could not understand the rest of her words. He took hold of the offered food, then winced.

Nameeda caught his hands in hers, folding out his fingers so she could see the bloodstained wrappings. She took a soft intake of breath. "Your poor hands," she said, her brow pinching together. Du Mu closed his fingers and squeezed, assuring her he was alright. He did not want her to be sad, he realised. He wanted to protect her from such feelings. That knowledge pulled on something deep inside, filling him with that strange sense of familiarity and warmth.

Du Mu's smile faded, and he glanced around nervously as he pulled his hands back. Tamuk had been much friendlier with him since the incident with the bird, but he still didn't think the other boy would like Nameeda holding his hands. "Where Tamuk?"

"Hunting," she said, then caught him by the furs again. "Come." Du Mu kept a firm hold on his meal as Nameeda towed him off in a different direction. They wove around the many dwellings, Du Mu tearing chunks off Nameeda's offering as they went, relishing the instant relief in his empty belly as he did so. The scent of warm hides was thick on the air as the heat of the glowing circle in the sky beat down from above. They reached the edge of camp, but Nameeda did not stop. She struck out across the open ground towards the river. A small stand of trees appeared to be her target.

Du Mu felt instant relief as they ducked under the branches. The browning leaves above sheltered him from the heat of the day. The furs were too hot on his shoulders and he could feel the sweat prickling on his face. A breeze picked up, blowing cool air off the water of the river into his face.

Nameeda drew him to the water's edge. "Sit." She pushed down on his shoulders until he did as she directed. Du Mu hastily swallowed the last chunk of his food as Nameeda took hold of his hands, beginning to unwind the bindings the frightening older woman had put in place.

His companion sucked her teeth as she beheld the raw and blistered skin beneath. The flesh burned as she traced her fingers over the damage. Du Mu winced and tried to pull them away.

"Khalvir," Nameeda admonished.

Du Mu's face stiffened.

"You don't like it?"

Du Mu shook his head.

"Then what else can we call you?"

"Du Mu."

"You know what that means?"

Du Mu jerked his chin. Nameeda had made it perfectly clear from the start. It meant 'boy'. But Du Mu found it fitting. He was just that. He had no name, no family. Not until he learned the truth about himself.

Nameeda sighed. "I can't just call you boy. Khalvir will do until we find something better."

Du Mu made a face but said nothing.

"Here," Nameeda said, and guided Du Mu's hands down into the cold flow of the river. Du Mu let out a breath as the water stroked and soothed his burning flesh, eventually numbing it. He left them there even when she let go. They sat in silence for a long time, listening to the trees whispering overhead. Du Mu closed his eyes. This felt... right. The proximity of the trees, the sigh and rustle of a protective canopy.

His shoulders slowly unwound as he breathed in the scent of sap and leaf mould.

"You like it here?"

Du Mu opened his eyes to see Nameeda watching him. "Yes."

"I come here," she said. "When I need quiet. You're welcome here, too."

"Thank... you," Du Mu said. The words still felt strange on his lips, but he was getting better.

Nameeda smiled, then straightened, looking regretfully back towards the camp. "We need to go. Halima will be waiting. Come with me." She pointed at his hands. "They need more wrapping."

Du Mu really did not want to face the severe woman called Halima. He didn't think she had forgiven him for hurting Nameeda's wrist upon their first meeting, for she still treated him with cool suspicion. But he didn't really have anywhere else to go, and so he rose and followed Nameeda back to camp.

The great shelter was quiet when Du Mu and Nameeda arrived. Halima was sitting beside a young boy. He had pale brown skin and reddish-brown hair. He looked a few seasons younger than Du Mu. And frail. There was a sickly cast to his skin. His expression, however, spoke of his displeasure at the attention he was currently being given by the surrounding women.

Halima's expression... Du Mu frowned. He didn't know her well, but he had never seen such a vulnerable expression on the formidable woman's proud dark face before.

"What is wrong?" Du Mu whispered to Nameeda.

Nameeda winced. "Mahasu is the son of Halima and the Chief. Not well. It causes Halima pain."

"Oh." Du Mu could not think of what else to say, but his dislike of the woman softened. Nameeda stepped away from Du Mu's side to crouch next to Halima and Mahasu.

Something bumped Du Mu's elbow. It was the little red-headed girl who had helped tend him in the frightening healer's tent. She shot him a grin as she trotted past, carrying an armful of herbs. She went before the mother and son, offering her load in a hopeful manner, talking brightly and rapidly.

But Halima's mouth only twisted, and she waved the girl away with a sharp word. The twinkling light in the little girl's eyes dimmed, and her bottom lip jutted as she withdrew, hugging her gift, before slinking away. Du Mu wanted to reach out, to offer her some comfort, but the look in her black eyes as she glanced up at him in passing stilled his hand. The desolation he saw there frightened him.

But Du Mu could spare no more thought to the little girl, for Mahasu was now pointing in his direction, frowning and asking a question of his mother. Nameeda beckoned him over. Du Mu hesitated. Halima's expression was far from welcoming, but Nameeda was insistent, and so he moved forward until he could crouch at their sides.

"Witch?" the young boy asked, pointing at Du Mu.

"No," Halima said. "Half-witch."

The boy blinked, surprised, and spouted a steam of words too rapid for Du Mu to follow with his burgeoning understanding. Mahasu looked between Du Mu, his mother and Nameeda when Du Mu failed to respond to his questions.

Nameeda touched her ear and then spoke to the younger boy. "He can't understand well." She kept her reply slow and simple, so Du Mu would be included. "And he can't remember. He was injured." She tapped the back of her head.

The frail boy frowned. Du Mu could see little resemblance to his terrifying father. "He can't remember?"

The ever-present sense of loss tore through Du Mu's chest afresh. "No."

Halima's son shook his head, as though unable to imagine such a thing and somewhat disappointed that his curiosity would not be satisfied.

"We call him Khalvir." Nameeda waved a hand.

Du Mu made a face, which unfortunately Halima caught. "What's wrong?" she asked shortly.

Nameeda hid a smile. "He doesn't like that name. He'd rather be called 'boy'."

Halima grunted, scowling. "I won't bother next time, then."

"Halima gave you the name," Nameeda explained.

Du Mu blinked, startled. "You name me?"

"Yes," Halima answered. Du Mu absorbed that for a moment. He had assumed Eldrax had given him the name, but he realised now that the leader had not once called him so. Only Du Mu. Boy. Some of his resentment towards the title eased.

Mahasu peered at him, the need for sleep and curiosity warring on his drawn face before he yawned. Halima was there in an instant, guiding him back to the furs. The boy looked as if he wanted to protest. His skin flushed as he tried to bat his mother away, but he was too weak to resist and fell back to the furs.

Nameeda pulled Du Mu away as Halima planted a kiss on her son's forehead, her hand wrapped protectively around his as she crooned a soft song. Du Mu's heart squeezed tight as he beheld the scene, inexplicable tears starting in his eyes. The feel of cool leather intruded upon his senses and he realised his fingers were clutching the mysterious pouch at his waist.

"Mahasu is Halima's only child," Nameeda muttered at Du Mu's elbow.

Du Mu nodded, his throat still too thick to risk speaking.

"Come. Let me." Nameeda pointed to Du Mu's raw hands.

He allowed her to sit him down upon a pile of furs while she found the materials she needed and quickly and skilfully rebound his palms.

"There," she said, satisfied.

A stiff breeze from the entrance to the shelter suddenly ruffled Du Mu's hair. His muscles locked down when Eldrax ducked through the gap in the billowing hides. Out of the corner of his eye, Du Mu saw Halima go rigid.

For the first time, the clan leader did not glance in Du Mu's direction. He strode straight past and loomed at Halima's side, staring down at their son. The pair exchanged a few words. Eldrax did not raise his voice, but Du Mu could see from the harsh lines on his face that he was not pleased. Mahasu seemed to sense his father's presence and leapt awake, jerking to attention. More words were exchanged, ending with Eldrax waving a hand dismissively.

"I can do it, father!" Mahasu's voice suddenly cried out.

"No!" Halima protested.

But Eldrax quelled her with a glance. Du Mu only caught a few of his words. "If he... hunt, then... no use to me, woman," he growled, before walking away. "Get him on his feet."

Everything in Du Mu screamed at him to keep his head down as the Chief passed, but still he could not find it in himself to bow and he held the fearsome leader's gaze boldly. Eldrax slowed and, to Du Mu's surprise, the hard expression on the pale face lifted. The black eyes travelled over him. "You looking much stronger, boy," he said in Du Mu's tongue. "That please me. You not been wasting the extra food I send you." He caught sight of Du Mu's wrapped hands and a smile tugged at the corners of the wide mouth. "Rannac tells me you make a fierce hunter, that you everything I could hope for." Du Mu forced himself to hold still as the clan leader leaned over to take his shoulder gently in his grip. "The Old Wolf yet to be wrong. I look forward to seeing you grow, boy. I suspect we will do great things together, you and I."

Du Mu swallowed but remained silent. Since the wounding of his leg and his subsequent healing, the Chief had been nothing but benevolent towards him. Du Mu suspected it was because of the Chief's protection that Lorhir and the others had not dared to lay a hand on him yet. Although it also stoked their resentment. But even after all the kindness the Chief had now extended, Du Mu still could not rid himself of the shiver that travelled down his spine whenever he met that glittering, black gaze, or the adrenaline that shot to his limbs, preparing them for fight or flight.

"Keep learning well... Khalvir," Eldrax said with one last squeeze of his shoulder. "I need you strong. The time is coming when you will need to prove yourself to me. Do I have your loyalty?"

Du Mu knew what he was asking. Rannac had told Du Mu if he wished to remain with the clan, if he wished to keep his head, he would have to swear his life to Eldrax as his leader. The thought turned his stomach. He could not swear himself to this man. He shook his head slowly.

The black eyes flared before the Chief smoothed his face before speaking in his own tongue. "There is still time."

Du Mu remained still and silent as the great Chief disappeared out of the shelter. It took him a few moments to realise Nameeda was staring wide-eyed at his face. She could not have understood what the Chief had said to him, but his favour had been clear on his face and in his contact. This was obviously not something she witnessed every day.

"Nameeda!" Halima barked, snapping them out of their combined shock, and then let out a stream of words that sounded like a command. Nameeda nodded.

"She says it is time for you to leave. This shelter is no place for a male."

Du Mu glanced pointedly at Mahasu, but let it pass. He rose, nodding his thanks to Nameeda for tending to his hands, before turning to leave. The Chief's words ran around his mind. If he didn't escape soon, he would have to bow to Eldrax or forfeit his life as a rogue on Hunting Bear territory. Fear shivered through his chest.

He was almost at the opening in the hide when a rustle of movement caught his eye. Du Mu froze when he beheld the huddle of women in the far corner of the shelter. He had not been this close to the witch-women since the first days following his capture.

They were not looking in his direction and did not appear to be aware of him. "Hello," he called softly as he started forward, hope fluttering to life in his chest.

A hand caught him by the arm and propelled him out of the shelter. "No!" he cried. "I need to talk to them. I need to know."

He had spoken in his own tongue, so he knew Halima had not understood his verbal plea.

"Stay away, boy. The Chief orders it for your safety."

"He lies!" Du Mu protested. "They not hurt me."

Halima's eyes softened ever so slightly. "He does not lie, boy. Not about this."

Du Mu balled his fists, the ache inside tearing away at him. "I need to know," he choked. "I do not belong."

"No. You don't."

Du Mu's eyes flew to the tall woman's face.

"You heard right. You do not belong here. I wish you gone. Far away."

"Wh-why?" This was not his home. He had no affection for Halima, but the open rejection still hurt, resonating with a deep part of his self.

Halima's hard mask cracked, and she reached out to touch Du Mu's chin. For an instant, Du Mu wanted to lean into that touch. The touch of a mother. "So young," she said. "Darkness should not mark your eyes." She drew breath, seeming to debate whether to speak. "I know my Chief, boy. He has been my mate since I was barely out of girlhood. I see and hear things others do not. You are right not to be fooled by his words. He plans for something. I know. Something that will put us all in danger should he get what he seeks." Her dark eyes pierced him. "You are what he seeks, boy. And that frightens me. I beg you. Leave us. No matter what it takes, return to where you came from. For your own sake, if not for ours." She gripped his chin. "Heed me well, for this is my only warning to you. Run, boy."

And with that, she disappeared back into her shelter and to her son within, leaving Du Mu very much alone in the gathering darkness. The temperature was plummeting in the absence of the Light Bringer. Du Mu's breath plumed upon the air, but the shiver that ran down his spine had nothing to do with the cold.

***

CHAPTER 14

PATIENCE

Eldrax watched as the boy disappeared into the darkness.

"Will he swear loyalty?" Tanag's voice sounded at his side.

"No."

Tanag hissed. "Rannac is failing. You cannot do any more to win his favour, my Chief. Ungrateful brat. You should kill him. You could have three of your own witch-children in the bellies of the elf-witches you Claimed. We do not need this rogue."

Eldrax shifted his feet. "I cannot know that, Tanag," he admitted grudgingly. "Until I am certain, I need this spawn of Juran to live. And so I will continue to show him favour. I will continue to treat him like a son. The longer he stays here, the further his ghosts stray from him. I can no longer see the forest in his eyes."

"He has not given up yet," Tanag warned. "I have seen him wandering when he thinks he is alone, watching the sentries. He intends to escape. Don't trust him, my Chief. This act of submission is nothing but a ruse to gain trust enough for us to let our guard down."

Eldrax snickered. "I'd be disappointed if he was so meek as to give in so easily. Breaking a weak spirit would bring me little satisfaction.

Rannac hopes to take him on his first hunt soon. That would present him with the perfect opportunity to run." Eldrax sucked his teeth. "I will order the Old Wolf to delay. The more time the boy spends in camp, the closer he will become to his new companions, and the harder he will find it to leave. What are fading ghosts to the warmth of a girl's hand? The companionship of brothers? You will witness his vow to me, Tanag. And to have Juran's son bow..." Eldrax savoured the thought. "His doom awaits, and I can expend all the patience I possess to see him walk willingly into its jaws. It is only a matter of time."

***

CHAPTER 15

FAILURE

"*Will you stay with me?*"

This time, in the darkness of his mind, there came no answer.

It was strange how the thud of flint embedding itself deep into wood had become the most satisfying sound in his known life; but Du Mu could not help but feel a fierce joy as he watched the spear haft shiver into stillness in the centre of his target.

"Is he ready?" Tamuk was at Rannac's elbow. "Surely he is ready by now."

Du Mu flexed his hands. The protective wrappings had long since been removed. He ran his fingers over the toughened skin marking the ridges and hollows of his palms. He did not make it apparent that he was also waiting breathlessly for Rannac's reply.

The silver orb in the night sky had waxed and waned and waxed again since the night of Halima's warning to escape. He had been patient. He had passed every test Rannac had thrown at him. Tamuk had taught him to follow a trail, Rannac had taught him to strike a target, even blindfolded. He had attuned his ears to pick out the slightest rustle of the brave target bearer's movement, and could strike true without the use of his sight.

In this, he surpassed even the more experienced boys. Du Mu was not aware how, but somehow he always knew where the target was, a faint shimmer in his mind's eye, telling him just where the target bearer would be. He knew Rannac was deeply impressed by this, and that it was not usual. Eldrax himself had appeared on the edges of the proving circle to witness his skill. The Red Bear's eyes glowed with an increasingly greedy fire.

Outside of his inner thoughts, the silence stretched. Du Mu raised his gaze to Rannac, trying to keep the anticipation from his face and appear calm, as a hunter should. The older warrior's gaze swept over him, studying every part of him with a critical eye. There was a quiet pride lurking in those piercing grey eyes as Rannac finally dipped his chin. "He is ready. Tamuk, prepare Lorhir and Galahir. A herd of elk was sighted a day's travel from here. We will leave at first light."

Tamuk grinned at Du Mu. "At last! You're in for some fun now," he said, and disappeared off to do as Rannac asked of him.

Yes, Du Mu thought, with a composed nod in Tamuk's direction. *We will see.* On the inside, his heart was pounding. He had done it. He had waited so patiently; battled against his growing doubts, grasping with all his might, refusing to let go of that feeling in his heart that someone, somewhere, was waiting for him. Now the day had finally arrived. He was being taken on a hunt. He would no longer be surrounded by sentries, hunters, women and children, never without at least one set of eyes on him, watching, either in curiosity, suspicion, or scorn.

Out on the Plains, he would just have Rannac, Tamuk, Galahir and Lorhir to contend with.

Du Mu ground his teeth at the thought of Lorhir. He had already accepted Rannac would be a challenge, but he would have to be extra cunning if he wanted to escape the notice of that sly jackal. Lorhir would watch for anything he could use against him. The thought that they would be forced together on this journey with so few others to separate them tightened Du Mu's stomach.

Rannac nudged him in the shoulder. "You have done well, boy. It is time to prove your worth."

"Yes, Rannac," Du Mu said, keeping his gaze down so Rannac would not detect the lie lurking in his eyes.

"Tomorrow, you will provide for your clan, as one of us."

I am sorry, Rannac. I am not one of you, Du Mu thought, but he nodded silently.

"Go on, get some sleep." Rannac dismissed him. "You need a sharp mind on the hunt. Make no mistake, boy, Tamuk speaks of fun, but it is a dangerous game."

I'm counting on it. The memory of the incident with the giant bird was still fresh in Du Mu's mind, even now. He did not know what a real hunting trip entailed, but if it was as fraught with danger as stealing those eggs, it might just distract his companions enough for him to slip away.

"You must keep your wits about you at all times," Rannac cautioned. "Never let your guard down."

"I won't," Du Mu promised, and let a faint grin slip onto his face. "You have taught me too well."

"Ah, away with you!" Rannac shooed him off.

Du Mu left the training circle and let the smile die as his heart contracted. He had not meant to, but he had grown close to the warrior. Rannac had watched over him and cared for him like a stern father since the moment he had woken in his care. Du Mu trusted him as much as he trusted Nameeda. The knowledge that he was about to betray him was harder than he could have ever imagined.

Wrestling with himself, Du Mu headed straight for the shelter where he slept with the other hunters. He was so caught up in his thoughts, he almost collided with Nameeda, who appeared to have been waiting for him.

"Sorry," he grunted hastily, catching her in his hands as he knocked into her, struggling to halt his momentum before he toppled them both to the ground. So much for keeping his wits about him.

She laughed at his clumsiness, pushing him back until he found his balance. He stood, looking bashfully at her.

"Tamuk told me Rannac is taking you on your first hunt tomorrow."

Du Mu dipped his chin. "Yes."

She beamed. "I'm proud of you, Khalvir," she said.

"Thank you," he responded, meaning for so much more than the praise. His throat tightened, knowing this would probably be the last time he would see the girl. "I... could not have done it without you, Nameeda" Hesitantly, Du Mu stepped forward and wound his arm around her. She stiffened in surprise. "Thank you for everything."

He let go of her then, separating himself, and strode on without looking back. He felt her eyes follow him until he walked out of sight.

Despite Rannac's admonishment to rest, Du Mu did not sleep. His mind worked, recalling the routes he had taken from the forest where Eldrax had found him to the Hunting Bear camp, fearing he might have forgotten the way. Then other fears intruded. If all went as planned and he made it back to the forest he had woken in, what then? How was he to find his answers? He did not even know what he was seeking. He cursed his misfortune in failing to get near the elf-witch women. But it was too late for that now. He was sorry he would have to leave them, but he had to get away. Halima's warning still weighed heavily on his heart. She had told him to leave before it was too late, and leave he would.

Knowing sleep was beyond him, Du Mu rose before the light of day touched the sky. Tamuk was snoring softly close by. Du Mu nudged him awake.

"S'matter," the other boy asked, struggling to lift his head from the furs and focus his eyes. "Khalvir?"

"Me," Du Mu grunted.

Tamuk groaned, his half-raised head dropping back. "S'not light yet. Go back sleep," he slurred.

"Oh, get up, Tamuk," another voice cut in harshly. "If we have to take this grasping rogue out on a hunt so he can start filling his own belly, I want to get it over with."

Du Mu glared as Lorhir shifted in the thick shadows, bearing several spears. He threw one to Du Mu. He caught it deftly and lowered the tip towards Lorhir. Tamuk rolled to his feet, snatching another spear from Lorhir. "Alright! Let's get out of here before the wrong blood gets spilled. Galahir," Tamuk nudged the nearby pile of furs with his toe. "Get up, we're leaving. Galahir!" Tamuk's nudge turned into a full-blown kick, causing the pale-haired boy to leap awake with a cry of alarm on his lips. "We're going."

"Ea above," Lorhir grumbled as he followed Tamuk from the shelter. "The rogue and the half-wit. We'll be lucky to catch a snail."

"Close your mouth," Tamuk snapped as Galahir scowled at Lorhir's back, but kept his own mouth closed. Du Mu could almost feel the heat of the half-Thal boy's shame radiating from his brawny body. Du Mu did not know Galahir well, the large boy did not speak often and Du Mu had not had the want to get close to anyone besides those he had needed to rely on since his arrival in camp. Nevertheless, he felt sorry for Galahir. He understood what it felt like to be the bottom of the pile. And Galahir did not enjoy the protection of the Chief.

The cold air outside stripped away the bleariness playing around Du Mu's eyes from his sleepless night, and he breathed in the clean scent of the Plains calling to him from beyond the sprawl of shelters. Today was the day he would regain his freedom. Nervous excitement tingled along his spine as he followed his companions to the edge of the camp.

There they waited in the quiet of the predawn, each of them lost in their own thoughts. Tamuk and Galahir yawned more than once, but the only constant sound came from Lorhir as he sat running his thumb ceaselessly across the flint tip of his spear, testing its sharpness. His calloused skin rasped over and over. The sound was just beginning to grate against Du Mu's nerves when Rannac loomed out of the shadows. Upon his wiry shoulders were several leather bags. Du Mu guessed they were filled with rations for the journey. Without a word, Rannac tossed the loads to Galahir, who slung them over his thick shoulders.

"Here," Du Mu held out a hand in offering. "I will carry one."

"I've got them," Galahir said, ducking his head.

Du Mu knew Galahir could carry the combined load easily, but he had his reasons for wanting to take one of the supply bags. If he was to strike out on his own, he would need food. "I know. But I like to take my share."

"That and more," Lorhir muttered.

Du Mu rounded on him. "You—!"

A spear thrust between them. "Enough." Rannac did not raise his voice, but the command in his tone could not be ignored. Scowling at one another, Du Mu and Lorhir stepped back. Du Mu turned to Galahir.

"I meant my share of the load." He extended his hand again.

Galahir's gaze flickered to Rannac, who nodded. "He needs to build his strength. Give him half the load, Galahir."

Galahir eyed Du Mu in a way that was mildly insulting. He arched an eyebrow. He might not be as thickset as Galahir and some others, but he wasn't *that* scrawny. Not any more, at least, thanks to Rannac's training and the favour of the Chief.

The pale-haired boy handed Du Mu two of the bags. He tried not to grunt as he felt their weight. Galahir had made them appear much lighter. Du Mu hefted them into place over his own shoulders, balancing the load. The weight, although already a strain, was reassuring. He did not know how long it would take him to find the forests of the south. He would most likely get lost several times before he found his way.

Dawn was breaking over the eastern horizon when Rannac gave the signal to move out. The grizzled warrior strode at their head. Tamuk waited until Lorhir moved ahead of him behind their leader before inserting himself between Lorhir and Du Mu. Du Mu was grateful. He wasn't sure if he could resist jabbing the hated tormentor in the back with his spear if he got close enough to him.

"Are you nervous?" Tamuk asked over his shoulder as they travelled.

The interruption mildly irritated Du Mu. He had been occupying himself by taking in the landscape, noting the recognisable landmarks and drinking in the Plains' raw beauty in the strengthening light of the day. "No," he replied.

Tamuk laughed softly, as though he didn't believe him. "I remember my first hunt. And I was nervous. First time out beyond the safety of the camp. Only four others to stand between me and the dangers of the Plains."

"Dangers?" Du Mu glanced around at the empty landscape.

"Oh yes," Tamuk flashed a grin. "Forget the hunt itself. Wolves are not bold enough to attack the camp, but a few hunters exposed on open ground... And let's not mention spear cats or other men. It hasn't been unknown for other clans or rogues to ambush the unwary." He arched an eyebrow. "A chance to thin out a rival's numbers is not one to pass up."

Du Mu glanced around somewhat more warily now, imagining another group of armed men lurking in the dips and hollows, just waiting to pounce.

Tamuk laughed again. "Relax, Khalvir. None of the other clans would dare risk provoking the Red Bear by killing his hunters in his own territory. Not unless they wanted to be wiped from the face of the Plains."

But Du Mu wasn't part of the Hunting Bear clan. As Lorhir liked to point out, he was a rogue, sworn to no one.

Tamuk turned and punched Du Mu's shoulder companionably. "Don't worry, my friend, I'll watch out for you." He grinned.

Du Mu attempted to smile back, but could not. If all went as planned today, Tamuk would certainly not be there to watch his back.

The Light Bringer rose higher in the sky, uninhibited. Du Mu soon wished for cloud cover as sweat beaded on his face. Rannac had set a ground-covering pace and Du Mu was glad Tamuk had taken up a conversation now with Lorhir, as he wasn't sure he could have spared the breath. The loads on his shoulders felt as if they had doubled in weight since he first hefted them. He stumbled, but quickly righted himself and gathered his will, gritting his teeth against the growing pain in his shoulders, the burn in his trembling legs. He would not show weakness to Rannac, and especially not to Lorhir.

A nudge on his shoulder brought Du Mu's head up. Galahir. The strain must have shown on his face, for the other boy offered an encouraging smile. He pointed a pale finger at the sky above and the position of the Light Bringer. "Rannac will stop soon," he murmured.

Du Mu twitched one corner of his mouth, wiping the sweat from his face with the fur on his arm. He did not mind that Galahir had seen through his pretence. He found himself at ease in the large boy's good-natured presence. Those clear blue eyes did not weigh and measure him, nor find him wanting.

"Halt," Rannac called a moment later, raising a fist.

Galahir flashed Du Mu a grin and promptly sank to his haunches, unslinging his own loads from his shoulders. Letting out a silent sigh of relief, Du Mu unburdened himself. Rannac swept by, looking as fresh as he had when they left camp. He did not look at Du Mu; he did not even break stride, but his hand flashed out and squeezed Du Mu once on the shoulder. Du Mu could not help the glow that fluttered to life in his heart, knowing he had pleased Rannac with his efforts.

Sinking down next to Galahir, he took a long swallow of water from the skin at his waist and then dug himself out a couple of strips of dried morsels.

A prickle ran up his spine. Du Mu stiffened instinctively. Turning, he froze. He had not realised they had come so close to the dark forest on the borders of the mountains; closer than he had ever been. It crouched there, like a living beast. A whisper brushed past Du Mu's ear. He frowned and looked around, but all of his companions were silent, busy filling their bellies as much as they could before Rannac signalled it was time to move on.

The voice brushed past his ear again. No, not his ear. His mind. It was coming from the forest itself. Du Mu stared. The dark line filled his vision, a black, inescapable maw sucking him in. And something inside him responded, uncoiling like a snake, broiling and hissing, as it was tugged towards the beckoning trees.

"That is the Forest of the Nine Gods." Galahir's voice shattered the spell. Du Mu flinched and snapped his head around, startled to find he was still in the same position with the Light Bringer shining overhead, surrounded by his companions.

This was the first time he had heard the threatening forest named. He had not understood enough of the Cro's tongue to ask when he had first arrived, and then he had been too caught up in gaining the skills he needed for this very day to think much on the strange tree line and the way it called to him sometimes. "The Forest of the Nine Gods?"

Galahir nodded. "You have yet to hear the stories told by our Dugnamtar. But it is told that the Nine Gods that created us went to live in those Mountains after they abandoned us to die in the Great Winter of Sorrow."

Du Mu cocked his head.

"Did the witches not tell you about the Great Winter of Sorrow?" Galahir raised his eyebrows. "Surely the tales of that dark time have not been forgotten?"

"Maybe not," Tamuk interjected. "But he has." He nodded at Du Mu. "Try to keep up, Galahir."

Galahir flushed but did not respond. He kept his focus on Du Mu. "It was many, many lifetimes ago now. An evil time. The gods destroyed the land in fire and brought about the Great Winter of Sorrow, all in an attempt to be rid of us. And they nearly succeeded. There were once nine Peoples, you see. Now, thanks to the gods' cruelty, there are only four left." Galahir ticked off his fingers. "The Cro, the Thals, the Deni, and the elf-witches."

"But why would the gods do that?" Du Mu asked.

Galahir shrugged. "We do not know. They grew tired of us, I suppose." He nodded towards the black tree line. "That forest is the start of their territory. It is said to be guarded by monsters and spirits that will steal your soul if you dare to cross into the trees." Galahir shuddered.

"Has anyone seen these monsters?"

"They say Rannac has," Galahir whispered, nodding towards their leader, who had moved a distance away and was keeping watch. "It is said a great Chief once provoked them. The shattered bones of his clan still litter the Plain."

A shiver ran down Du Mu's spine. He looked towards the tree line again, trying to quell the fear curling through his soul. *Spirits that will steal your soul if you dare to cross into the trees.* Was that what he was hearing whispering against his mind?

"No man will tread there," Galahir concluded. "It is forbidden."

"Gather." Rannac had returned, his voice shaking Du Mu and Galahir back to the present and the task at hand. Du Mu was relieved. He wanted nothing more than to leave the forest far behind and never look back. He rose hastily to his feet, forcing himself to turn his back on the trees and the faint, ghostly whisper.

"Do you want me to take those?" Galahir nodded at the supplies at Du Mu's feet. In answer, Du Mu lifted his chin and swung the leather bags back into place on his back. It was a relief, however, to find that their weight reduced now that the hunting group had satisfied their thirst and hunger.

Rannac took point again, but this time, he beckoned Du Mu forward with him. "This is your hunt," he said. "We are approaching the area where the herd was last sighted. Lead us to them."

Du Mu swallowed, suddenly conscious of all their eyes weighing on him. Tamuk had taught him a few tricks, and he had always succeeded in their games, but Lorhir had not been looking down his nose at him then.

"It is elk we're after. Big animals. Cloven hooves."

Du Mu dipped his chin, showing he understood, then stooped to study the ground, reading it as he had learned. "That way," he pointed once he was certain he had divined all that the hard earth could tell him.

Rannac gave no clue whether Du Mu was correct in his reading. He just waved him forward impassively. This was a test.

It was not easy. Du Mu struggled to remember all the nuances Tamuk had taught him to look for. He studied every little scuff, every broken blade of grass, he analysed every smell and sound. Soon, he found himself caught in a tangled web of trails. How was he supposed to know which animal had left what trail?

He heard Lorhir laugh scornfully on more than one occasion and mutter something about how it was a good thing the clan wasn't relying entirely on him to feed them. Du Mu hissed through his teeth, raking his hands through his hair. He had to find what they sought. It was his only hope of getting away.

At last, Rannac gave an impatient sigh. "Tamuk, take point. We have to find the beasts before we lose Utu's light." Another snicker from Lorhir, but Rannac quelled him with a glare. "Khalvir, watch Tamuk."

Cheeks flaming, Du Mu did as he was told. He soon realised Tamuk had not simply been bragging when he claimed to be the clan's best tracker. The trails spoke to him in a way Du Mu could not yet understand. It was not long before Tamuk halted, his fist in the air, and signalled that their quarry was close. The wind shifted and Du Mu thought he could discern sporadic grunts and snorts carried on the breeze.

Rannac gestured for them to stay low. Du Mu watched as their mentor assessed the breeze, sniffing the air, then motioned with his hand. Lorhir and Galahir broke off, half running in low crouches until they were out of sight. Du Mu's heart sank when Rannac signalled he should keep close. He had hoped to be sent with Tamuk or Galahir.

Patience, patience, he told himself as he crept forward on Rannac's flank. They mounted a small rise and looked down. A vast herd of large creatures spread away before them.

"Elk." Rannac pointed to them.

Du Mu stared at the animals, taking in their sharp hooves and swift-looking legs. Many of them sported crowns of deadly antlers. The healed wounds on his leg throbbed. The hatchet bird had come close to killing him. What would happen once they roused these animals?

His mouth was dry as Rannac stalked forward, right to the edges of the grazing herd. His grey eyes raked over the beings before him, searching. "There," the warrior spoke on a breath. "That is your target, Khalvir. Strike true."

Du Mu looked across and saw a young creature browsing among its fellows, its soft eyes peaceful. His eyes widened, darting between the unsuspecting creature and the weapon in his hand. He almost dropped it, forgetting everything Rannac had taught in that one instant. *Monster, monster, monster.* The word echoed in his head. "No!"

The herd's sentry's head bolted up, alerted by Du Mu's shout of denial. The creature's high-pitched warning split the air, bringing the rest of the herd to attention. Rannac cursed, but his words were drowned out as the sentry's call was taken up, passing from animal to animal. The ground began to rumble. The vast herd fled, galloping and leaping away from the hunters that lurked in the grass.

"Throw!" Rannac shouted at Du Mu. "Throw, damn you, before it's too late."

But Du Mu was frozen. The haft of wood in his hand fixed uselessly in place. The panic he had caused buffeted across his senses, and he had to fight the urge to clap his hands over his ears. *Monster!* The voice in his head screamed.

Rannac swore, thrusting him to the side. Du Mu watched, numb, as together, Tamuk and the older warrior let fly with their own weapons. He flinched when the spears struck a trailing animal, the cruel flint tips burying themselves deep in the other being's flesh. Du Mu thought he felt a brief flash of pain, as though he himself had been struck when the elk bellowed and crashed to the ground. Rannac and Tamuk were out of hiding in a flash, sprinting towards their downed victim.

Left standing alone, Du Mu took a breath, then another, but the numbness would not recede. He tried to think past the echo he had just heard in his head, to remember his purpose. Rannac and Tamuk were occupied, focused on the animal they had felled. Du Mu stumbled back, forcing his legs to move. This was the opportunity he had waited for. There was nothing between him and the open Plains. *I'm coming!* He called out to the missing part of himself that his soul yearned to be reunited with.

"Khalvir." Rannac's voice was a growl in his ear. The warrior's half-hand clamped down on Du Mu's shoulder. This time, there was nothing affectionate in the contact. Rannac's fingers bruised his flesh. "Where are you going?"

Du Mu stared up into the furious face and his words failed him. Without waiting for an answer, Rannac dragged him towards where the wounded elk lay. Du Mu was not strong enough to resist, and he was still too stunned and sick at heart by what he had just experienced to even try to fight as Rannac deposited him next to the bloodbath.

"What happened?" Even Tamuk's face was unfriendly.

"I-I," Du Mu stammered. "I did not know. I did not realise. I thought..." He trailed off.

"What?" Tamuk demanded. "What did you think? That we'd just be poking the elk to steal eggs from under them?"

Du Mu's face flamed. "I-I don't know."

"Here," Rannac thrust a long flint knife into Du Mu's fingers and pushed him towards the downed elk. "Provide for your clan. Finish the hunt. Cut its throat."

Gating a sob between his teeth, Du Mu faced the helpless creature. His inner senses screamed as he experienced her pain and helplessness. Her flanks heaved, her wide eyes wheeled in terror. She knew, she knew what he was there to do.

Monster, monster, monster.

The knife slipped from Du Mu's fingers. "No," he answered both the echo and the faces staring at him. "No, I won't be a monster."

"Oh, get out of the way!" Tamuk thrust him to the side, drawing his own flint knife. Without a moment's hesitation, he plunged the blade deep into the elk's heart. The terrible twitching stopped as she sagged, her eyes falling blank, no longer vital. Dead.

Galahir and Lorhir were approaching fast, confusion on their faces.

"Come with me, now!" Rannac caught Du Mu by the furs and dragged him away from the carcass before they could ask questions. "Take that back to camp," he snapped at the other young men. "Do not wait for me. If Eldrax questions, tell him I will return before Utu sets again."

Du Mu felt a chill run up his spine when he heard Rannac say 'I' not 'we'. He had never seen Rannac appear so angry. The fear of what was going to happen next returned some feeling to his limbs as Rannac continued to drag him by the scruff of his furs.

Then he stopped. "Hold still, boy," he said gruffly.

"What are you going to do?"

"Teach you a lesson. Give me your wrists."

"No." Du Mu tried to fight, but Rannac was too strong. He threw Du Mu to the ground and pinned his wrists behind his back. Glaring over his shoulder with his cheek in the dirt as the hurt and betrayal burned through him, Du Mu saw the warrior draw a length of twisted material from a pouch in his furs before he used it to bind Du Mu's wrists together. Then he unwound the protective leather strips he wore around his wrists.

"No!" Du Mu protested again, guessing Rannac's next action. But with his hands bound, he could do nothing as Rannac bound the leather around his eyes, depriving him of his sight.

"On your feet." Rannac's hand clamped around his elbow, pulling him back upright. "Now come with me."

Du Mu said nothing as he stumbled along in Rannac's wake, but the numb shock of betrayal was wearing off. Anger stirred at his centre.

He did not know how long they walked, but when Rannac finally stopped and pulled the leather from Du Mu's eyes, the light in the sky had waned. They were standing in a loose stand of trees. And he did not know where he was. The dark tree line of the Forest of the Nine Gods could no longer be seen. He glared up at Rannac. "Have you brought me here to gut me, too?"

Hurt flickered across Rannac's face before it was banished. "No," the older man growled. "Though the Red Bear may gut us both if I do not get through to you, Khalvir. If you are to be a part of the Hunting Bear..."

Rage blazed through Du Mu. "That is not my name! And I do not want to be a part of your clan! I want to go home." And with that, he lunged, barrelling past Rannac, making a last, desperate effort to get loose. He was on the ground again before he made it two strides, as he expected. "Let me go!" he cried.

"There is nowhere for you to go. The Hunting Bear is your only hope."

"No." Du Mu's shout of denial turned into a sob.

"Yes. You must accept it. I vowed for you, boy. I vowed to Eldrax that you would not betray him on my own life."

Du Mu stopped struggling and flipped over on the ground to stare up at the older man. "Why?"

A range of emotions flickered through Rannac's grey eyes as he looked down on Du Mu. His mouth opened and closed several times before he swallowed and composed himself. "I am very good at judging worthy young men. I saw something in you I believed would benefit the clan. But for you to fulfil that potential, you must learn the lessons of the world. You may hate me for this, but it is for your own sake. And mine. If you will not hunt, the clan will turn on you. And when they do, you will face a far worse death than starvation." With that, Rannac pulled Du Mu from the ground and tied the loose end of his bindings to the thick branch of a nearby tree.

"Rannac."

The warrior did not respond. He kept his eyes averted from Du Mu. He drew his hunting knife, and Du Mu tensed, but Rannac simply threw it to the ground, embedding the tip in the earth, just out of

Du Mu's reach. "You can use this to free yourself. But by the time you manage that, I will be long gone." Rannac leaned Du Mu's spear against another tree. "I am going to leave you alone now, Khalvir. There will be no clan to feed you. Nobody to help. If you want to eat, you must kill. We'll see how monstrous you consider killing is when you are mad with hunger." And with that, he turned and strode away.

Panic seized Du Mu's heart as the full weight of his situation settled around his shoulders. "Rannac!" he shouted. "I am sorry. Please."

Rannac paused, but didn't turn. "Quiet now, otherwise you will not last the night. Stay in the area. You are on the edges of Hunting Bear territory. Stray and you will face the mercy of a rival clan. Quiet now, boy. The Chief and I have matters to attend to, but I will find you when I return. Until then. Survive."

"Rannac," the whisper slipped from Du Mu's lips. He strained against his bonds as the older man walked away from him, his wiry shoulders bowed as though under a great weight.

Survive. The word rang peculiarly around Du Mu's head as the Light Bringer vanished below the horizon, leaving him utterly alone in the dark. *Survive.*

Salty tears swelled in Du Mu's eyes and dripped into the uncaring leaves below.

***

Chapter 16

MASTER OF THE PLAINS

E ldrax walked at the head of ten of his most loyal men, men like Tanag who had supported his leadership even while his cursed father still lived. The strongest of his fighters. Although intimidating, they were not enough of a force to be a threat to another clan on their own territory, but sufficient to protect the Chief should their neighbours not listen to reason.

They had travelled west, following a branch of the river. The land had become less rugged the further they moved from the Mountains of the Nine Gods. It had rained the previous day, making the ground slick. The heavy clouds had drifted on and steam rose from the damp ground to meet an unveiled Utu.

Rannac walked silently at his elbow. His old mentor's eyes were tight, the set of his shoulders tense. "What is wrong, Old Wolf?"

Rannac pressed his lips together, clearly choosing his words before speaking. Eldrax guessed that the memory of a snapped leg was holding his tongue in check.

"They will never agree to this," Rannac said at last. "Another Chief will never submit to your rule. It is not the way of our People."

Eldrax hefted the skin containing the carved stone, the skull, and the mangled arm of one of the dead rogues. He was pleased with how his and Tanag's deception had worked. Tanag had come upon the small band of nomads flirting with the edges of Hunting Bear territory while on a patrol of the borders. It had not been a difficult task for Eldrax and Tanag to kill the five rogue men and the two women who had travelled with them.

Eldrax spared a moment of regret for the women. They had been strong and spirited, and could have made proud additions to the Hunting Bear ranks, but Eldrax had needed their silence more than he had needed their future progeny.

The hardest part had been recreating the damage he had seen the Watchers inflict on the Black Wolf. It had been messy work, involving heavy axes and crushing stones. Work that had made even Tanag pale. But the grizzly deed had served its purpose. The staunch Rannac had been convinced that the Gods were an imminent threat, poised to strike, and to defend against such a threat meant bending the unspoken rules of the Plains. But it appeared the ruse had not banished all of his doubts.

"Kiduku will bow or he will die," Eldrax said in response to the Old Wolf's fretting.

"You will kill another Chief, unprovoked?"

"If that is what it takes to save the land from the gods."

Rannac's jaw worked. "Why now? No living man has seen them since the Great Winter of Sorrow. What have we done to provoke them?"

"What did we do to provoke them the first time except live?" Eldrax growled. He halted and turned to face Rannac. "And what does it matter?" he demanded. "Are you going to lie idle, questioning the workings of a god's mind while they rain fire down on our heads? Are you going to stand by and watch them do to the women and children of the Hunting Bear what they did to the Black Wolf? To Halima?" Eldrax raised an eyebrow. He wasn't a foolish man.

His prod was rewarded by the barest twitch. "We could form an alliance, join our forces together, but leave the other Chiefs in charge of their own clans."

Eldrax barked a laugh. "And when the time for battle comes, who will lead? Several warring Chiefs all with their own ideas and fighting traditions? No Rannac. The men of the Plains must be united under one leader. This is the only way."

Rannac ground his teeth together, Eldrax could see his mind twisting this way and that, but in the end, the raknari leader jerked his chin once.

Eldrax turned on his heel. His patience with Rannac's doubt was wearing dangerously thin. And he needed his old mentor. At least for now.

A scout ran back towards Eldrax's group. Mahasu. Such a disappointment. He had thought when he had Claimed Halima as his chief mate and matriarch, that such a formidable woman would bear him worthy children. Strong boys who would become fearsome warriors to follow in his footsteps and spread his legacy through the lands. Instead, all she had gifted him with was a string of dead children and this one sickly boy. The insult rankled.

"The Ravens are camped downstream, my Chief," the boy panted, his thin face flushed. "Half a day's travel."

Eldrax acknowledged him with a curt nod and signalled his followers to double the pace. He wanted to reach the Ravens and look Kiduku in the eye before Utu set. Tanag, Rannac and the rest of his fighting force were silent now, their weapons slung across their backs in inoffensive positions, and Eldrax drew out a small antler strung with white feathers. A symbol of peace. If Raven sentries were to witness their passage, it would not do to cause unnecessary complications by sparking a fight before he wished, or spook the Ravens into flight. He was in no mood to hunt them down again. He wanted their fealty now and he would have it. One way or the other.

Utu was tipping towards the west when the sound of warning drums in the near distance told Eldrax that he and his company had been sighted. The Ravens were preparing for the arrival of the Red Bear. Eldrax spared a moment to imagine the fear and uncertainty running through the other clan upon hearing of his approach.

Gritting his teeth, he held out his peace totem as the cluster of shelters came into view. Half the size of the Hunting Bear clan, the Raven Clan was nevertheless a formidable fighting force. Kiduku was already standing before his home, his raknari warriors arrayed at his back.

"Red Bear," Kiduku called out as Eldrax brought his group to a halt a respectful distance from the other Chief. From there, he weighed his rival. Keen, pale brown eyes narrowed over the high cheekbones and broad nose. A shock of tawny hair flowed down the muscular back in a long braid. Kiduku was not a large man, but his dark Cro skin bore the marks of a lifetime of battles. Battles he had walked away from. His opponents had not. "What brings you to Raven lands?"

Eldrax did not waste time. "Kiduku, I come before you bearing a grave warning. Hear me well. The gods are awakening."

Kiduku's pale eyes widened, and a ripple of shock at Eldrax's blunt declaration passed through his men. Then the shock passed and soft laughter jittered through the opposing force. A smile played about Kiduku's own mouth. There was a twist of mockery in his voice as he spoke. "The Red Bear must have lost his mind. The gods are long gone. They no longer walk the land."

The growing laughter at his expense went through Eldrax's heart like a flaming brand, the red mist of a blood rage played at the edges of his vision. His mother's own laughter sounded as though her cold, dead lips were pressed against his ear. *They mock you. They think you a fool, my son.* Eldrax's lips peeled back off his teeth, his hand twitching towards his heavy fighting club on his back.

"Eldrax," Rannac said. He did not raise his voice, but that tone that still had the power to cut through Eldrax's rage enough to give him pause. "Don't. They have not seen what we have."

"They soon will," Eldrax snarled. Unslinging the skin containing his evidence from his shoulders.

The smile vanished from Kiduku's face as he silenced his followers. He had clearly seen the murderous flash in Eldrax's eyes and thought better of antagonising the leader of the most powerful clan in the known land. Eldrax snorted and threw the skin before Kiduku, spilling the damning contents at his feet.

The rival Chief stared down at the arm, the skull and the stone, his rich skin losing colour before Eldrax's eyes. He stooped to lift the stone, studying the carved image, so lifelike in its terrible detail.

"They are coming for us, Kiduku," Eldrax said softly. "They mean to slaughter us all. And they will, unless you do exactly as I say."

Kiduku drew his gaze away from the strange stone, visibly composing himself as he narrowed his eyes at Eldrax. "As you say?"

"You must join your clan together with the Hunting Bear under my rule. All the clans must accept me as protector, lest they wish to perish."

A flurry of sharp protests travelled through the ranks of the Raven. Weapons shifted. Eldrax felt Rannac tense at his side. Kiduku looked

Eldrax straight in the eye as he spoke. "I thank you for your warning, mighty Red Bear. The Ravens will prepare for any attack that might befall us, but I cannot submit myself to your rule. I am the Chief of my clan and I have earned the right to lead it by the lores of our People."

Eldrax let a long, hard silence sit between them before he spoke. "Short-sighted fool. That is your answer?"

Kiduku lifted his chin. "Go now, Eldrax of the Red Bear, and I will allow you to leave my territory unmolested."

He was brave, Eldrax would give him that. Such a pity. "Then you leave me no choice. As the saviour of mankind, I will do what I must." He turned, assessing his fighters. Kiduku was a warrior to be reckoned with, but he was no match for Eldrax himself, no man was. But Eldrax was not the one who needed to eliminate the Raven Chief.

"Urbat," he barked. A head and shoulders taller than Kiduku, Eldrax's warrior stepped forward upon his Chief's command. His dark red hair flared like fire in the dying rays of Utu's light, taut skin glowing as he removed the furs from his torso, displaying a rugged and powerful body honed for one purpose alone.

"I, Urbat of the Hunting Bear, Challenge you, Kiduku of the Raven, for control of your clan and the territory you walk."

Kiduku's eyes widened. "No. That is not our way. I have the full support of my clan. I have given them no cause to doubt my leadership. They will not follow you, a man they do not know. I reject your Challenge, Urbat of the Hunting Bear." Kiduku spat on the ground.

"If you do not accept," Eldrax said. "Then I will return with the full force of my clan and slaughter every man, woman, and child in your pathetic camp. I will do the gods' work for them."

Kiduku's face flushed as his men shifted nervously behind him.

Eldrax laughed. "If you know you cannot stand against me, how do you expect to stand against the gods?"

"I will not allow my women and children to be murdered, but I cannot bow to you, Eldrax. Only over my corpse will you take control of my clan." He shifted his gaze back to Urbat. "It seems I must accept your Challenge, Urbat of the Hunting Bear."

Eldrax saw Rannac's shoulders rise and fall with a heavy sigh.

Kiduku cast aside his upper furs and whirled his arshu fighting staff as he stepped forward to meet Urbat in the space between the two opposing forces. Eldrax watched as his warrior and the rival Chief circled one another, each sizing the other up, feigning and dancing, testing for both skill and weakness. Urbat had youth, power and reach on his side. And Rannac had trained him. Eldrax knew no better teacher. It was one reason the Old Wolf still breathed. If the older Kiduku had an advantage here, it was in experience. But Eldrax was not one to leave his fate to chance. Should the fight go against Urbat, Tanag had his orders.

Witches were not the only spoils Eldrax had seized from the shin'ar forests of the south. It had always perplexed him that the witches had so many toxins available in their jungle home that it never occurred to them to fight back when he raided their tribes. He supposed he should be grateful. It would be a bad day for the Cro should one of them ever realise that.

Eldrax could see Tanag carefully concealing the toxic dart in his fist.

The clash of wood and the rattling of sharpened antler tips shivered through the evening air as Urbat and Kiduku came together. Kiduku's wiry arms shook as they locked weapons, Urbat bringing all of his considerable power to bear. Unable to match such strength, Kiduku disentangled himself and whirled away.

The deadly dance played out before Eldrax's eyes. His own muscles twitched in response to Kiduku's attacks, itching to be the one to end him. The fighting pair slashed and parried, cutting at one another with savage ferocity. Furs and skin were rent, blood and sweat poured, the ground slicked with the salt and fluid of their struggle.

Twice it appeared Kiduku would get the better of Urbat. The Raven Chief fought ferociously, clearly seeking a swift end to the fight before Urbat's youth and vigour got the better of him. Eldrax prepared himself to give the signal to Tanag. But each time, Urbat fought back with the tenacity of a cornered bear.

And so the fight wore on. Eldrax watched as the prolonged fight Kiduku had hoped to avoid slowly sapped the strength of his rival. He no longer took the offensive, it was all he could do to keep Urbat's attacks at bay. At the last, Kiduku's foot slipped on the churned ground and the Raven Chief went down on one knee. He could not regain his feet to muster a defence in time and Urbat's weapon smashed into Kibuku's spear arm. Eldrax heard the bones crack before Kibuku's howl of pain drowned the sound out.

Shouts of dismay from the gathered Ravens lifted the air. A woman's voice raised above the rest and Eldrax saw a tall female figure attempt to run to the downed Chief before she was caught and restrained by Kiduku's warriors. She was tall enough to carry Deni blood. Eldrax ran his tongue across his bottom lip, approving. She would make a worthy mate for Urbat once this was over.

And over it was. Kiduku cried out for mercy, but Eldrax had ensured mercy had no place in his warriors' lives. Without hesitation, Urbat swung his weapon, smashing the antler tips into his opponent's head. Blood sprayed, and Kiduku's twitching body fell to the ground.

Silence fell over those gathered. Only the quiet wails of the woman held in a Raven warrior's arms broke the stillness.

"Bow to your new Chief!" Urbat roared to the stunned Raven clan. At first, they did not respond, but then they took in the sight of Eldrax. He watched as their shock receded and the realisation that there was no way out sank in. Accepting this new, unknown Chief from a foreign clan was the only way to protect their women and children. And that was a raknari warrior's sole purpose. One by one, the Raven men sank to the ground and bowed.

Eldrax moved forward and clasped Urbat by a bloodied shoulder. "This clan and territory is now yours," he said, then tightened his grip. "Yours, but never forget who gave it to you. When I call, you *will* respond to me."

"Yes, my Chief," Urbat intoned. Eldrax could feel the quiver of his warrior's muscles under his hand. He knew that the excitement of a battle won could only be sated by one thing. He nodded to Kiduku's grieving mate.

"Good, then take what you need."

Without another word, Urbat rushed forward to pull the tall woman from the grip of the warrior who held her, drawing her out before all.

"I am your Chief!" Urbat cried again. "And I claim this woman as mine. If any man wishes to Challenge for her, step forward now."

None of the Raven men rose to their feet. They kept their eyes on the ground as Urbat wasted no time. He threw the woman onto her hands and knees before seizing her hips in his bloodstained hands and plunged his quivering body deep inside her, roaring his pleasure and victory to the sky.

Eldrax smiled as he watched Urbat Claim his first spoil as Chief. The Ravens were now under his control. It was only a matter of time before he seized the title of Master of the Plains.

***

Rannac brooded beside the campfire, twisting a stray stick of wood over and over in his fingers. Eldrax had gone to hunt with half of their remaining number. Mahasu had accompanied him, refusing to stay behind, but the rest of the band remained under Rannac's charge to set up camp.

The fire now crackled and danced against the shadows, and the rest of the men talked quietly amongst themselves. Akor was sitting to one side, a frown pinching the light brown skin of his brow together. He did not speak. Rannac could almost suspect that the young man was avoiding his gaze, though he could not guess why. And so Rannac was left alone with his own thoughts. They were not good company. Rannac spun the stick faster, trying not to dwell on what had passed the previous day with the Ravens.

When he and Eldrax had first stumbled upon the butchered remains of the rogues, the sight had filled Rannac with a mortal terror. The Watchers were abroad and that could mean only one thing. Their masters had awoken. And if that was so, then no one was safe. Eldrax was right. Only by standing together did the Cro have a hope of surviving what was to come.

Rannac knew it was necessary. He knew it. But he also knew that it was wrong. In saving their People, how much would be lost? The reality of what Eldrax had set out to do weighed heavy on his heart. Each Cro clan, while of the same People, held so many rich traditions, unique knowledge and learning. Now all of that was at risk, as Eldrax sought to stamp his rule over all the Plains. The leaders of the other clans would no longer be chosen from within the ranks of their own families to replace the old. Now they would be dominated by outsiders.

Eldrax's own loyal subjects.

Rannac had taught them all. Each one of these men that had grown with their Chief since boyhood was great in their own right. Each one was different. Except in one thing. They had all shared Eldrax's ambition, even Akor. It was why they had been chosen.

The Ravens would learn fast not to question or antagonise their new leader in any way.

Rannac shifted his thoughts away from the unpleasant task of bringing the clans together and turned them instead to Khalvir. He found no relief there. The sound of hurt and betrayal in his young voice as he pleaded with Rannac not to leave him still tore at his heart. They had hurt and betrayed each other. Rannac recalled how he felt when he caught the boy trying to run. He had assured Eldrax the boy was settled. He had been wrong.

And that left him with no choice. Rannac had to break the boy if he was to make him. He had to learn that the Hunting Bear was his only refuge for himself.

Would he be alive when Rannac returned to him? He hoped so. If not, if Khalvir could not let go of the elf-witch beliefs and achieve a kill, then he would have been no good to the clan, anyway.

Rannac threw the stick he had been worrying between his fingers into the fire and watched it spit and burn, twisting as the heat of the fire corrupted its form.

A whistle in the gathering darkness announced Eldrax's return. Rannac rose to his feet as his Chief loomed into the firelight, laughing with three of his warriors. Over one broad shoulder, Eldrax carried the carcass of an antelope, which he threw down in triumph next to the flames. "We feast in honour of Urbat!" he announced. The others let out whoops of approval and descended upon the kill, pulling loose their skinning knives.

Rannac did not move.

"Not hungry, Old Wolf?" Eldrax raised an eyebrow.

Rannac shook his head. "Not tonight."

Eldrax's eyes narrowed. "I have your support, Rannac?

"Of course, my Chief."

"Good. I would hate to think you did not stand at my back, Old Wolf. I am only doing what is needed."

Rannac dipped his chin, ducking his eyes so Eldrax could not see the shadows of doubt that lurked there. He watched the men hungrily preparing the carcass. It was then that he noticed one of their number was missing and his heart gave an uncomfortable squeeze. "My Chief, where is Mahasu?"

In the corner of his eye, Rannac saw Akor's head come up.

Eldrax glowered back into the shadows and the dark land beyond. "The weak fool took off. Hunting the buck."

Rannac's hands contracted into fists. "But he did not have a spear. He was armed only with a hunting knife."

"Oh, I know," Eldrax said, "but he wouldn't listen. He disappeared into the darkness. I would not waste time going after him. Good riddance."

Rannac felt the blood drain from his face. Without saying one more word to Eldrax, he snatched up his spear and bounded into the shadows, half aware that Akor was on his heels. He had promised Halima he would look out for the boy. He had thought he would be safe with his father. Once again, he had been wrong. He cursed the child.

"I always knew his need to prove himself to our father would be his undoing," Akor hissed.

In the dark, it was almost impossible to retrace Eldrax's trail. Rannac ran low. Now and then, he risked a soft call. "Mahasu?" But there was no answer. He did not dare risk calling any louder. He and

Akor were now far from their company and the protection of the firelight. Wolves and worse stalked these lands, hoping for an easy meal. Rannac ran faster not caring if Akor kept up.

At last, they stumbled upon the site of Eldrax's kill. Even in the blackness, Rannac could make out the grooves and cuts in the earth made by the panicked herd of antelope. The scent of spilled blood was still thick in the air. They could not linger here. Where had the boy gone? Rannac scoured the earth for answers, touching with his fingers, searching for the boy's trail.

Before he could find it, the sound he had dreaded shattered the stillness: the blood-curdling shriek of a child in mortal peril.

"Mahasu!" Rannac bolted headlong into the dark. The sharp cackle of a hyena turned Rannac's blood to ice. A howl, a yelp of pain, and then there was nothing but silence. "Mahasu!"

Rannac slewed to a halt at the end of Mahasu's trail. But the boy was gone. All that remained at Rannac's feet was a torn remnant of bear-skin and the shadow of blood staining the ground.

Akor's soft tread sounded behind him as he caught up. "We're too late," he murmured before muttering a prayer to the gods for his half-brother.

The strength went out of Rannac's knees and he collapsed to the ground, burying his face in his hands. Whatever was he going to tell Halima?

***

CHAPTER 17

SACRIFICE

Du Mu pulled against his bonds. The skin at his wrists was raw from his struggles. Night had fallen and Rannac was long gone. The warrior had left him. Abandoned him, tied to a tree with a knife placed just out of reach. His shock and fear had long since burned out. Now all Du Mu felt was fury. He fought, thrashed, and strained against his bonds, uncaring as the bindings cut into his flesh. But he could not reach the tool that would grant him his freedom. At last, exhausted, and alone in the darkness, Du Mu collapsed to the ground.

He dozed, his mind fleeing the confines of reality. At one point, the sound of a soft tread caused him to stir. His eyes flickered, and in his half sleep, Du Mu thought he saw a being standing over him with hair as black as a raven's wing under the silver disc in the sky above. Dark, glittering eyes peered at him out of a pale face; skin whiter than he had ever seen. Du Mu's heart leaped. Was this one of the spirits Galahir had spoken of, come to steal his soul?

"Wh-who are you?" he slurred in his sleep.

"*Shalanaki,*" the being whispered, the voice soft and comforting. Du Mu felt a peculiar sense of familiarity steal over him in his dream-like state. His eyes drifted closed, and he sank deeper into unconsciousness.

The heat of the Light Bringer pressing on his eyelids the next morning woke Du Mu with a start, scattering his dreams to the back of his mind. He had been sitting with Nameeda and Tamuk around a campfire, laughing about... he could not remember. Du Mu pushed himself up into a sitting position. He was still alone. Still inside the small copse Rannac had abandoned him in. His dream made Du Mu feel the isolation all the more keenly. He hissed through his teeth, rubbing his forehead with one hand.

And froze, his eyes growing wide as he held both of his hands up before him. Hadn't he been inescapably tied? The angry red abrasions on his wrists told him he was not losing his mind. Rannac had indeed tied him. Catching his breath, Du Mu cast about quickly and lifted the pieces of the twisted rope before his eyes. The rope had been cut. Rannac's knife and Du Mu's spear had been placed close beside him.

Du Mu gripped the severed ends of the rope, thinking back to his dreams and the spirit figure he thought he had imagined.

Not imagined, he thought with an unpleasant thrill. *Real.* A black-haired being with ghostly pale skin had stood over him while he slept in the night. It had freed him. Du Mu dropped the rope and looked about, scouring the trees and the Plains beyond for a sign of life. "Hello?" he called in his own tongue. There was silence but for the rustling of the leaves overhead. "Hello?" he tried again in Cro speak. No answer. Whoever the stranger had been, they had not remained close by. Du Mu was alone again.

Alone, cold, and hungry. The sense of betrayal filled him again, and Du Mu seized the severed rope and flung it as far as he could with a scream of frustration. Thrusting himself to his feet, Du Mu snatched up the hunting knife and his spear, and stared out at the open wilderness before him. He sucked in a few deep breaths, tasting the icy air of the dawn, letting it temper his anger and fill him with a cold, hard purpose.

This was what he had wanted. He was free. He never expected to gain his freedom in such a way, but he wasn't about to argue. The only thing he lamented was the loss of the rations he had expended so much effort to carry. No matter. Now there was nothing between him and the journey south. He did not care about Rannac's warning. Other clans might be out there, ready to snatch a stranger, but they did not know where to find him, or even know of his existence. Rannac did. And Eldrax's warrior had promised to come back for him.

"Over my dead body," he vowed. He was not going back. He was going to return to the home he knew he had had in his mind.

How long before Rannac returned? He did not know. Sheathing the hunting knife in the tough furs wrapped around his left leg, Du Mu shouldered his spear. Gauging the rising Light Bringer's position in the sky, he adjusted his course and struck out. *Hold on, hold on for me,* he thought to the missing piece of his aching soul he still clung to.

The vast Plains felt that much larger when one was alone. Du Mu felt the vastness threaten to swallow him from existence. He kept his head low, his spear thrust out before him, alert to any noise or faint quiver against his senses. Now and then, Du Mu got the sense that he was being watched. Each time, he would freeze and rake the surrounding land with his eyes. But he saw nothing, just the innocently waving grasses and the empty, rolling landscape.

He passed by the occasional herd of elk and oxen. They raised their heads and snorted threateningly in his direction, squaring up to the lone boy, prepared to run him from their ground should he make the wrong move. But Du Mu wisely kept his eyes down, keeping his spear out of attack position, and suffered no more than the stamping of a hoof or the occasional mock charge.

Du Mu thought back to the violence of the hunt he had witnessed and shuddered. He did not blame the herds for being aggressive to one such as him.

Du Mu walked all of that first day without rest. If he stopped, there was nothing to distract him from the gnawing of his empty belly. And he was lonely. When moving, at least the sound of his own feet brushing through the grasses was a comfort, a companion. Had he ever been alone before? Nighttime came, and Du Mu huddled himself down against an outcropping of rocks, trying to fold himself inside his furs as much as he could. His breath plumed on the air as the soft breeze pinched the end of his nose.

As the temperature dropped, Du Mu found himself longing for the warmth of a campfire. The silence made him miss Nameeda and Tamuk bantering at his sides. The ground bit at his body, making him feel the absence of the comfort of a shelter, a pile of furs, and the warmth of several other bodies slumbering around him.

Everything that he had left behind.

What was calling him ahead? Du Mu strained until he thought his mind would burst, but he could not picture what he was running to. The pain of hunger and cold made it harder to focus on that nebulous, ever-fading call within his soul, to see the shadowed images that taunted the edges of his vision, only to flee, laughing, whenever he tried to turn towards them.

Du Mu buried his face in his knees and willed himself to go to sleep. He hated the doubt Eldrax, and now his own weakness had sown in his mind. But once the seed had been planted, he had been unable to dig it out. It had buried itself there, insidiously taking root, sinking deeper with each day that passed.

Hunger kept sleep at bay. Du Mu dozed in fits, startling awake often. Sometimes his heart would leap as he imagined he saw a shadowed figure standing in the near distance, watching him silently, but he then would blink and the figure would dissolve into an outcropping of rocks, a browsing herbivore.

It was with sore eyes that Du Mu greeted the Light Bringer when it finally peeked over the eastern horizon. Harsh as it was on his sleepless eyes, Du Mu savoured the sight of the bright disc, for he would not have it for long. Thick black clouds were forming in the southern skies. The wind picked up, tugging restlessly on the grasses around Du Mu, ushering the threatening, rain-filled mass before it.

The storm broke before the Light Bringer was at its zenith. Rain lashed down, pounding the land and the travelling boy beneath. It took only moments for Du Mu's furs and leathers to be soaked through, increasing their weight on his already tiring body. The roar of the sky's fury deafened his ears as the ground grew slick beneath his feet. Du Mu kept his head down, not bothering to swipe his dripping hair from his eyes. It required too much energy.

Hunger. The gnaw in his belly was all-encompassing. Almost three days had passed since he had eaten. When the light waned once more, Du Mu had become so desperate he yanked a handful of grass from the ground and stuffed it in his mouth. It did not help. That night he wretched the contents of his stomach up against the rocks he sheltered against.

Nights and days passed in a haze as Du Mu continued to stumble along. Only the faint call of the unknown kept him on his feet. *I'm coming. I'll make it back.* He chanted over and over. *I'm here.*

The Light Bringer was riding high overhead on the fifth day of his journey when Du Mu's blurring eyes caught something in the distance. White stood stark against the browns, greens and greys. So desperate was he, that Du Mu bolted towards it without caution, almost stumbling on his hands and knees in his haste. A pile of cracked bones greeted him. In a frenzy, Du Mu clawed through them, searching for a remaining scrap of flesh, anything that he could eat. But his hunt was in vain. Whatever had killed this creature had already taken its share. Scavengers had done the rest. There was nothing left.

Du Mu collapsed to the ground in defeat, too exhausted and overcome to move further. Several tears leaked past his control and rolled down his haggard face. Sniffing, he tried to hold back his panic. He was going to die, and there was nobody to save him.

A large ground-dwelling bird chose that moment to bob out of the grasses before him, perhaps hoping to peck a morsel from the bare bones of the old kill. He caught sight of Du Mu lying in the dirt and froze. The bird and the boy regarded one another for one heartbeat, and then the bird fled. Du Mu was on his feet in the same instant, knife in hand. A sudden strength shot to his depleted limbs, powering his pursuit of the bird.

No, not a bird. Food. His deprived mind stripped all other identities away. The fleeing object before him was what he needed to live, and he was going to catch it. With a cry, Du Mu threw himself forward. Quick as a striking snake, he snatched the bag of meat and feathers from the ground, deaf to its protests. He did not think. His knife flashed and there was a spray of blood. The struggling bird fell limp in his hand.

A delirious laugh escaped his lips. *Food. Food. Food.* He sliced open the still-twitching carcass, baring the muscle within, and descended upon it, tearing great chunks free with his teeth and swallowing.

Du Mu hummed his pleasure as the warm flesh filled his shrunken stomach. He could feel a trickle of his strength returning with each wet mouthful. But as his strength returned, so too did his reason. By and by, Du Mu became more aware of the blood sliding down his chin, the wet slimy texture of the animal's body in his mouth, the dead eyes as they rolled in the dangling head next to his face.

With a soft cry, Du Mu dropped the almost-stripped carcass. He wretched once but clapped a hand over his sticky mouth, unwilling to lose his meal despite the horror. Du Mu doubled over, drawing long breaths through his nose against the nausea until his full stomach settled. When he was sure he was once more in control, he straightened and fled the accusing stare of his victim, not stopping until he stumbled upon a babbling stream. Dropping his knife and spear, he plunged his bloody hands into the icy flow, splashing his face over and over until he was sure every trace of the bird's blood had been washed away. Then he sat there, shivering.

He had done it. He had done what Rannac had wanted. Du Mu had killed to feed himself and proven himself strong enough to survive. But, though he felt very much alive now, Du Mu couldn't help but feel a part of his soul had died. *Monster.* The word echoed around his head, but in opposition, a command layered in several voices screamed louder. *Survive!*

Du Mu put his head into his knees and wept, feeling the jaws of some distant fate, one he always seemed to know was there, close about him. If he was to obey those voices, a monster he had to be.

Du Mu sniffed back his tears and turned his face south. Could he go back there now, having sacrificed this part of his soul? Once again, he tried and failed to picture what he was trying so hard to return to. It was becoming harder and harder to believe his once vehement convictions.

Du Mu had never felt so lost. The vastness yawned around him, mocking his foolishness. He was very much alone.

Or was he?

Du Mu sat upright, stemming his tears long enough to hold his breath, listening hard. Yes. He hadn't been mistaken. He was not the only one crying. The sound of soft sniffles brushed faintly against his ears on the breeze.

"Hello?" he rasped over the hissing grasses.

The sound of crying ceased. Whomever was out there had frozen, startled into stillness by his call.

"I won't hurt you. Please." Du Mu staggered to his feet and stumbled into the prevailing wind from where the sound had been carried. "Hello?"

Du Mu almost did not see him. His tawny furs blended him into the earth as effectively as a deer fawn, concealing him until Du Mu tripped over his foot.

"Mahasu!" Du Mu cried, staring down at the child.

Eldrax's young son stared back at him out of red, tear-stained eyes. "K-Khalvir?"

Du Mu was too stunned to wince at the name. "What-what are you doing here?"

"I was hunting with my f-father." Fresh tears spilled loose from the dark eyes. "I was trying to impress him. And, and hyenas came and," Mahasu's voice broke off into a sob. He pulled aside the furs on his thin arm, revealing a bloody wound. "I managed to get away, but then I couldn't find m-my way back."

Du Mu's heart gave an uncomfortable squeeze and his eyes darted about the landscape. Eldrax had been near. He could so easily have stumbled into the dread Chief and found himself dragged back to camp. But against that fear, another part of himself that he would not admit to wished that it had been so; the part that longed to be returned to solid warmth and company. To reality. Du Mu shook his head.

"D-do you have any food?" Mahasu blinked up at Du Mu hopefully, echoing his own previous need. Du Mu swallowed, forcing the dead bird from his memory, and shook his head. Mahasu diminished before his eyes and the boy clutched his belly. "I-I need to get back to camp. Take me home, Khalvir."

Du Mu stiffened. "No," he blurted before he could think.

The younger boy looked as if he had slapped him. "No? But you can't leave me here! I lost my knife!" A desperate glint came to Mahasu's eye as he rose to his feet, drawing himself up to his full height. "Take me back, or my father will gut you for leaving his son to die."

Du Mu bristled at the threat. *He already left you to die himself.* He set his chin. "No. I will not take you, for I am not going back. Find your own way." Du Mu moved off, resuming his journey.

"Khalvir!" Mahasu cried, fear stealing his bravado. "Don't leave me!" The shout turned into a sob that tore at the heart. "Please, stay."

I can't, Du Mu continued stepping forward. *Besides anything else, your own mother wanted me gone.* He wondered, not for the first time, at Halima's warning.

A rush of feet told Du Mu that Mahasu was in pursuit. The boy caught hold of his furs, beseeching him. "Please. I don't want to be alone."

Du Mu halted and stared down at him. "I'm not going back," he repeated.

"I-I know," the boy stammered. "But I don't want to be alone. Please."

Du Mu blew out a breath and then carried on walking, Mahasu clinging to his side. He did not know what he was going to do with the boy. Perhaps they might come across another of his clan's hunting groups, and Du Mu could send him running for them. But then he would have to trust that Mahasu would not betray him. He ground his teeth together at the impossibility of the situation he was now in.

"Where are we going?"

We? "I'm going south."

"Why?"

"I don't want to talk about it!" Du Mu snapped, losing patience. "If you're going to come along, be quiet."

Mahasu drew himself up, and for the first time, Du Mu saw a hint of his giant father. "Who are you to order me around?"

"The one carrying the spear, that's who."

Mahasu fell silent. At least he wasn't stupid.

They walked in silence as the Light Bringer passed slowly overhead but after a length of time had passed; it seemed Mahasu could no longer hold back his curiosity.

"Why are you out here alone? Did you get separated from your hunting group, too?"

"No. Rannac tied me up and abandoned me."

Mahasu sucked in a shocked breath. "Why?"

Du Mu ground his teeth together. "I would not hunt."

He could sense Mahasu's confusion. "Why?"

"I—" Du Mu's temper flared. "I don't know. I did not want to kill. I did not want to be a monster." His throat closed.

"Monster? For eating?"

"Please be quiet."

But Mahasu couldn't keep it up for long.

"Witches are strange," the child muttered. He blinked up at Du Mu. "Can you heal the injured?"

"What?"

"Talk to animals and trees?"

"Why ever would you think that?" Du Mu asked irritably.

"You're a witch. Or at least half a witch. Are you magic?"

Du Mu snorted. "No."

"Huh, father will be disappointed."

"I don't care."

"Where did you come from?"

"South."

"Is that why you're travelling that way?"

"I thought I told you to be quiet." Du Mu gave the boy a warning tap on the back of his head with the haft of his spear.

"Ow!"

The day passed in silence after that. Du Mu congratulated himself on his empty threat. But soon it became apparent that it wasn't the reason behind Mahasu's quiet. The boy's eyes were half closed as he stumbled ever more slowly in Du Mu's wake. The Light Bringer was only just touching the western horizon when Mahasu collapsed to the ground in an exhausted heap. "Khalvir, I'm hungry," he slurred as his eyes drifted closed. Du Mu stood, shifting from foot to foot, torn. He did not want to stop, but he also could not abandon Mahasu here alone. Du Mu sank down next to the child.

"Don't leave me," Mahasu's face was pale and wan as he reached out to clutch at Du Mu's furs in his sleep.

"No," Du Mu sighed as he took up watch, his spear leaning against his shoulder.

The sound of the boy's soft breathing filling the air. Despite the complication he presented, Du Mu drew comfort from Mahasu's company in turn. It was strange, but in watching over this child, the aching hole in his chest had eased. It felt natural to be protecting someone, anyone, like a part of his missing centre had been given back to him.

Mahasu slept until the predawn of the following day. Du Mu dozed lightly at his side until the child's eyes fluttered open. "Mama?" he called, still befuddled by sleep.

Du Mu gripped his spear, guilt shooting through him. He had the ability to return Mahasu to his clan. To his mother. He knew the way back as far as where Rannac had left him. He had no doubt Mahasu would know the way from there. Instead, he was leading the boy further away towards the ghost of a feeling. Du Mu pinched the bridge of his nose and rolled his eyes closed.

He did not look at the younger boy as he got to his feet and continued on his path. He was doing his best not to think. Mahasu scrambled after him.

They travelled in silence again as the Light Bringer climbed higher. Scattered herds dotted the landscape as they passed by. Du Mu's stomach rumbled painfully again. The meal of the bird had long since worn off, but he kept his eyes averted from the animals. He wasn't that far gone yet to wish a repeat of his encounter with the fowl. He had failed to pay attention to Mahasu's condition, however.

A groan was his only warning before there was a dull thud and he turned to find Mahasu had collapsed in a swirl of dust.

"Mahasu!" Du Mu threw himself on his knees beside him and lifted the boy by his shoulders. His head lolled back. He did not even have the strength to lift it.

"Hungry..."

The boy was dying, his young and fragile body unable to endure the deprivation. Du Mu's eyes went to the herd of creatures browsing peacefully in the distance. "I-I can't," he stammered to himself.

Anger and accusation flashed through Mahasu's dark eyes, but he was too weak to fight and he simply sagged back in defeat, accepting his fate. Accepting death.

Du Mu could not accept it. If he did not let go of his aversion, this child would die and he alone would be responsible for his death. Du Mu dropped his head as his choice was made for him. What was his soul when weighed against an innocent life? He had a responsibility to look after Mahasu, no matter the cost to himself. Mahasu was his clan. Du Mu sucked in a breath.

Lowering the boy to the ground, he gripped his spear and stood up. "I'll be back. Hold on for me."

Du Mu took off at a run, sprinting towards the herd in the distance. The animals loomed larger the closer he got, and Du Mu felt a shiver of doubt break into his determination. One wrong move and the herd would charge the lone threat and trample him to death. He did not have a hunting group to support him. He did not even have any experience. All he had was a single spear and his wits.

Du Mu slowed to a halt. Rannac had tested the wind before approaching. Du Mu did this now. He needed to move where the breeze would carry his scent away from the herd. Shifting into a crouch, Du Mu crept around until he was in the perfect position. Once there, he flattened himself onto his belly, letting the grasses hide him from the occasionally lifting heads and swivelling ears.

Now what?

Choose a target. Du Mu's throat went dry. He had to choose who lived and who died. He closed his eyes, doing his best to sink into the frame of mind that had seized him in the madness of starvation. These were not living individuals with thought and feeling. All he could allow himself to see before him was food. Food to save a boy's life. Food to slake his own growing need. He focused on the gnawing of his own stomach to aid the illusion.

Du Mu opened his eyes. Stone cold now, he scanned the bodies before him. He dismissed the largest specimens. One of those would be impossible to bring down alone and carry back to where he had left Mahasu.

There. A small individual had strayed too far from the protection of the others. And it was within striking distance. Du Mu bolted up onto his knees and closed his eyes, using only his remaining senses. It made it easier. All that lay before him was the lump of wood Rannac had had him pierce day after day. Just an unfeeling lump of wood. Du Mu focused on its centre, breathing out in one long release of air as he threw his arm forward with his full weight behind it.

The spear left his hand.

There was a beat of silence, then a dull thud.

The scream that followed went straight through his own heart. The wood became a living being.

But Du Mu did not have time to dwell on what he had done before the thunder of hooves shook the ground. The herd scattered. Du Mu darted forward, his eyes fixed on his hapless victim. The calf's legs were still flailing as he came upon it. He had missed the heart by a whisper. Du Mu drew his hunting knife. "I'm sorry," he whispered, and drove the razor-sharp tip into the centre of life. He would not let her suffer.

Mahasu. He kept the thought of the boy firmly in his mind as he lifted his kill. Du Mu grunted under the weight of the calf, struggling to balance himself as he heaved it over his shoulder. It reminded him that while Rannac had worked hard to build his strength; he was still a long way from becoming a man. Setting his will, he staggered back towards where he had left Mahasu.

He had to stop to drop his load often. In the end, Du Mu resorted to dragging the kill through the grass, leaving a streak of blood behind him.

Mahasu was in exactly the same position he had left him in. He barely flickered his eyelids when Du Mu called his name. Hastily, Du

Mu drew his still-bloody hunting knife and carved a dripping chunk of meat from the calf. He brought it before the fading child.

"Mahasu, here, I brought you food. Eat now." He pulled the boy up into his arms, supporting him as he held the still-warm piece of flesh to the boy's lips. A trickle of strength appeared to flash through the boy as he caught scent of the nourishment. His pale hands came up, guiding the morsel to his mouth as he took bite after bite. Each motion became increasingly vital. At last, Mahasu dropped back with a contented sigh and fell into a deep sleep.

Du Mu let him. He needed to rest and restore his strength. The gnaw in his own stomach turned to an ache, but he was not yet hungry enough to see the bloody, cooling carcass as appetising. Wrapping his arms around himself, he sat and waited for Mahasu to awaken.

It was a strange cackling call on the far horizon that had Mahasu leaping from his sleep. "Hyenas!" he gasped. His dark eyes swept around, taking in the carcass and then the trail of blood leading to their position. "You dragged it?" he asked incredulously.

"You try carrying it!" Du Mu snapped back. "What's wrong?"

"Hyenas, scavengers. They're following the scent of the blood. Quick." The boy heaved himself to his feet and then began scouring the ground. "Help me look."

"Look for what?"

"Black root," the younger boy cried, combing through the under-growth with desperate fingers. "Here!" He yanked a plant with dull red leaves from the ground. Black fleshy roots dangled from the foliage. "Pick up that carcass! I don't care how heavy it is. Move."

Du Mu bristled against being ordered around by a boy seasons younger than himself.

"Do you want to get eaten so badly, elf-witch?" Mahasu demanded. He no longer appeared a boy now. He was an experienced son of the

Plains with all the no-nonsense bite of his mother. Du Mu stooped and hefted the carcass back into his arms. "Good, now move." Mahasu broke the roots in half and a foul stench filled the air.

Du Mu wrinkled his nose as his eyes watered. "That's awful."

"That's the idea. It'll cover our tracks. No hyena will put its nose near black root juice. It'll burn their nostrils. Move, Khalvir. Hyenas travel fast."

Du Mu did not know what a hyena was, but he could see the lurking fear in Mahasu's eyes and knew he'd be a fool not to heed what he said. Mahasu might be younger, but this was his domain. Du Mu set off as fast as he could under his heavy load. Mahasu came behind him, smearing the grasses with the stinking juices of the black root.

Du Mu travelled until his legs would no longer hold the weight and he dropped the carcass to the ground.

"That should be far enough," Mahasu panted. What little colour he had regained in his cheeks had disappeared again. "Now we have to build a fire. No predator will risk coming near a fire without good reason. Not when there are so many other creatures to eat."

Du Mu helped the boy gather a pile of grass and sticks from a nearby cluster of trees, surrounded by a ring of rocks. Once they had a satisfactory horde, Mahasu pulled forth two pieces of flint from his furs and struck them together, showering sparks over the dried grasses until one caught and orange tongues flickered to life. Mahasu kept feeding the dancing figures until he had a true blaze crackling before them. Heat washed over Du Mu's face. He closed his eyes and sighed. He hadn't been warm since before he had followed Rannac out on that doomed hunt.

Mahasu sat back, exhausted. "N-now we wait. When it is hot enough, we can cook that." He nodded towards Du Mu's kill. He rubbed at the arm bearing the bite mark restlessly.

Silence lapsed between them as the cackles of the hyenas grew steadily louder, hunting for the kill they thought to steal. A few yelps sounded.

Mahasu laughed faintly. "Th-they found the black root."

Du Mu permitted himself a smile. "You're very good at this," he said.

Mahasu snorted. "Tell that to my father." He shook his head and looked hungrily towards the dead calf. "If I had brought that back, there would be a feast and celebration in honour of my first kill."

"Feast?"

"You've never heard of a feast?" Mahasu blinked.

Du Mu shook his head.

"Well…" and Mahasu launched into a story of the celebrations he had witnessed. His explanations morphed into other stories as they cooked hunks of the calf flesh over the fire. The scent of wood smoke and sizzling meat filled Du Mu's senses as they made their own feast. Mahasu told of his life in the Hunting Bear clan. His joys, triumphs, together with his sorrows. Overlaying all was the overwhelming sense of belonging. Du Mu could hear it in his every word. It made his heart ache. He wanted to feel that sense of belonging, too. His face turned towards the south and the smile that had formed on his face in response to Mahasu's latest tale died on his lips.

"You want to go back home, Khalvir?"

"Yes."

"Where is that?"

"I don't know."

"You don't remember?"

Du Mu bowed his head. "No."

Mahasu's brow pinched together. He rubbed at his arm again. "Then why are you trying so hard to go back if you can't remember?"

There it was, out in the air. Du Mu hitched a breath. "I-I don't know," he whispered.

"I miss my mama," Mahasu sighed, his voice sounding once again like the young boy he was as he drifted towards sleep. Moments later, his soft snores rose to accompany the crackles of the fire, leaving Du Mu alone with his thoughts.

The Light Bringer sank from the sky and Du Mu remained sleepless. Countless other lights winked in the vast blue-black emptiness overhead. He thought of Mahasu's tales and found himself longing for Nameeda and her unwavering kindness. He missed Tamuk and his brotherly support. And Rannac, the warrior who had placed his own life in the balance for him. And how had he returned all that kindness? He had chosen to leave them behind. Du Mu stared south. The land ahead stood stark, cold, and empty.

"Mama." Mahasu began to thrash in his sleep. "Mama."

"Shhh," Du Mu placed a hand on him, trying to quiet his young companion, then cursed. Mahasu was hot. Too hot. Tearing aside the furs on the boy's arm, Du Mu gasped. Even in the faint light of the twinkling eyes above, he could see that the bite wound was inflamed. "Mahasu?"

The boy groaned. "Khalvir. I don't feel... I want my mama. I need my mama."

Du Mu's resolve shattered. *I'm sorry,* he thought to the silent call at his centre as it cried out in response. *I have no choice. I don't even know if you exist. This boy needs me.* And with that, Du Mu turned his back on his path. Scooping Mahasu into his arms, he whispered. "Hold on, Mahasu. I will take you to her. I will take you home."

CHAPTER 18

TORN

Du Mu only stopped long enough to snatch brief periods of sleep and to rest his aching body. Mahasu tried to walk as much as he could, but exhaustion would take him often and Du Mu would carry him until he could force his body no longer and he also needed to stop for rest. The journey seemed never-ending, and Du Mu began to fear he had lost his way. But on the fourth day of travel, Mahasu's fading spirit sparked.

"I recognise those rocks," he whispered, pointing from where he lay across Du Mu's aching shoulders. Du Mu let out a silent prayer of thanks to whatever power was watching over them. The knowledge that they were almost at their goal lent strength to Du Mu's weakening limbs, and he increased his pace. Mahasu's illness was worsening. He had to get him to the frightening elder who had stitched his leg soon after he arrived in camp.

"Hold on, Mahasu," Du Mu panted when he felt the boy's body go limp against his. "You'll see your mother soon."

When the dark, forbidding line of the Forest of the Nine Gods came into view on the horizon, Du Mu no longer needed Mahasu's guidance. The camp of the Hunting Bear was close. He just had to find the river and it would lead him in.

The Light Bringer was high in the sky above when Du Mu found the sandy banks and paced along them. He mounted a rise, then paused, letting out a laugh as the sprawl of shelters unfolded in the near distance before him. The sight eased his heart. Ahead of him lay life and laughter. Healing and comfort. Du Mu's eyes picked out the individual shelters and, with a faint thrill, he realised he could name each one.

"We-You're home, Mahasu!" he said. The boy made no answer as he slumbered across Du Mu's shoulders. There was no time to waste. Forgetting his exhaustion, Du Mu raced ahead towards the camp. A rolling beat thudded out. The sentries had raised the alert. Faces appeared before the outer shelters, spears held at the ready. Du Mu thought he recognised Rannac among the warriors.

"Rannac!" he rasped as he drew near.

He was close enough now to see the older man's eyes widen. Rannac handed his fighting staff to the warrior closest to him and ran out to meet Du Mu.

"Khalvir," he gasped as Du Mu let himself collapse at his feet, utterly spent.

"Mahasu," Du Mu forced the words out. "Bitten. Wants Halima."

Du Mu thought he saw Rannac blink back a sudden sheen of tears, his face twisting with emotion for one fraction of a heartbeat before it disappeared behind his stoic mask. He stooped and lifted Mahasu from Du Mu. "Can you walk?" he asked.

Du Mu answered by pushing himself back to his feet. He stumbled along at Rannac's side as they made their way back to camp together.

"Mahasu!" A cry went up. Du Mu almost did not recognise Halima's voice as the matriarch of the clan rushed to seize her son from Rannac's arms.

"Mama." Mahasu's voice quavered. "It hurts."

"It's alright," Halima whispered. "You're safe now. Thank you." She turned her dark, tear-stained eyes to Rannac.

Du Mu felt Rannac's hand on his shoulder. "It was Khalvir who brought him home."

Halima's gaze flickered to him. "You came back," she whispered.

"Yes."

Du Mu read each emotion as it passed over her face. Consternation, gratitude, fear, respect, sympathy, accusation, each warring with the other before her expression relaxed into resignation and she kissed her returned son on the forehead. "Thank you," she murmured. "I know what this cost you."

Du Mu bowed his head to the proud woman, striving to feel nothing but gladness for the reunion in front of him and to ignore the ache of his own loss deep within. Without another word, Halima carried Mahasu away. Du Mu assumed she was headed to the frightening healer.

Rannac's hand was still warm on his shoulder. Du Mu closed his eyes briefly. He had not known how much he had missed the man's regard until this moment. "You saved the boy's life. Halima will never forget it."

There was a long pause. Everything hung in the silence between them. Du Mu did not know what to say. His exhaustion clouded his thoughts.

"Forgive me, Khalvir, for what I had to do." The older warrior broke the silence first.

Du Mu kept his gaze fixed ahead. "I know now why you had to do it," he said so quietly he wasn't sure if Rannac had heard him.

"You hunted?"

Du Mu dipped his chin.

He heard Rannac's release of breath. "You kept yourself and Mahasu alive, like a true man of this family. I am proud of you, Khalvir."

"Thank you," he whispered. Du Mu still hadn't really processed what had taken place over the last few days. He had taken lives. He had turned his back on the chance to return to the forests of the south and find his missing centre. And the most confusing of all: his heart hadn't broken when he had done so.

"Go and sleep, boy," Rannac pushed him in the direction of the hunters' shelter. "You have earned it. Mahasu will be safe now."

Du Mu barely registered what the older man said. He barely remembered entering the hunters' shelter. Already asleep on his feet, Du Mu pitched forward onto a pile of soft furs and knew no more.

"Khalvir, wake up!"

Du Mu grumbled, gripping a fur and pulling it over his head. "Go away."

"I didn't understand that, but I think I can guess. C'mon, Khalvir, Utu is nearly at her highest!" And the fur was ripped back. Du Mu blinked up into Tamuk's grinning face. "You do have eyes."

Du Mu stared up at him.

"Ah, you're actually pleased to see me. I can see it on your face. Not such a blank stone like the rest of the witches anymore. You truly are becoming one of us."

The corners of Du Mu's lips twitched. "Hello, Tamuk."

"Here, I brought you something." The other boy held out a large, seared bird leg.

Du Mu's empty stomach clenched, and he seized the leg and descended upon it, humming his thanks to Tamuk.

"Tiki sent it. The entire camp is spinning tales of how you saved the Chief's son."

Du Mu froze mid bite. "All I did was return him to camp." He didn't mention how he almost hadn't. If Mahasu hadn't told of it, then he wouldn't, either. Then an awful thought dawned on him. What if Mahasu couldn't speak? The boy had been deathly ill. What if he was... "How is Mahasu?" Du Mu asked.

"Sleeping. If you had not found him and brought him home when you did, he would be a feast for the vultures by now."

Du Mu swallowed his bite of meat so he wouldn't have to dwell on that image.

"Are you ready now?"

Du Mu looked up, questioning.

Tamuk raised his eyebrows and nudged him with a toe. "You might be the hero of the day, but don't think for a moment that Rannac will let you rest easy. He wants you in the proving circle now. Bring your spear. You might have learned to hunt, but that does not mean you know how to fight." Tamuk moved to mock punch Du Mu in the head. Du Mu automatically ducked, only to receive a gentle jab in the ribs, proving Tamuk's point.

Du Mu sighed. He hadn't thought to return to this life. But until he sorted through his tangle of turbulent emotions and knew which path was the right one, he had no choice but to do what was required of him. He got to his feet and stifled a groan. His body felt like a bull ox had trampled on it.

When he emerged from the hunter's shelter, it was like his first few days in camp again as he made his way to the proving circle with Tamuk. All eyes turned to follow him along with the whispers. Du

Mu kept his head down until he reached the circular clearing within the camp where Rannac had put Du Mu through all of his training so far. Rannac was already waiting, spear in hand. Du Mu tried not to let the resignation show on his face.

"The raknari are the defenders of the clan," Rannac said as Du Mu came before him. "They are chosen because they are the most skilled with the spear and learn how to control an *arshu* staff. They fight for and defend the clan under the Chief's wishes. Few boys are chosen to become raknari, and it falls to the rest to feed the clan, to be hunters, as you now are, Khalvir. But even a hunter needs to know the basics of how to fight with a spear and help protect that to which he belongs. Do you understand, Khalvir?"

Before his abandonment, Du Mu would not have felt the weight of Rannac's words. Now, after learning the importance of putting another's life before even his own soul, Du Mu understood. "Yes," he said.

"Then defend yourself." And with no more warning than that, Rannac lunged.

Du Mu still had many skills to gain. His attacks and defences were woefully inadequate against Rannac's vast experience. But he was fast, and he learned. He made sure never to make the same mistake twice. Each time Rannac put him into the dirt, he stayed up all the longer the next time. He was pleased to see he wasn't the only one dripping in sweat when their bout eventually came to an end.

"Getting old, Rannac?" Tamuk teased his mentor, then promptly quieted when the butt of Rannac's spear clipped him around the ear. "He's got ability," he quickly changed the subject, rubbing his ear and nodding at Du Mu. "You should put an *arshu* in his hand."

Rannac shook his head. "The Chief has not expressed a wish for Khalvir to join the raknari. The Red Bear has other plans for him."

"A waste," grumbled Tamuk. "We could use him. He's even faster than Lorhir." Tamuk's eyes strayed longingly to where another group of male adolescents were sparring with the long, double-ended staffs.

"If you want to defeat Lorhir, Tamuk," Rannac said, "you need to stop standing around and work harder."

Tamuk flushed and slunk away to where his peers mock battled.

"He's right," Rannac said once the other boy was out of earshot. "You would make a formidable raknari warrior, Khalvir."

Du Mu glowed, the praise lifting the fatigue from his shoulders. But as he gazed up into the lined, wolfish face, Du Mu could see the weight of sorrow there, even a sheen of tears. "What's wrong?" he dared to ask.

"You just remind me of someone I knew long ago."

"Who?"

"It doesn't matter. But he was a formidable warrior, too. No man could meet him in battle and live to tell a fireside tale."

"Was?"

"He was killed before you were born."

"By who?"

"Not who. What," Rannac said. And a chill ran up Du Mu's spine as the older warrior's grey eyes shifted towards the dark line of the black forest in the distance. "Now," Rannac said, and his tone had changed, once again sharp and direct, calling Du Mu's attention back to the present. "I want you to observe the young men as they spar. As much can be learned from watching your potential opponents as it can from fighting them. Watch them well, boy."

Du Mu did as he was told. He trained his eyes on every movement. Even to his inexperienced eye, he could see Lorhir, while physically weaker than the rest, was by far the most skilled, weaving like a snake through striking weapons. Galahir was struggling to hold his own, a weakness Lorhir was quick to take advantage of. A curl of anger coiled through Du Mu's gut as Lorhir targeted Galahir mercilessly.

"My Chief." Rannac's greeting brought Du Mu's head around. The red-headed leader was striding towards them.

Eldrax ignored his raknari leader. He had eyes only for Du Mu. "Rannac tells me you made your first kill."

Du Mu nodded solemnly.

"Then you are a man, now." One of the huge, pale hands thrust towards him. Clutched in the Chief's grip was a carved hunting knife. Du Mu looked up at Eldrax, unsure of what was expected. "Well, take it," the great red-haired man said gruffly. "It is a gift to mark your first hunt and for the safe return of Mahasu. You have my favour."

Du Mu blinked and reached for the offered weapon with shaking fingers. "It's beautiful," he whispered as he studied the intricately carved bone that made up the hilt, flowing seamlessly down into the razor-sharp flint blade. "Thank you." He almost but couldn't quite bring himself to say 'my Chief'. The words lodged in his throat, and the omission was not lost on Eldrax. Du Mu saw the molten black eyes cool to hard stone. Fortunately, the moment was covered by the sudden rolling of drums.

"What is happening?" Du Mu cast around.

Eldrax grinned. "A Claiming. Wakadi wishes to prove himself worthy of Dami. Bring the boy, Rannac."

Du Mu felt Rannac's eyes sweep over him. As usual, they missed nothing. "The boy is weary, my Chief. It is probably better for him to rest. I have much more to teach him when Utu rises again."

Du Mu saw the light of reason flicker out in the Chief's eyes as Rannac contradicted his wish. "Bring him," he growled. Then his mouth twisted. "If he is to be a man of this family, it's time he learned one end of a woman from the other." He barked a laugh as he strode away.

Rannac sighed as Tamuk ran up with Galahir only one step behind. Both sported fresh cuts and bruises. Tamuk did not seem to notice the injuries, however, as he said, "A Claiming?"

"Yes," Rannac said. "Enough training for this day. Now is the time for rejoicing. This will be Khalvir's first Claiming celebration. Tamuk," he pinned the other boy with a stare. "Careful with the vision water."

"No promises," Tamuk grinned as Rannac walked away with a resigned shake of his head.

"What's a Claiming?" Du Mu asked as soon as they were alone.

Both Tamuk and Galahir laughed nervously, and a delicate shade of pink flushed across Galahir's pale cheeks. Tamuk coughed. "You'll soon find out. Come, let's find Nameeda. It's about to begin."

Nameeda. Du Mu felt a lift in his weary heart at the mention of her name, further tearing the two forming halves of him apart. He hadn't seen the girl since he returned to camp.

The Light Bringer was already beginning to wane towards the western horizon as Khalvir followed Tamuk and Galahir towards the centre of the camp and the biggest circle of open ground that swept out before the chief's own shelter.

A crowd had gathered at the edges. Excited murmurs and whispers travelled around the circle. Heads craned, seeking a better view. The clan was waiting for something to unfold. Du Mu went after Tamuk and Galahir as they ducked under elbows and made their way to the front.

Once there, his eyes widened, heat rising to his face when he witnessed the sight before him. A woman stood at the centre of the circle. She was completely naked but for a drape of leather around her waist. Her breasts were bared to the sky, her smooth skin marked with curling lines of red paint. They stood out boldly against the dark colour of her flesh, highlighting her every curve and hollow. She held her head high, proud, under the gazes of the gathered clan.

Du Mu wanted to avert his eyes, but at the same time, could not look away. A strange sensation curled through the pit of his stomach, tightening his loins. The flush in his face deepened.

Halima was at the naked woman's side, her hand upon her shoulder. Behind Halima were several young girls, Nameeda among their ranks. She threw a quick smile in Tamuk and Du Mu's direction, but Du Mu was too distracted by the onslaught of mixed emotions and new sensations cursing through his body to respond.

Halima placed her hands on the young woman's head in benediction, guiding her to kneel upon the ground, and then melted back with her girls to disappear among the watching faces.

"Glad to see you again, Khalvir," Nameeda's voice sounded next to Du Mu's elbow a few moments later. There was a reserve in her grey eyes as Du Mu met her waiting gaze. He knew then that she had figured out he might not return. *So, you came back*, was implied heavily in her tone.

Du Mu ducked his head, feeling a twinge of shame for throwing all of her kindness back in her face. "Yes," he answered the unspoken words. He did not say *for now*. But he guessed she had heard his meaning just as clearly as he had heard hers. She pressed her lips together, then her suspicion dispelled, and she threw her arms around his waist. Shocked, Du Mu curled one hand hesitantly around her shoulders, his mouth forming into a smile as warmth spread through his heart, beating back the longing deeper inside.

"That was for saving Mahasu," Nameeda said, then broke away and moved to Tamuk's side, taking his hand.

A hushed anticipation had fallen over the gathered clan, and Du Mu returned his focus to the circle in time to see a man, stripped to the waist, step into the clearing. Like the woman who knelt patiently at the centre, the man's skin was decorated with swirling red marks. In his right hand, he brandished one of the long staffs tipped at both ends with curving, lethally pointed, antler prongs. An *arshu*.

"Do you think anyone will Challenge Wakadi's Claim?" Galahir asked, blue eyes fixed on the spectacle unfolding before them.

Tamuk made a noise in the back of his throat. "Yes. Dami is much desired. This will get bloody before the spoils will be won." Tamuk grinned rather roguishly at Du Mu. Nameeda jabbed him in the side. "Ow!"

But before Tamuk could form a protest, Wakadi's voice cried out. "I am Wakadi! And I lay Claim to this woman. If any man wishes to prove himself a more worthy mate," Wakadi swung his weapon. "I invite his Challenge!"

There was only a moment's silence before another male shrugged into the circle, stripping off his upper coverings and brandishing a spear.

"I, Nada, answer your Challenge!"

Tanag snorted. "What does a hunter hope to achieve fighting a raknari?"

"He must think Dami is worth the risk," Nameeda said. "He is bigger than Wakadi."

It was true. The new male was a full head taller than the first, but he did not handle his weapon with the same fluid assurance. Even Du Mu could see it.

"That doesn't matter," Tamuk said. "Wakadi will destroy him."

Tamuk's prediction proved brutally accurate. After testing Wakadi's defence with a few feigned jabs, Nada charged. But never once did the spear tip come close to marking the raknari warrior. Du Mu suspected Nada only lasted as long as he did because Wakadi wished to prolong his humiliation. The warrior toyed with the other man like a wolf with a deer fawn before finally pitching him, bloodied and bruised, into the earth.

Eldrax's booming laugh lifted over the rest of the cheers as Nada tried and failed to rise. Two other men had to dart out of the crowd and drag the wounded and exhausted man out of the circle.

Wakadi prowled the perimeter like a cat, whirling his arshu, eyes burning as he called out his challenge again. Another man came forward. This challenger also bore an arshu and moved with the same assurance as Wakadi.

"Ahhh," Tamauk hissed. "Now we will see a fight!"

The two raknari warriors circled one another. The violence of their clash was beyond anything Du Mu had yet seen. This fight was no mere sparring match. This was a struggle that would only be won when one man was too bloodied and injured to continue. Or until one perished. Du Mu watched, horror-struck, as the two men savaged each other. Clan brothers, kin. But none of that mattered in this heated moment while the naked woman knelt between their twisting, straining bodies.

At last, Wakadi threw down his latest Challenger, striking the other man's arm so hard with the haft of his weapon that the bone cracked. With his spear arm broken and the fingers of his other hand bloodied from a previous strike, the Challenger submitted, bowing out of the circle while grimacing in pain.

Wakadi moved around the circle again. This time, he limped, his body torn and gleaming with sweat as he rasped out for a third time, "I am Wakadi! And I lay Claim to this woman. If any man wishes to prove himself—"

"Enough!" Eldrax's voice cut off the rest of Wakadi's Challenge. "You have proven your worthiness, Wakadi. By my word, you have earned the right to the Claim. Take your woman."

"Why would he stop him challenging another man?" Du Mu asked curiously. He knew the Chief to have a love of violence. It seemed odd that he would stop the proceedings when Wakadi himself had been prepared to face another in battle.

"The Chief is wise," Tamuk said. "Wakadi just proved himself against a very formidable opponent. If the Challenge was joined again, it would not be a fair fight. Wakadi is exhausted and injured. If the Chief did not judge him worthy now and let the Challenges go on, in the end, a lesser man, not worthy of standing in Wakadi's presence when he was at full strength, might win with a single blow. And what would that prove? It would simply allow a lesser man to Claim Dami. And that is not what the purpose of a Claiming is. It is a tradition passed down by our forefathers in order for the best men to prove themselves worthy."

"Worthy of what?"

Tamuk's eyes widened. "The right to father children on the best women, of course." He pointed to the centre of the circle where Wakadi was now standing before Dami.

"You have Challenged and proven yourself worthy of me, Wakadi," she said. Her eyes bright with an emotion Du Mu could not place. Anticipation? But there was also a nervous undertone to her words. "I accept your Claim." She raised her hands and stripped the bloodied furs away from Wakadi's waist, leaving him completely naked before her. His manhood jutted out before him as Dami moved to take up a position on her knees and elbows. Wakadi then knelt behind her, his hands moving hungrily over her body, lingering in places and eliciting moans that deepened Du Mu's flush. His hand dipped down between her legs, working for a moment until Dami's moans turned to a beg. A few stifled laughs ran around those gathered. Du Mu felt nothing but confusion. Then Wakadi removed his hand, seized Dami tightly around the hips, and thrust his manhood deep inside her.

Dami's moans of pleasure turned into a yelp of pain, her face contorting as Wakadi withdrew and then slammed his hips forward again.

"He's hurting her!" Du Mu hissed, appalled by the now loud cheers and whistles of encouragement.

Tamuk laughed and ruffled his hair in a condescending manner. "Ah, innocent boy." Du Mu batted his hand away, furious.

"Oh, calm down, Khalvir," Tamuk said. "It happens. Dami can't have mated before. It won't last long."

He was right. Dami's gasps of pain soon morphed back into mewls of pleasure as Wakadi continued to move, his own groans of ecstasy echoing hers. That strange curl of heat tightened in Du Mu's stomach again, making his own body respond, much to his confusion and shame. Tightly packed as the crowd was around him, Du Mu could not move and he was forced to remain, watching as Wakadi's strokes became shorter and faster, until his body convulsed and he threw his head back, roaring to the darkening sky above.

Drums rolled in harmony with the cheers as the warrior collapsed over the woman before him. They both laughed together as she turned to throw her arms around his neck.

"I love a happy Claiming," sighed Nameeda, appearing rather misty-eyed.

"So does Khalvir by the looks of things," Tamuk snickered. Du Mu thought he would die of embarrassment right there. He tried to retreat, but Tamuk caught him by the arm, taking pity on him. "It's alright, brother," he said. "You shouldn't be ashamed. Happens to us all. It's a good thing! At least you know you won't have a problem when you come to Claim yourself a mate!"

Many questions flew around Du Mu's mind, but as his body calmed, he knew one thing for certain: he would never, in his whole life, do what he had just witnessed. He cringed at the mere thought. But the way he saw Tamuk squeeze Nameeda's hand in that moment, Du Mu knew performing a Claim was the foremost thought in Tamuk's mind.

"Happy or sad Claiming, there'll soon be a new mouth to feed in camp. It's a good thing you know what to do with at least one of your spears, now, eh, Khalvir?" Tamuk waggled his eyebrows suggestively.

"More mouths?" Du Mu frowned, then wished he hadn't spoken as all three of his companions' brows shot towards their hairlines, even Galahir's, who until now had kept out of Tamuk's teasing.

"You really do not know where babies come from?"

A fresh flush under Du Mu's skin gave him away.

"No wonder there aren't many witches left!" Tamuk said incredulously.

Nameeda elbowed him. "What you saw wasn't just for pleasure," she explained. "Wakadi gifted his seed to Dami. If it quickens in her belly, she will give birth to a baby in a few turns of Nanna. A new member of the clan."

"Ah," Du Mu said, knowing his face was still red as fire.

He saw Wakadi lift Dami into his arms, sharing a passionate kiss with her as Eldrax cried out. "Wakadi has Claimed his new mate. She is his and his alone. Tonight, we feast in their honour!"

Tamuk and Galahir whooped with the rest of the clan. Joy and contentment radiated out around Du Mu. It permeated through him, making him feel warm and at ease.

Fires blazed, the scent of sizzling meat filled the air, and drums pounded out a rhythm Du Mu had never heard before. Its purpose was not to alert, or to call, it was simply there for the pleasure of listening to it.

Du Mu followed his friends around the celebrating clan, eating the delicious meats that slaked his hunger, filling his belly and letting the awful memory of starving alone out on the Plains fade away. Du Mu relaxed, for the first time, letting himself feel everything around him without resistance. He laughed aloud at the tales Tamuk spun for them, making his companions stare at him in amazement. Du Mu noticed the egg hunt misadventure he had been a part of when he first arrived in camp was now a tale of daring and bravery.

"So who do you think could have cut the bindings?" Galahir asked as Du Mu finished recounting his adventure out on the Plains. "A spirit?"

"Don't be foolish, Galahir," Tamuk said. "A spirit from the forest would have stolen his soul or gutted him while he slept."

"Then what?"

Tamuk shrugged. "Pale skin? Most likely a Thal. They stray into Cro territory sometimes."

A Thal. Du Mu frowned, trying to picture the figure he had glimpsed in his half-sleep. He had never seen a pure-blooded Thal. Only half Thals like Galahir and the Chief himself. Why would a Thal have helped him?

A skin travelled around the crowd and Tamuk seized it as it came by them. He took a long draught.

"Tamuk," Nameeda warned as he held out the skin to Du Mu. "He's never tasted it before."

"Then it's about time he did," Tamuk said. "We're celebrating. Here, Du Mu, try this."

Du Mu took the skin and held it hesitantly to his lips before taking a sip. The liquid scorched all the way down his throat; the fumes hitting him in the nose. Taken off guard, Du Mu choked.

Galahir crowed and slapped him on the back. Du Mu winced as his bones rattled. "Every time," the large boy chortled, then took the skin and drew a long swallow of his own.

"What is it?" Du Mu asked, his voice slightly hoarse.

Nameeda grinned. "Vision water. We make it from fruit." She took her turn with the skin, taking a smaller sip than either Tamuk or Galahir.

The drums continued to pound, and the burn in Du Mu's stomach from the vision water spread through his body, making his muscles feel curiously loose and further easing his mind. He watched as Tamuk suddenly threw aside his latest stripped bone, his eyes brighter than they had been before the vision water, and stood up, dragging Nameeda with him. She went willingly.

"Come on, Khalvir!" she called as she and Tamuk began to sway and stamp in time with the music. Du Mu shook his head. He didn't know how. But Nameeda wasn't taking no for an answer and pulled him up as she and Tamuk passed by, then thrust him at the nearest free girl, who eagerly snatched him up and pulled him around.

Du Mu awkwardly tried to mimic her movements, swirling with the rest of the twisting clan. The drums went on, pounding dizzyingly against his blood, the vision water's curious effects continued to spread, and Du Mu's body responded, his awkward movements becoming more assured as he ceased to think and simply twisted and swayed in time with the beat, weaving through the other dancers as part of the complex pattern. His heart drummed against his ribs. He was one with the Hunting Bear Clan. Their joy was his, and his theirs. Was this what it felt like to be home?

Fingers against his skin jolted Du Mu back to reality. The vision water had not robbed him of his senses completely, and he realised the girl he was moving with had slipped her hands boldly under his furs. He choked and scrambled back in alarm.

Du Mu stared, consternated, as a wounded expression crossed the girl's face. But the moment only lasted a heartbeat before a hand pushed Du Mu unceremoniously to the side, and Lorhir swept the girl up around the waist, a triumphant smile twisting upon his spiteful face.

Anger shot through Du Mu, but before he could react, Tamuk caught his arm, laughing off the incident. "I really need to teach you about females. You had the chance to learn where to put your other spear then." He clapped Du Mu on the back, shaking his head disparagingly.

Du Mu couldn't help but let out a chagrinned laugh, though his cheeks were blazing again, which only caused his companions to laugh more. But he did not mind. Their laughter was not cruel, it was the pure sound of camaraderie and friendship.

"More vision water, I think," Tamuk said, his dark eyes passing over the pulsing crowd. He disappeared among them for a moment and then returned carrying another water skin. This time, Du Mu knew what to expect. Now that he anticipated the burn, he decided it was actually quite pleasant, warming his body and mind. He felt giddy, everything around him taking on a peculiar haze. He had never felt so carefree.

A shout went up. A group of younger children rushed past, throwing what looked like a small animal's skin between them, competing and wrestling until, with a cry of triumph, one would take possession and dash away with the others in swift pursuit. Du Mu watched with interest until one boy grabbed the skin, but in his enthusiasm, he wrenched the object with a little too much vehemence. As the boy he was trying to seize it from let go, the skin flew from both their grips, sailing through the air until it caught part way up the single standing tree amongst the shelters.

The young children groaned in disappointment, heartbroken by the premature end to their game. A few sniffed while the others looked up at the tall tree, faces forlorn.

Nameeda made a sympathetic noise. "I'm sorry," she said. "It's lost."

"No," Du Mu said suddenly. "I can get it." He got to his feet and started towards the tree.

"Khalvir, no," she caught his arm. "You've had too much vision water. It's too high up."

"I can reach it." And somehow he knew it. He had climbed lots of trees... before. Du Mu made his way to the base of the trunk, assessing the position of the lost skin, then jumped to catch hold of the lowest branches above his head, hauling himself up. The feel of the bark under his fingertips flooded his mind with the flickering, half-formed images that had all but left him. This was familiar, this was right, *this* was home.

The fissure in his heart tore even further apart. Du Mu shook his head, struggling to focus on the skin waving gently in the breeze. He mapped the branches in his head and began to climb. His mind could not remember ever climbing a tree, but his muscles did. This was effortless. Even the old, fading callouses on his hands, almost entirely replaced now by the new layers of skin created by his spear training, lay in just the right positions as he gripped the skin of the tree. Often, the branches of the tree were too far out of his reach, and Du Mu would leap to catch hold of them.

He heard gasps of fear from Nameeda and impressed whoops from Tamuk and the children whenever he made a successful leap. The vision water swirled through his veins, making him feel invincible. He was halfway to the skin now. He coiled, preparing to throw himself up to the next handhold.

"Careful, clumsy," a young girl's laugh sounded in his ear.

Du Mu cried out in alarm, recoiling. He grabbed air. Another cry tore from his lips as he tumbled away into the void beckoning below. His arms failed out, making any grab he could to break his fall. Branches whipped at him. A couple beat the air from his lungs as he crashed into them. Pain lanced through his left shoulder. At the very last, Du Mu caught a branch nearing the ground. His shoulder wrenched painfully as he broke his fall, before he let himself drop the last short distance, landing in a heap at the base of the tree with a dull thud.

His breathing was loud in immediate silence. His friends and the children stared at him for a full moment before Nameeda rushed forward.

"Khalvir!" She knelt at his side. Tamuk and Galahir were not far behind her. "Speak to me! How could you be so foolish?" she scolded. "You could have broken your neck."

"Wh-who spoke?" Du Mu forced the air back into his lungs.

"Spoke? No one. We didn't dare."

"A girl," Du Mu rasped, looking around, but all he could see were his friends and the young boys who had lost their skin. There was no one else there. He closed his eyes, shaking his head again. "Never mind."

Nameeda hissed, and Du Mu flinched as she probed his left shoulder with her fingers. "You've gashed your arm. It's bleeding. You need to go to Johaquin."

Du Mu's head was beginning to ache. "Not Johaquin," he groaned. The memory of the bone and thread piercing the skin of his leg was not something he would soon forget.

"Yes," Nameeda insisted. "That is deep. Tamuk, go with him."

"No," Du Mu sighed, pushing himself unsteadily to his feet. The continued pounding of the drums was now banging painfully against the backs of his eyes. He felt faintly queasy. "You carry on celebrating. I will go."

He brushed Nameeda off and staggered away into the surrounding shelters. Du Mu pinched the bridge of his nose. He could not get the sound of the girl's voice out of his head. Nor could he forget the emotions climbing the tree had brought forth. The sense of belonging with the Hunting Bear clan pulled his heart forward, stronger and stronger, but the call in his centre kept pulling him back, making him yearn for another home. One that he could not even picture in his mind.

A flicker of movement in the corner of his eye made Du Mu turn. A faint quiver inside told him it hadn't been the flit of a bird or a rodent that had drawn his attention. Somebody was hiding behind the shelters, trying to keep out of sight.

Gripping his injured arm, Du Mu paused for a moment. Nearly the entire clan, apart from the sentries, were in the centre circle, celebrating the Claiming. Why would someone be out here trying to hide? Without thinking of the danger, Du Mu moved to investigate, following that odd quiver inside him, the faint flicker of warmth up ahead. It was the sensation he always honed in on whenever Rannac covered his eyes in spear training, the reason he always knew where the target was, even when he could not see it. Du Mu wasn't just relying on his ears like the other boys. There was another sense inside, unknown and buried, that allowed Du Mu to *feel*.

There. A small figure crouched in the shadow of a shelter, face turned towards the blazing firelight coming from the centre of camp. The flickering light illuminated the features of the stranger.

Du Mu gasped. It was one of the witch-women who had accompanied him from the south. A woman he had strived to speak to since the moment he arrived in camp. His heart hammered in his chest as he took a step forward. This time, there was no one watching, no one to stop him. This time, he was going to get his answers.

The elf-witch stiffened and spun around, though Du Mu was sure he had not made a noise. Her eyes widened at the sight of him and she made to flee.

"No, wait!" Du Mu called, his old tongue slipping effortlessly past his lips. "Please! I won't hurt you. Don't run."

The elf-witch turned and waited like a crouched animal, staring him full in the face. Du Mu felt the hairs on his neck prickle as he met those large indigo eyes. A part of him expected the warm light of welcome and it was like a slap in the face when a cold, baleful light pierced him instead. He shifted, suddenly uncertain.

"Please," he said. "You know me. You know who I was. Help me."

"Forbidden filth," she spat. "That is what you are. My tribe sisters and I are here because of you. Kadaa is with child with that red-haired monster's spawn because of you. Ninmah is shamed."

"No! Please, I had nothing to do with your capture. I was taken, just like you. Help me. I can get you get out of here, I know the camp. I am on your side."

The elf-witch straightened from her crouch. The cold light in her eyes did not waver, but now there was also a look of cool speculation as she said, "If you are indeed on our side, Forbidden, then you will help us now. Perhaps then I will tell you what you wish to know."

Du Mu hesitated, then nodded. "I will help you, please. Tell me what I must do."

"Do nothing. If you stand by and do nothing to stop what is about to happen, then you will have proven whose side you are truly on."

The uncertainty swept through Du Mu as his senses quivered. "And what is about to happen?"

A deafening howl splitting the air answered in the elf-witch's stead. It was quickly joined by another, and another, until the whole night was alive with a sound that turned the blood to ice.

"Wolves!" The cry sounded from the centre of camp, spinning Du Mu around.

The rhythmic beating of the drums ceased before they reawakened, striking out a frantic warning roll as screams of panic ripped through the gathered clan.

"They gathered themselves together for the feast," Du Mu heard the elf-witch speak over the din. "But it is they who will be devoured." She laughed.

Du Mu spun back to face the elf-witch, but she had vanished like a ghost.

His heart was hammering in time to the warning drums, the screams piercing his soul, as he leaped forward, racing back towards the centre of camp. He thought he saw the shadows moving all around him, large creatures running in the concealing darkness. Growls and snarls accentuating the screams and the sound of running from up ahead.

His wounded shoulder throbbed as he ran, but he ignored it. He had almost reached the centre of camp when a large grey form on four great paws padded from between two dwellings in front of him. Du Mu froze. Sharp ears cocked forward as a pair of golden eyes gleamed, staring out of a large, thickly furred and pointed face.

And Du Mu relaxed, a sense of calm and safety washing over him in the presence of the wolf. He grinned and stretched out his hand. Here was something from his lost past. He knew it. He *knew* this animal. This creature was a friend.

"Khalvir!" He did not recognise the female voice hissing at him from the shadows. "Khalvir, what are you doing? Run!"

"Why?" Du Mu answered, taking a step towards the staring wolf with his hand still outstretched. Visions of wolf pups rolling around in his lap blurred through his mind. "He won't hurt me."

"Khalvir, no!"

The wolf snarled, revealing a row of dagger-like fangs. Du Mu did not have a chance to cry out, his muscles locked down in shock as the creature lunged for his arm. He pulled it back just in time to save his hand. But the jaws closed on the loose furs at his wrist and Du Mu was yanked to the ground with irresistible force. Fierce golden eyes, teeth, and fur filled his vision. The wolf's hot breath saturated his face.

"No!" someone roared. There was a yelp. The heavy body pinning Du Mu to the ground flinched and shuddered. "You'll not have him! He is mine!" Then the wolf was ripped off him. Blood showered upon Du Mu's face. He blinked and looked up into Eldrax's furious eyes as the great Chief hurled the dying predator away. Then Eldrax was in his face, hands hard on his shoulders. Du Mu nearly cried out at the pain in his left.

"What were you doing?" Eldrax shook him hard. "You fool! I gave you a knife, and you stood there like a woman!"

"I-I," Du Mu stammered. He felt like sobbing. He had known. He had been so certain. The visions evaporated, taunting him, leaving him alone with reality. "I thought..."

"Nothing!" Eldrax shook him hard again, black eyes blazing. "I have told you, boy. I have told you! Forget what you think you know. It is nothing but a trick planted in your mind by the witches. This is the second time I have had to save your life."

A plaintive cry for help cut off the rest of the Chief's tirade. Eldrax released Du Mu and spun around, sprinting off towards the continued sounds of pleading.

In a daze, Du Mu staggered to his feet and stumbled after the Hunting Bear leader. His thoughts and emotions, past and present, battled together for dominance, tearing him apart. He was floating, cut loose from reality. He had thought he had known.

"Mama!" The cry brought his blurring eyes forward. A group of children pressed back against the wall of a shelter. It was the same group of boys who had played with their rabbit skin with such joyous abandon what seemed like only moments before. Three wolves were closing in, cornering them for the kill. "Mama!"

Eldrax did not hesitate. Outnumbered though he was, he threw himself upon the wolves, hunting knife slashing. He caught the first by surprise, dispatching it quickly with a blade to the heart. Its nearest companion snarled, abandoning its hunt, and leaped to avenge its fallen pack mate. It barrelled into the giant man, baring him to the ground. Over and over they rolled, blade and teeth flashing. The third wolf did not even blink in their direction. It continued to stalk towards the cowering children as though blind to the struggle unfolding right beside it. Its mouth gaped.

"No," Du Mu whispered. "No. Leave them." There was another flicker in the corner of his eye. He turned his head in time to see the elf-witch standing in the shadows, her indigo eyes alive with a malicious light as she watched the wolf close in on the infants. She saw him watching, and he felt rather than saw her smile. *Do nothing,* he thought he heard her voice in his head. *Do nothing and I will tell you everything.*

Fury surged through Du Mu's veins. "No!" he screamed. The battle inside him resolved, and the haze lifted. Everything became startlingly clear in that one terrible moment. Eldrax was still fighting the second wolf. He would not be in time to save the children. A spear leaned against a nearby shelter. Du Mu seized the haft, aimed, and let the weapon fly with a cry on his lips.

The flint tip buried itself deep into the wolf's side, killing it instantly. Eldrax roared, wrapped his arms around the other creature's throat, and snapped its neck.

Silence.

Only the beating of Du Mu's heart and the frightened whimpers of the children filled the emptiness. He looked to where the elf-witch stood. She stared back at him, hatred twisting her face, before she melted away into the shadows. Du Mu knew at the core of his being that he would never see her again.

Eldrax heaved the body of the wolf off himself and rose, spitting upon his dead foe. He then stepped to Du Mu's side and gripped his shoulder as they stared at the bloodbath and cowering children. "Do you see now, boy?" he hissed in his ear. "Do you believe me now?"

✳✳✳

CHAPTER 19
BLOOD FEUD

Rannac's heart was troubled as he made his way through the camp. The attack by the wolves had left the clan shaken. The elf-witches were now under tight guard in the Chief's own shelter. Only two remained, one that was by now obviously pregnant by the Chief, and the other who Rannac suspected was related by blood to the expecting witch. The other two had fled the camp in the chaos of the attack. Eldrax had sent his best hunters to track them down. They would not get far, but Rannac doubted they would find the murderous pair alive.

He could not dwell on what had happened, however, for a far more pressing matter was at hand. Once the dead from the attack had been buried, Eldrax had summoned Rannac to his shelter. It was time to bring another clan to heel in preparation for facing the final destruction.

"Who?" Rannac had asked, as the niggle of reluctance in his heart threatened to show on his face.

"The Eagles," Eldrax had said.

The sense of foreboding that had filled Rannac's heart upon hearing those words had refused to ease. The Eagles. Rannac remembered them all too well. A minor clan, Eldrax had all but wiped them out seasons before. Young, untried and out of control, he had been driven mad by the need to possess Khalvir's mother. The Eagles had been unfortunate enough to lie in the path of his rampage.

By the time Rannac and Murzuk had hunted Murzuk's errant red-headed son down, the damage had already been done. All the men in the Eagle clan had lain dead, their Chief Rikal kneeling wounded at the young Eldrax's feet, his mate stripped naked in the snow, the Red Bear threatening to violate her before Rikal's eyes unless he told him what he wanted to know.

Rannac had felt sick to his stomach. Eldrax had torn aside the lores of the Plains, endangering what was most sacred between clans and sparking a blood feud over the empty promise of a children's tale.

Murzuk had put his errant son back in line and spared Rikal and his clan women their lives. But it might have been kinder to finish them. The Eagle clan had been all-but destroyed, leaving only frightened women and a few small children to their old, beaten Chief. It had been unlikely Rikal's clan could survive the winter without the men to provide and protect. That was the reason Rannac had drawn Murzuk's attention to Rikal's sandy-haired half-Thal son and urged him to take him. He had thought he was saving the boy from a slow and painful death, brought on by starvation.

Galahir, like Khalvir, did not know of his origins. He had been too young to remember the horror of his birth clan's demise for long. And like Khalvir, the Chief did not want the half-Thal boy to learn of his beginnings, for that might divide his loyalty. And once Eldrax believed a man's loyalty to be divided... Rannac shuddered.

And his prediction had not come to pass. The Eagles had not perished. Rannac had seen their totems fresh on the borders of their traditional territory with his own eyes. And now he was about to face

Rikal again. And this time, he *would* witness the Eagle Chief's death. For Rannac knew, if any Chief was to bow before the Red Bear, it would not be Rikal.

The thought of what was to come still weighing heavily on Rannac's mind when he came to the proving circle. Khalvir was already there waiting for him with his spear in hand. Rannac took a moment to appreciate how far Khalvir had come from the scrawny, angry, and frightened child they had found in the shin'ar forest.

Fire still burned in his green eyes, but now it was tempered with determination and purpose. His body was no longer thin. He had grown at least half a hand since he had lived among the Hunting Bear and had filled his rangy frame with the promise that was to come. Long, smooth muscles ran under the light, reddish brown skin. The beginnings of a beard teased around his chin. Before Rannac stood a man. A man who now had to pledge his blood to Eldrax. Or die.

Rannac gripped the spear in his hand. He still could not guess where the boy's heart truly lay. Most of the time, Khalvir was still as impassive as a stone. All Rannac could do was hope that when the time came, Khalvir would choose the right path. For both their sakes.

The green eyes looked up at him as he came near, and they tightened with a question. Rannac realised the heaviness of his thoughts had been weighing on his features. He did not have the advantages of an elf-witch upbringing where all emotions were shared internally. Khalvir knew there was something wrong.

Rannac did not wish to speak of it, however. The less Khalvir knew of what the Chief was doing, the better. He was just beginning to see the Chief as someone more than a blood-thirsty monster, and Rannac did not wish to damage that when the time for him to swear the blood oath to Eldrax was at hand.

"I won't be sparring with you today, Khalvir," he said. For the first time, the boy did not stiffen or wince at the sound of the name he had been given. It was a noticeable change that had taken place since the elf-witches had called the wolf pack into camp. It gave Rannac hope that the boy's allegiances were shifting in the right direction. "The Chief wishes me to join him in patrolling the edges of our territory."

"Another patrol?"

Rannac pressed his lips together. "Winter is nearly here, hunger will make rogues more bold. We have to defend what is ours if we are to feed the women and children."

Khalvir dipped his chin in understanding. "Akor?"

There was both a hope and a reluctance on his face as he asked after Eldrax's son. It was clear Khalvir had grown to like Akor. Akor had often taken a hand in his training whenever Rannac was unavailable, but the bruises the boy received during such training explained his reticence.

"Akor is coming, too." Rannac reached out and gripped his shoulder in farewell. "Keep watching the other boys. Go hunting with Tamuk. Listen to the stories of our clan." He hesitated and then threw out a test. "You will be a man of this family soon, before all."

Khalvir's eyes flickered. There it was. The edge of reluctance that refused to fade. Rannac gritted his teeth. He pressed the boy's shoulder once and then moved away. In the end, the choice was Khalvir's. Rannac could not make his mind up for him.

Eldrax was waiting at the edge of camp with five of the most physically imposing of the raknari at his back, Akor among them. All were ready to supplant the rightful Chief of the Eagles. Rannac quashed the reluctance inside his chest. Eldrax had discovered more evidence of the Watchers emerging from the borders. Rannac had dared to argue with his Chief again on the wisdom of relocating the Hunting Bear camp. But his concerns had been firmly rejected.

"When the gods come for us, it makes no matter where we are, Old Wolf," had been Eldrax's answer. "There will be no running. I will meet them and end them on the borders of their own territory."

And so what choice was there? The Watchers could not be stopped by one clan alone. And no Chief would stand willingly with the Red Bear. Sometimes, to defend the clan meant sacrificing that which was most dear. It was a harsh lesson Rannac taught all the young men he trained. *Nothing* came above the safety of the clan. Halima's face flickered through Rannac's mind.

As soon as Rannac took up his customary position at Eldrax's right hand, a place reserved for the leader of the raknari, the Red Bear signalled with his battle club and set off across the Plains, heading east towards Eagle territory.

The journey took several days. Along the way, evidence of Thals flirting with the border of Hunting Bear territory put Eldrax into a foul temper. It wasn't the trespass itself that blackened the Chief's mood. The Red Bear hated the Thal People with a vicious vehemence that Rannac had rarely witnessed. Any reminder of the Chief's own mother was to be destroyed on sight. Rannac was surprised Eldrax had kept the carved spear created by her hand and not burned it the moment he tore it from Khalvir's hand in the witch forest. But Rannac had long ago accepted he would never fully understand the workings of the Red Bear's mind.

The borders of the Eagle territory lay two days beyond the reach of the Red Bear's own. Rikal was wisely keeping to a safe distance. Totems of the Eagle screamed their presence from the landscape, warning away stray wanderers and rival clans. Eldrax crossed them with his fiery mane thrown back, head held high as though he were already the master of these lands. Rannac gritted his teeth.

"Keep your wits about you," Rannac hissed to the men walking in his wake. "The sentries will see us soon, if they haven't already." Eldrax, a full head and shoulders taller than most men, with his bright red hair and a company of his biggest warriors, was hard to miss, even for the most unobservant scout.

Even so, they remained strangely unchallenged as they travelled deeper and deeper into Eagle territory. Rannac felt the hairs pricking along his arms and kept a ready hold on his *arshu*.

A copse of trees and the beginnings of the foothills sheltered the Eagle camp on either side. The position gave it shelter from the wicked winds that drove across the Plains.

"The gods! How did the scouts not see this?" one man rasped in a low voice, uncertainty colouring his tone. Rannac did not turn to see who spoke, he was too busy absorbing the sight before him.

He had known the Eagle clan had survived Eldrax's butchery, but he had never expected this.

A vast camp faced them. Almost the size of the Hunting Bear's own settlement. Rannac gripped his *arshu*.

"Eldrax, we should turn back," he cautioned.

But the Chief's eyes were ablaze, greed and fury warring on his face.

"Rannac is right, father." It was Akor who spoke.

"Are you a coward, Akor?" Eldrax asked, and Rannac heard the dangerous undercurrent of his temper bubbling just beneath the surface of the soft tone. "Maybe you do not deserve the honours I plan to bestow upon you."

Akor squared his shoulders, ignoring Rannac's warning head shake. "No, father. But there will be no honours for any of us if we're dead. This is a trap. I know it."

Eldrax snorted disdainfully. "I will not allow my power to be Challenged. The Eagles will bow before me like all the rest. Their Chief cannot refuse a Challenge." And he strode forward towards the eerily silent camp, giving the others no choice but to follow.

"No, father!" Akor made to grab his father's arm. Rannac closed his eyes as his heart cried out. His muscles twitched with the need to prevent what was to happen, but he could do nothing. There was the swift rasp of a stone knife and a grunt of pain. Rannac opened his eyes and watched with a silent tear tracking down his face as Eldrax pulled his hunting knife from deep within his son's gut.

"I am to be the saviour of Mankind," Eldrax said, deadly calm as Akor coughed up blood and sank to his knees. "That is the penalty for questioning my rule. I am the Red Bear. I fear no one."

With a dismissive snort, Eldrax turned away to speak to the other warriors standing stunned behind him, behaving as though nothing of consequence had happened. Rannac could hold back no longer and rushed forward as the dying Akor fell back into his arms. "Easy, easy, boy," he said softly.

"Are any of my other raknari warriors going to shame their Chief?" Eldrax challenged the rest of his fighters, the bloody knife still dripping in his hand. They all squared their broad shoulders, hardening their eyes as they faced their Chief.

"Red Bear!" they cried, voicing their loyalty to the man who would give them what they all desired. Power.

Cold fury curled through Rannac's gut as Akor's blood spilled over his hands. This was a young man he had trained from boyhood, just like Khalvir.

"Come, Rannac," Eldrax ordered. Fortunately, the Chief did not look in his direction, for Rannac wasn't sure he had entirely masked the animosity he was feeling from his eyes. "Leave him!"

Snarling silently on the inside, Rannac laid Akor gently on the ground, laid a hand on his forehead in farewell, and then rose to his feet, pushing his grief down deep, though it took all of his practiced will. He didn't have a choice. If he refused to follow Eldrax, he would share in Akor's bloody fate.

It was with one less warrior now that Eldrax's band moved towards the Eagle's stronghold.

"That is far enough, butcher," a voice called out. A woman's voice. And from between the shelters ahead of them melted a fighting force outnumbering theirs by two to one, all bristling with arshu staffs and spears, their faces concealed by skull masks arrayed with eagle feathers. Rannac's eyes experienced a thrill of shock when he realised most of them were women.

"The Chief of the Hunting Bear clan only wishes to speak with the honoured leader of the Eagle clan," Rannac called out. "Where is Chief Rikal?"

A stunned silence fell over the opposing warriors. They had all become very still.

"Fool," Eldrax hissed furiously at him before another gravelly voice called out with a sardonic laugh.

"Your Chief has not informed you, Old Wolf, that Chief Rikal died painfully on the Plain while he watched his beloved mate and my dearest friend violated and murdered before his eyes."

Rikal was dead?

"No," Rannac whispered, his eyes going to Eldrax as realisation dawned. "You killed him? Your father ordered you to let him live. There was no reason."

"My father was a weak fool!" Eldrax snarled in Rannac's face.

Rannac searched the twisted features, seeking any sign of the young boy that had been, of his mother, but he could not find any. All he could see was the black soul of a brutal and dangerous man who would do anything to seize power. He had not changed. Rannac's heart wept as his hopes turned to ash. Eldrax was still the blood-maddened young man, broken by his father and abandoned by his mother. A deadly enemy to all who walked the Plains. Including those who followed him. Rannac felt something fracture inside him.

Eldrax turned away. "Who are you, woman?" he demanded of the voice who had addressed them.

The ranks of Eagles parted, and a thickset part-Thal woman strode out from between the ranks, draped in black wolf furs decorated with eagle skulls, while a shock of black feathers erupted from the back of her head, lending to her height and formidable presence. Eldrax bared his teeth at the sight of her.

She was not young. The passing of seasons, grief and hardship lined her pale skin. Her hair under the array of feathers was as grey as the sky above. There was little merriment in her black eyes, only a calloused stare that glittered with untold hatred for the Red Bear standing before her. "I am Yatal," she spoke. "I am the Chieftess of the Eagle Clan. How do you like it, Red Bear?" She indicated the camp and the warriors behind her.

Rannac heard Eldrax's teeth grind together and knew he would like nothing more than to rush in and snap the part-Thal woman's neck, but for once, common sense held the Chief of the Hunting Bear in check. They were vastly outnumbered.

"I come to offer a warning, Yatal," Eldrax growled between his teeth. He threw his carved stone and skull before the Eagle leader's feet. "The Watchers have emerged from the Forest of the Nine Gods, released by their masters. I come to offer you salvation, join your clan with mine under my rule and we will defeat the gods who seek to bring about our destruction!"

The by now familiar stunned silence fell over the gathered Eagles in the wake of Eldrax's bold claim. Then Yatal laughed. "You have truly lost your mind, Eldrax. The gods are no more." She studied the evidence Eldrax had brought. "These are nothing more than rock and bone." She threw the objects back at the Hunting Bear leader. "Not unless I saw the living gods themselves approaching with their promise of death would I submit my clan to your bloodthirsty rule." She spat in Eldrax's direction.

Eldrax's pale skin burned red. "Then I will take your clan by force. You are a fool to think a frail woman can stand between me and my destiny. Vinax!" The warrior Eldrax had summoned stepped forward.

"I, Vinax of the Hunting Bear, Challenge you, Yatal of the Eagles, for control of your clan and the territory you walk."

Yatal's small eyes widened.

"Answer the Challenge and your clan will live," Eldrax said. "Refuse and I will return with the full might of the Hunting Bear and finish what I started on the day I killed Rikal."

All amusement fled the Chieftess' eyes. A chill ran up Rannac's spine as he beheld her face. For the first time, Rannac thought Eldrax had met his match.

"Then unleash your full might upon us, Red Bear," she said. "For I will not answer your Challenge. The Eagle survived your brutality once, and we shall do so again. Your warriors will fall upon our spears!" She raised her fist in the air and the formidable clan at her back echoed her declaration. The chill Rannac felt turned into a shiver.

"Leave now... if you can." A dark smile curled across Yatal's wide lips. "You made a grave mistake coming here, Red Bear. It is not the gods that come for you. It is I! Bring me his head."

Eldrax held his ground for a handful of heartbeats, and Rannac feared he was going to fight. But then, his face white with fury, the Chief gave the command he had only given once in his life. "Fall back."

Rannac thanked whatever benevolent god that existed as he turned and fled with the rest of Eldrax's group as the Eagles gave chase, charging over the open ground between the two opposing forces, baying for blood. Eldrax's men had a good start, but their lives would come down to whomever could last the longest. Already, several of the swiftest Eagles had gained on Udo, the slowest of the warriors in Eldrax's forces. The Eagles fell upon him like wolves, hacking and stabbing at the Hunting Bear warrior, who fought like a spear cat until he disappeared under a mass of bodies.

Dry mouthed, Rannac drove his legs faster. His eyes raked the landscape, searching for a path that might lead to salvation. The foothills held their only hope. In the maze of cliffs and craggy rises, they might lose their enemies long enough to make it back to Hunting Bear territory. It had worked for them once before when they had needed to escape the Watchers Eldrax had roused all those seasons ago.

"Into the foothills!" Rannac cried to his remaining brethren as a hail of spears thudded to the ground at their heels. He heard a roar behind him and turned his head in time to see a spear graze Eldrax's thigh. He stumbled and Rannac's heart leapt to his mouth as three Eagle warriors caught the Chief.

But, even wounded, three warriors were not enough to subdue the might that was the Red Bear in a blood rage. Roaring like the bear he was named for, Eldrax threw his enemies off, his heavy, pronged battle club impaling and crushing their bodies with the force of his blows, leaving behind only bloody mangled corpses in his wake.

"Into the foothills!" Rannac cried again. He waited for Eldrax to pass in order to guard his back, then ran on. But before he took two strides, a hand caught hold of his leg, sending him down in a heap.

Concealed in the tall waving grasses, Akor lay slowly bleeding out from the wound his father had dealt him. His fading black eyes met Rannac's. The pounding of feet drew closer and Rannac pressed himself down into the grass beside Akor.

"Faster, he's getting away!" Rannac heard one of the Eagles cry as they raced past his place of concealment. Then they were gone. Rannac let out a breath.

"Rannac," Akor slurred, reaching out with a bloody hand. "Rannac."

"Shhh," Rannac hissed. "The Eagles."

The young man shook his head, his grip becoming insistent. "Listen, listen." His voice no more than a breath. "I need you to hear." Rannac leaned in close. "M-my father. Tricked you. Tricked the other clans."

"What do you mean, Akor?" He hardly dared to ask.

"Th-there was no threat. Th-the rogues, the remains, m-my father and Tanag killed them t-to make you believe in the threat." Akor shook his head. "The g-gods aren't coming for us. E-Eldrax i-is the one hoping to provoke a war with the Watchers. H-he is taking over the clans for n-nothing."

Rannac could not feel his lips as he asked: "Why would he do that?" He could smell the scent of shed blood thick on the air. The cries of dying men. "Why would he do this?" But in his own heart, Rannac knew the truth. He had already come to the realisation. For power, there was no sin Eldrax would not commit.

"Rannac, y-you must stop him," Akor rasped with the last of his breath. "He is going to kill us all."

***

Chapter 20

RAKNARI

Rannac did not return. Du Mu spent his days with his friends. He went hunting for small game with Galahir and Tamuk and sometimes Mahasu. He learned how to close his thoughts down in order to protect himself against the pain echoing through the back of his mind as he deprived another being of life. His new brothers taught him how best to gut and clean a kill.

He kept up his practice with his spear, sparring whenever Tamuk and Galahir had the time to spare. When they were training with their fellow raknari, Du Mu would sit with Nameeda, listening to her speak of the happenings in camp while watching the matches unfold in the proving ring. He paid particular attention to Lorhir as the slender boy defeated all challengers his own age, and even some of the older men.

After days of such observations, Du Mu felt the motions of the combatants had become second nature. His fingers itched to hold one of the fighting staffs of the raknari and test himself.

"You're doing it again."

"What?"

Nameeda's lips twitched as she finished knapping the piece of flint she had in her hands to a razor edge. "Twitching your shoulders. You're not the one fighting Lorhir right now, Khalvir."

Khalvir. It had crept up on him, but he found he no longer hated the name. But there was still some part of him that fought against it, resisting with all of its might. *That is not who I am,* it screamed, but with a smaller and smaller voice. Du Mu frowned. The protest sprang from the same part of him that had believed the wolves to be harmless. He shuddered at the memories of that night. The memory of the screams, the flashing of teeth, the snarls that had made his blood turn to ice. The vision of the torn bodies of those who had fallen before the men had driven the attacking predators away would stay with Du Mu for the rest of his life.

He had thought he had known the truth. Instead, Du Mu had seen the man he had always seen as a cold-bloodied enemy, single-handedly save the lives of children from those his inner being had told him were friends. He no longer knew what the truth was. No longer trusted that fading inner voice.

The sound of drums broke through Du Mu's inner turmoil. He leaped to his feet with Nameeda. Behind them, the sounds of sparring ceased. Someone was approaching camp.

The training raknari rushed by, calling orders to one another as they headed towards the outer edge of the shelters. Du Mu and Nameeda followed on their heels. When they reached the last of the shelters and nothing but the open Plains stretched before them, Du Mu came to a halt and waited.

In the distance, Du Mu picked out a faint movement. He fixed his gaze upon it as it drew closer, taking on form and colour. "It is the Chief," he said to Nameeda, catching the flare of red at the head of the column of men coming towards them. As the words left his mouth, the pounding drums changed their rhythm from a warning to one of greeting.

"Something is wrong," Tamuk murmured, his arshu gripped in one fist. "The Chief went out to patrol with six men, including Rannac. I only see three."

A dull thud went through Du Mu, and he strained his eyes, trying to pick out any sign that would tell him Rannac was among those returning. Gruff and as unforgiving as the wiry raknari warrior might be, he had become the centre of Du Mu's new existence. Without him, Du Mu feared he would be cast adrift again.

The small group travelled slowly. One of the three was being dragged behind the other two, Eldrax and...

"Rannac," Du Mu breathed a sigh of relief.

The Red Bear was limping as he made his way toward camp. When the three men finally made it past the sentries and came to the first of the shelters, Du Mu could see a deep gash had been opened in the clan leader's thigh. But the pain did not appear to register on the rough, pale face. The Chief's features were cold as stone, his eyes like two burning embers. There was no thought or benevolence behind that black gaze. Just murderous fury.

Rannac's face appeared to have gained new lines. He somehow appeared smaller than the last time Du Mu had seen him, as though an immense weight had been placed on his shoulders and he was struggling to bear it. He stared straight ahead, seemingly unable to meet the gazes of those around him.

Du Mu recognised the man being dragged as a member of the raknari, but did not know him. The furs at his chest were soaked crimson. Blood bubbled at his mouth with each rattling breath he took. A silence fell over the gathered clan as they watched the small procession pass. Du Mu saw what everyone else did. The young man's life was at an end.

"Boy." The Chief's voice rumbled through the stillness like a crack of thunder and the hairs on Du Mu's arms lifted as though he had been struck by the lightning. The Chief's black gaze was now resting upon him. The rest of the clan's attention turned. Du Mu found himself facing stares on all sides.

"Come here, boy." Eldrax crooked a bloody finger. Du Mu's muscles had bunched, ready for flight, but he stepped slowly forward, trying to ignore the flash of fear he saw in Rannac's grey eyes. "I have been patient long enough," the Chief growled as he drew near. "It is time you proved yourself worthy of my generosity. Heal him." The Red Bear pointed down at his stricken son.

Du Mu blanched, a cold sweat breaking out on his forehead. "I-I can't, I don't know how," he said. He suspected the Chief had run mad with grief. "Perhaps Johaquin, she is the ashipu."

The black eyes flared. Eldrax lunged and Du Mu was not fast enough to prevent him from seizing the scruff of his neck and thrusting him towards the doomed man. "You think me a fool, boy?" the Chief snarled. "You think that crone could heal this? You are a witch-child. You have power. Use it!"

"I-I don't know how!"

Eldrax thrust Du Mu onto his knees with bruising force beside the dying warrior. The light was already leaving the man's half-open gaze. "Lay your hands on him, tell his wounds to heal!" The Chief ripped aside the furs at his own chest, revealing a mass of scarred skin that had clearly once been ripped open and healed back together. "The Scarred One brought me back from death. I know it can be done! You will do it now or I will snap your worthless neck!"

Helpless, Du Mu laid his hands on the wounded man's chest. He did not know what he was supposed to do. What power did he have? He flinched, tears leaking from his eyes as Eldrax bellowed. "Heal him!"

"I-I can't," Du Mu whispered as the final breath shuddered from the man under his hands. "It's too late."

The next thing Du Mu knew, he was off the ground, Eldrax's fingers squeezed around his neck. "I saved your life. I gave you food from my own hunt. I protected you. And this is how you reward me?" The Chief's hot breath saturated Du Mu's face as he snarled out each word. The crushing fingers around Du Mu's neck tightened. Du Mu brought his hands up, trying to pry them away as he choked for air.

"My Chief!" He thought he heard Rannac's protest and somewhere, Nameeda was shouting.

"No power, not even enough to save your own life. Worthless." The fingers squeezed until Du Mu thought his bones would crack. He was going to die. Spots danced before his eyes.

That was when it happened. The strange fire inside his chest flared to life. Like a sleeping beast, it uncoiled, hissing and unfurling its claws. But it came up against a wall, tethered, unable to break free. It roared and spat inside him, fighting harder. Du Mu glared into the Chief's burning black gaze.

The shrewd eyes widened. "Ah, there it is! Come on, boy. Let it out."

Du Mu bared his teeth, a terrible rage burning through him. His vision hazed red and a trickle of the heat broke from the bonds that held it. Loosed, it raced to the surface.

Eldrax let out a cry of pain. The hold on his neck released, and Du Mu fell to the ground in a barely conscious heap. He coughed, dragging air back into his starved lungs. Bruises were already forming around his throat. Rannac appeared at his side, supporting him as Eldrax laughed. Du Mu brought his blurring eyes up in time to see the Chief studying his hand disdainfully.

"Is that all? A bee sting? Bah!" Eldrax dropped his hand and came towards Du Mu again.

Then Rannac was there, standing between them.

"Move Rannac. If that is all he can do, he is of no use to me!"

"So far. You do not know what this boy may become and you will never find out if you end him now."

Du Mu's hand went to the abused flesh on his neck. He was still too stunned to feel any emotion as the exchange went on.

"On your head be it, Rannac. If you want to keep him, then take the worthless wretch. Just keep him out of my sight. And he is not to be fed. He will eat only what he catches himself. The rogue will take no more food from the clan's mouths."

"Thank you, my Chief." Rannac bowed, but there was an edge Du Mu had never heard before in the older warrior's tone.

Rannac slipped his arm around Du Mu's shoulders and lifted him to his feet, baring much of his weight as he carried him swiftly away from the gathered clan and the furious Chief.

"I-I thought he was going to kill me," Du Mu gasped.

Rannac shook his head, his gaze still curiously removed. "No. I've seen Eldrax's face when he is going to kill. He was trying to force you. And he did. You hurt him, Khalvir. It is not what he wanted, but it was enough to stay him for now, otherwise nothing I said would have saved you."

"But I don't know what power I have! What does he want from me, Rannac?"

Rannac did not answer. His features may as well have been chiselled from stone. Du Mu balled his fists. He had not controlled what he had done. It had been like a reflex. He had failed to save the wounded warrior, instead; he had caused the Chief himself pain. But Eldrax had liked it?

Du Mu's strength was returning as they finally walked through the entrance to the *ashipu* dwelling, and he was about to protest, but the look on the older man's face quelled him.

"Johaquin!" Rannac barked, bringing the old *ashipu* healer from the shadows of her domain. "His neck. Check there is nothing broken."

The old crone crept up close, peering at Du Mu's throat with her one good eye. Du Mu tried not to draw away, holding his breath against the smell emanating from her, as she lifted her clawed fingers to prod and stroke his flesh.

"Just nasty bruising," Johaquin croaked. "Painful, but won't threaten his life."

Rannac nodded. "I want him to stay here tonight, under your care."

"N—" Du Mu began, but Rannac forced him down onto a pile of furs.

"I have to return to the Chief before he does anything more to jeopardise our safety. I will return for you in the morning. Do not leave or stray back into the Red Bear's path until I have decided what to do with you."

"Yes, Rannac," Du Mu muttered as he stared hard at the ground.

"Do not leave this tent," the older warrior ordered him again before stalking away.

He wasn't left with his troubled thoughts for long. Nameeda, Tamuk and Galahir were at his side before the hides at the entrance to the shelter had stopped billowing from Rannac's departure.

"Are you alright?" Nameeda asked, her hands immediately going to his neck.

Du Mu winced. "I think so."

"Sorry." Nameeda dropped her hands.

"What did the Chief want from you?" Galahir pressed. "You should not withhold what he wants, Khalvir."

"I withheld nothing from him!" Du Mu flared, causing Galahir to shrink back. "He wanted me to heal that man." Du Mu worried his fingers over the pouch at his waist, feeling the objects inside slide tauntingly under his fingers.

All three pairs of eyes widened. "Like in the stories of the witches? Can they actually do that?" Tamuk asked.

"Ninkuraaja."

"What?"

"Ninkuraaja. The witches. That is what they are."

"How do you know that?"

Du Mu frowned. "I-I don't know. It just came to me." His fingers worked faster over the leathery bag.

"Can *you* heal people?"

"No!" Du Mu dropped the bag. "The Chief would not have tried to kill me if I could."

"If the Chief wanted to kill you, you would be dead," Tamuk echoed Rannac's words. "He is a hard man with a quick temper. There isn't one of us who hasn't fallen afoul of his displeasure and suffered for it. But it is the Red Bear's strength that keeps this clan safe, Khalvir. He protects us all. You will rise in favour again, you will disappoint him again." He shrugged. "That is the way it is. But something happened out there to make him angry and you were unfortunate enough to bear the brunt. He has lost four of the raknari." A frown slashed Tamuk's dark brow.

"What do you think happened?" Nameeda whispered.

"I don't know," Tamuk said. "But it can't be good. The Chief is on the warpath. Whatever it is, it is a threat."

Du Mu saw Nameeda pale and both he and Tamuk reached out to comfort her at the same time.

"Don't worry, Nameeda. I will protect you, whatever happens."

Du Mu wanted badly to offer the same promise to this girl, but he could not. He was no warrior. He was nobody. Just a boy without family or clan. A rogue.

"Khalvir?" A small voice broke in. Du Mu looked up to see Eldrax's young red-haired daughter coming towards him with a skin of water. "I have soaked some bark. Drink this. It will help with the pain."

"Go away, Selima," Tamuk waved a hand. "He doesn't want to try your worthless mixtures. Go and play somewhere else."

The black eyes flared with hurt and anger. "It's not worthless! I'm not worthless!"

Du Mu's heart contracted at her plaintive tone. He held out his hand. What harm could it do? "Will it help?"

Selima beamed. "Yes, I have watched. Injured antelope eat this bark all the time."

Tamuk rolled his eyes as Du Mu lifted the skin to his lips and took a sip.

"More," Selima urged.

Du Mu took a long swallow.

"Not that much!" The little red-haired girl snatched the skin away.

Du Mu made a face at the bitter taste as it slid down his throat.

Johaquin came looming out of the shadows. A carved stick bedecked with dangling feathers and skulls rattled in her hand. She caught Selima by her furs. "What have I told you, girl? I am the healer here!" Releasing her, the elder snatched the skin from the young girl's hands and tipped the contents onto the ground before her eyes.

"No!"

"Be gone! I told you to find me a rabbit skull, worthless creature. Go."

Selima snatched her now-empty skin from Johaquin's grip. The murderous stare she levelled at the old crone proved whose daughter she truly was. If Du Mu was Johaquin, he would be sleeping with one eye open.

Johaquin watched the girl until she backed out of the shelter, and then rounded on Du Mu's three companions. "You do not need to be here. Rannac asked me to watch the half-witch, not all of you. Be gone!" She lunged for them with her stick, jabbing. Du Mu knew either Tamuk or Galahir could have disarmed her in a heartbeat. But they raised their hands in defence and scurried to their feet.

"Alright, alright, we're going!" Tamuk turned for the entrance. "Rest, Khalvir. The Chief's tempers pass as swiftly as they come. The next time you see the Red Bear, he will be different. Just stay out of his way for now."

"That's what Rannac said."

"Rannac is wise," Tamuk flashed him a smile before ducking out of the shelter, Nameeda and Galahir hastening on his heels.

Du Mu hissed, folding over as they disappeared. His stomach had begun to cramp. Perhaps he shouldn't have taken that water after all, but the pain in his neck had indeed begun to subside.

He lay back on the furs, breathing deeply against the discomfort in his stomach. Try as he might, he could not shake the memory of the raknari warrior fading under his hands, and the fury in the Chief's eyes when he could not do what was expected. His hatred for the Chief had started to lessen in his time with the clan. Now his fear and uncertainty burned back to life.

Tamuk and the rest of Du Mu's friends accepted the Red Bear's bouts of violence and temper in return for the protection he brought the clan. But Du Mu did not know if he could accept that. He did not know if he could follow such a man. He ran his fingers idly over the pouch at his waist again, listening to the faint call that still existed inside, pulling him away, pulling him back.

I don't even know if you are real, he thought to the silent voice. *Who are you?* But there was no answer, and Du Mu's path remained uncertain. Did he trust his heart, or the word of a man whose brutality both frightened and sickened him? A man whose truth had been proven time and again? The same man who had saved his life? Du Mu groaned.

The silent call inside him was all he had left. The only hope he had that there was something else out there waiting for him. *Who are you? Where are you?* The weight of sleep stole over him, overcoming even the discomfort in his belly. Du Mu fought against it, trying to think, but it flowed over him, dragging him under. The last thought Du Mu had before he lost consciousness was the promise that he would never again take any water Selima offered.

"Will you stay with me?"

"To the end."

Indigo eyes flashed in the darkness, filled with warmth, trust and acceptance.

The boy's heart swelled with a love that encompassed every part of him. He needed nothing more. The warmth at his centre grew.

"Stay with me." The voice begged.

"I will," the boy responded, confused by the sudden, desperate edge.

"No. Come back. You're breaking your promise."

"No!"

Pain. The warmth in his heart was now a burn, searing through every part of him. He couldn't breathe.

Du Mu awoke gasping. Blackness swirled in his mind. For a moment, he thought he was still dreaming. A pair of indigo eyes glared through the darkness above him. Hands were at his chest, pressing down, but it felt as though they were reaching inside him, squeezing, burning at his very heart. He tried to struggle, but there was no strength in his arms.

"Oh no, Forbidden," the voice drifted through the air. "Tonight, I will accomplish what your mother failed to do and rid the Great Spirit of your threat."

The elf-witch was trying to kill him. "No!" he choked. "I, I'm not a..." His eyes wheeled, seeking help. He wondered where Johaquin was, but his thought was answered when he saw the elder sprawled on the ground. Dead or unconscious, he could not tell.

"Half-breed abomination. Your very presence is an insult to Ninmah. Now that red-haired Wove seeks to use you." A crazed light burned in the indigo depths. "By her grace, you will die by my hand."

Du Mu's heart stuttered. Fury blazed through him. A hatred like he had never known tore his last misconceptions apart. He glared at the face above him, burning the memory of his murderer into his mind's eye, from her dark hair to her evil indigo eyes. The heat at his centre flickered, trying, bound as it was to fight back. He saw the witch's face stiffen in shock.

"No," she whispered. "No, it cannot be." Her face twisted with renewed determination, her hands stiffened to claws upon Du Mu's chest. "I must rid the world of the evil you wield." Du Mu's heart fluttered once, twice, then stopped. Du Mu's vision hazed to black.

"Here you are, witch!" The bellow seemed to reverberate through the very ground. The witch's hands disappeared. Du Mu's silenced heart thumped back to life. Gasping, he opened his eyes in time to see Eldrax tearing the elf-witch away from him.

"You will not have him!" The witch screeched back. "You will not possess the Destroyer. The monster must die!"

Eldrax's gaze flickered towards Du Mu. "Destroyer?" A smile curled across his pale face. "I will possess whatever I wish, witch! I am the master of everything I see. That boy is mine. And so are you! Come with me." He folded the diminutive woman under his massive arm and bore her from the *ashipu* shelter. Du Mu heard her shrieks and denials raise the night air beyond the hide walls.

Du Mu was left alone in the dark with the unconscious Johaquin. He was shaking. His galloping heart refusing to quiet. He could not stand to be in this shelter a moment longer. His aching stomach churned. Scrambling to his feet, Du Mu fled through the hides. He did not care that Rannac had told him to stay. He needed to escape.

Reaching the edge of camp, Du Mu was violently sick in the grass. Dawn was at hand when he finally forced himself upright, angrily wiping the back of his hand across his mouth as he watched the growing light dance on the ripples of the river before him.

The witch had tried to kill him. The hate and disgust he had seen burning from her face sank into his very bones. Eldrax had spoken nothing but the truth. The witches had twisted his mind. There had never been another home for him. It was all a lie. *Monster. Abomination. I will accomplish what your mother failed to do.*

His own mother had tried to kill him for what he was. *Abomination.* The word reverberated through him. Past and present. He had been called such a thing before.

The fading voice inside shrieked, railing against the truth that had permeated his bones, still trying to corrupt him and drag him to his doom. With a snarl, Du Mu throttled it, silencing the voice, banishing the half-formed visions and the lies to a dark place where he would never again have to see them.

His snarl turned to a cry as he tore the leaf leather pouch from around his waist, flinging back his arm, preparing to hurl this last connection to his past into the churning river where it would be washed away forever.

But he could not do it. No matter how hard he tried. Du Mu could not let go. He could not let go of this one insignificant little thing. It felt like the witch was burning the heart out of his chest again at the mere thought of it.

Du Mu crashed to his knees and sobbed, folding his arms around the pouch. There was no other home for him.

There was no warning. The body collided with him with enough force to rattle Du Mu's teeth as he was thrown to the ground. The impact drove the air from his lungs. There was a laugh, and the pouch was ripped from Du Mu's unprepared grip.

"What's this?" An unpleasant voice grated across Du Mu's ears. He knew that voice. Lorhir stood above him, an arshu in one hand, Du Mu's leaf leather pouch in the other.

"Give it to me," Du Mu growled, trying to rise, but Lorhir just kicked him back down.

"I've never seen you without this thing. But as you now seem so keen to throw it away, I think I will keep it for myself now."

Laughter sounded and Du Mu realised he was surrounded by a group of Lorhir's friends. Slowly, he got to his feet and faced the other boy. "Give it back to me, Lorhir, and leave."

Lorhir laughed. "The rogue thinks he can give orders. I don't think so," he said. "It appears you no longer have the favour of the Chief, half-witch." Du Mu flinched at the title. "That means I can have my fun at long last." With that, Lorhir lifted the pouch, taking it in both hands, clearly planning to tear it in two. The sight sent an unpleasant echo through Du Mu's mind.

"No!" Du Mu lunged. The arshu whistled around. The haft cracked him in the arm and Du Mu once again found himself in the dirt. He hissed, as his fingers went numb.

"You want to fight?" Lorhir taunted. "Iniba, throw him a spear. Rannac tells me I should never attack an unarmed man, after all." More laughter and the hollow rattle of wood sounded as a spear landed close to Du Mu's side.

"Come on then, rogue," Lorhir hissed, holding out the pouch. "If you want it, come and take it."

Before Du Mu's better sense could break through his pain and clouded awareness, the spear haft was in his hand. Drunk on his grief and fury, he leaped to his feet. It was without thought that he made his first swing.

Lorhir swiftly sidestepped, bringing his arshu around to smack Du Mu on the back as he tumbled past, off balance.

Du Mu quickly regained his footing and came about to face his opponent again. His hands were trembling with the force of his emotions. The Chief had beaten him. The witch had tried to stop his heart for simply being. Now this cruel boy hoped to hurt and humiliate him. He would take no more. Du Mu set his feet. This ended here.

Through his rage, he struggled to remember all Rannac had taught him, to see the patterns in the attack. Shifting his hands to a wide grip on his spear, he sank into a half crouch, waiting for Lorhir to make the next move. He would not chase him.

Lorhir circled, stalking Du Mu now like the jackal he was. Du Mu shifted his feet, balancing his weight as he moved with his enemy. When Lorhir lunged, he gave no warning. The arshu whined through the air, blurring towards Du Mu's face. His breath caught as he brought the haft of his spear up to block the oncoming weapon, stopping the sharpened antler prongs short of ripping open his cheek.

There was a quiver, the strange sense inside Du Mu telling him that the audience was shocked. They had not expected him to be quick enough to defend against Lorhir's blow. But quick as he was, Du Mu was not a match for Lorhir's skill and the other end of the long staff cut his legs from under him, sending him sprawling to the ground for a third time. Shock turned into laughter, then gasps as Lorhir came on, striking.

Du Mu rolled, barely escaping the weapon that cracked into the ground where he had just been lying. Du Mu threw himself to his feet, heart pounding as Lorhir came for him again. This time, he managed to block two blows before Lorhir outmanoeuvred him. The taste of blood and dirt was bitter in Du Mu's mouth as he split his lip on a rock. Bruised and spitting, he staggered back upright.

"You are asking for punishment, aren't you?" Lorhir raised his eyebrows. "Don't you know how to stay down?"

Du Mu snarled, once more going on the offensive, jabbing and swinging with his spear. Lorhir parried his every strike and Du Mu's arms soon began to ache, but he kept on, driven by desperation.

But desperation was not enough.

"Alright, enough fun." In two moves, Lorhir knocked the spear from Du Mu's tiring grip. Du Mu stumbled. The arshu whistled around and this time he had nothing with which to block it. Pain spasmed through Du Mu's body as the deadly antler prongs scythed across the front of his right thigh, ripping apart his furs and opening three red lines in his flesh. Before the cry of pain had left his lips, Lorhir pounced. Twisting around, he caught Du Mu from behind, bringing the haft of his bloodied weapon up to Du Mu's throat and pulled back. The uncompromising wood cut into his shrinking flesh.

"Enough," Lorhir hissed in his ear as he struggled to free himself. "You are no match for me, and now everyone can see it. You are nothing but a pitiful rogue, with no place in the world."

As it had when he was in Eldrax's grip, the red mist descended over Du Mu's eyes. Blood-maddened, the beast inside uncoiled. A new need awakened. Violent, uncontrolled. The need to strike with anger, to take his vengeance and see his enemy bleed. The release was both frightening and a relief. Du Mu gripped the haft digging into his throat and heaved. Over the turns of Nanna, his strength had grown. He was more powerful than Lorhir. Crying out in his rage, he threw the other boy over his shoulder and smashed him into the earth.

Lorhir stared up at him, shocked and winded. But only for a moment. Lorhir had been trained from early boyhood as a warrior, and he regained his feet before Du Mu could land a strike. Du Mu twisted away from his opponent, snatching his fallen spear from the ground. He met Lorhir's next blow, the crack of wood on wood reverberating through the camp. Recreating Lorhir's previous move, Du Mu twisted the other boy's weapon away, disentangling himself, then made his own strike. Lorhir was fast, skilled, but now the beast had been awoken inside Du Mu. There was no move that Lorhir could make that he could not *see*. It was almost as if the other boy's thoughts had been laid bare for him to read. Every twitch of his muscle, every shift of his weight, quivered against Du Mu's senses. He was there to meet Lorhir's every strike before he even made it.

Lorhir's face was no longer taunting. The arrogance had melted away with the sweat and blood pouring from his flesh. Du Mu bared his teeth savagely as he saw the first flickering of fear in his opponent's eyes. When the opening came, he took it without hesitation.

Exhaustion sent Lorhir's blow wide. Du Mu caught the haft of his weapon and yanked him off balance, smashing the butt of his spear into Lorhir's unprotected flank at the same time. He thought he heard a faint crack beneath Lorhir's grunt of pain.

Du Mu did not allow him to recover. He kicked the wounded boy's legs out from beneath him, smashing him into the earth for a second time. But this time, he did not let him rise. Swiping his gifted hunting knife from the furs at his lower leg, Du Mu had the blade at Lorhir's throat before he could draw another breath.

"I am no rogue," he snarled down into Lorhir's stunned face, the truth of it snapping into place inside his heart, driving out the last vestiges of the call within. That other place did not exist. "*This* is where I belong."

A gravelly laugh sounded in his ear, startling him. "That you do, boy." Eldrax's large hands caught Du Mu by the shoulders, dragging him away from Lorhir as Rannac inserted himself between the pair. "That was a display worthy of a true raknari warrior. The first I have seen with true promise for many a season." Du Mu thought he saw Lorhir pale where he still lay on the ground as Eldrax shoved him roughly towards Rannac. "He will swear his loyalty to me now as a man of the Hunting Bear and you will train him to be raknari, Old Wolf. His use has been revealed. He will serve and protect this clan, keeping it safe from all who would bring us harm."

Eldrax strode several paces away and then knelt, waiting, like a crouching bear, his eyes fixed upon Du Mu. Tanag stepped quickly to the Chief's side and called out, "Before you is the Chief. Pledge your loyalty to him in blood and serve him from this day until the day you can serve no more! In return, you shall enjoy the protection of the

Hunting Bear Clan and its Chief until the day he can serve you no more."

Du Mu drew a deep breath, squaring his shoulders. He was ready. He lifted a foot, preparing to step forward, but Rannac caught his arm. His words were a mere breath in Du Mu's ear. "You don't have to do this."

Du Mu's eyes went to the crowd that had gathered, drawn by the sound of his fight with Lorhir, and his gaze settled on his friends. Tamuk stood beside Nameeda, Galahir behind them both. Eldrax's voice rang in his ears. *He will serve and protect this clan, keeping it safe from all who would bring us harm.*

"Yes, I do," he said. Breaking away from Rannac, he stepped forward. Blood was sliding freely down his leg from the wounds Lorhir had dealt to his thigh, but he barely felt the pain.

Lifting the carved hunting knife still in his hand, Du Mu sliced the skin on his left palm as he came to stand before Eldrax, staring down into those glittering black eyes.

"I am Khalvir," he spoke in a loud, clear voice. "And I pledge myself to you, Eldrax of the Hunting Bear. From now until I can serve no more, I give to you my life and loyalty." And with that, he placed his left hand on Eldrax's pale forehead, marking his new Chief with his own blood.

***

EPILOGUE

THE BEAR AND THE WOLF

Rannac approached Eldrax as he sat looking out at the setting of Utu. The golden rays set the Chief's fiery hair aflame. The Chief. The clan's leader. The violator. The one who would kill them all.

Rannac's mouth burned as he spoke. "I want to thank you, my Chief, for sparing Khalvir's life and giving him over to the raknari. He will make a formidable warrior. Perhaps even better than me."

"I'm hoping for it," Eldrax spoke without taking his eyes off the horizon. "I was denied the opportunity to test myself against the father. It seems fate has smiled upon me by giving me the son. It would be no test of skill to kill a weakling."

Rannac's flesh went cold. "My Chief?"

Eldrax shifted. "Did you really think I had spared his life?" He laughed. "Old fool. You did not see how that boy defied me when we found him. He denied me. The girl got away and I want him to suffer for that. But not now, when he is stronger, when he has something he cares about more than his own life. That is when I will strike. And I will enjoy every moment of his pain when I take everything that matters away from him."

The Chief's face came around. "Train him, Rannac. Train him hard. You knew Juran. Make his son better than he ever was before the time comes for me to exact vengeance. I wish to know who would have won between us."

Rannac stared into the black eyes and felt a final breaking inside him. "As you wish, my Chief," he said. But it was in words only. Eldrax was no longer Rannac's Chief. Rannac had no Chief. He would raise his brother's son. He would do as Eldrax asked and raise him to be better than his father ever was. But it would not be for Eldrax that he did it. When Khalvir fought, it would be to win. His father had been a great Chief. And a great Chief was what the Hunting Bear deserved.

Utu disappeared below the horizon, and upon the glowing sky spirit, Rannac made a vow. He would not rest until he saved the clans and his brother's son from Eldrax's madness. The Red Bear was going to fall.

***

THE END

Khalvir's journey will continue in *Call of The Warrior*, Book 2 of *The Raknari Trilogy*.

Also by Lori Holmes